Betrayed

Forged by Magic, Book2

M.P. Starkweather

PHOENIX ECLIPSE PUBLISHING

First paperback and e-book edition 2020 (Originally published as The Order of Orpheus)

Second paperback and e-book edition 2021

Substantive editing by Joe Fryman

Copy editing by Hayley Blair

Cover images by Depositphotos

Published by Phoenix Eclipse, LLC

Contents

romance that transforms

I want to dedicate this book to my two biggest fans, my husband Josh and my son Thom, who will probably never read any of my books. Thanks for pushing me to chase my dream. I love you both to the moon and back.

Acknowledgments

I would like to thank:

My author besties, who encourage me to keep writing, even when it's hard;

My amazing PA, Gwen, who is my twinsie;

My Alpha Team who tries hard to keep me on track;

My Editing Team who does their best to make sure my books make sense and have as few typos as possible;

My Cover Artist, Ravin DeMarco, who's responsible for the gorgeous images on the front of this book

and My ARC Team, who catch some of the things the rest of us miss.

one

q

I WOKE WITH A splitting headache in the middle of the night. I turned on my lamp and surveyed the room. Everything had been cleaned as much as possible, though the broken furniture was still piled in the corner. I should have known that Zoey didn't completely trust me, but I didn't realize it until I got back to my room with the book. It didn't take me five minutes to know it was a fake. But I hid it anyway, just in case Gill had been following me when I received the book.

I'd figured out a while ago he was working for the Chairman, but I didn't want to upset Kyro or scare Zoey. To be honest, I still wasn't sure I could trust them either. Zoey is straightforward enough, but it's so hard to tell with the others. And I was pretty sure it had been Kyro's idea to give me a fake book.

I thought I could handle myself, so when I walked out of the bathroom to find him standing in my room, I didn't even flinch. I wasn't worried because I didn't think he could hurt me, though the desperation in his eyes said he might just try. I squared my shoulders and prepared to stand my ground. Of course, he was no match for me physically. He began to wave his hands in front of his face in a strange pattern and hit me with a spell I had never seen before, knocking me out cold.

When I woke up, I wondered how the room got cleaned up, as I was sure that I hadn't done it. I decided to take a walk to the top deck to see if I could find Gill. We had some unfinished business to address. I climbed the steps to the deck slowly, my head still spinning from Gill's spell.

I heard talking as I walked outside. I figured it was Gill and Mack. I still wasn't convinced that Mack wasn't on Gill's side.

"I can't believe he would betray us like that. He was my best friend." Mack sounded distraught.

I didn't recognize the voice that responded. "I know, but you have to let that go. Something happened, and it must have changed him. What else could have caused this? There's always a reason why things happen."

I guessed that Mack wasn't talking to Gill but about him. Feeling more confident, I turned the corner and made my presence known.

"If a spell hadn't knocked me out, I would have had him. I'm guessing he got away?"

Mack turned to me, "Yeah, unfortunately. We couldn't get to him in time. And I'm pretty sure he hit you with more than just a spell. I had to stitch up a nasty gash in your head."

My hands automatically went to my hair. It didn't seem like anything had happened to it, so I started feeling my scalp. Sure enough, a line of stitches was probably five or six inches long on the left side just above my ear. I'd have to talk to Mack about that later when we were alone.

"Who are you talking to out here? Is Kyro or Zoey out here with you?"

"Nope, just me." It was the voice I heard before but sounded like it was coming from the water.

I moved to the edge of the boat and looked overboard. There was a blonde merman there, just hanging out by the ship.

"Oh, hi there. I'm Q. I got knocked out by Gill before he ran off, and I don't think I met you earlier," I stated cautiously.

"Hi, Q, I'm Mateo. Mack here was telling me about what happened. Are you feeling better?"

"Not at all. My head is killing me. I don't usually complain about pain, but this is awful. I think I'm going to have to sit down." I felt kind of dizzy and not sure which way was up. I sat down right there where I was. Mack came over and sat down beside me.

"Are you alright?" Mack asked as he put a hand to my forehead.

"I'm going to swim around the boat and make sure everything is still good while you check her out." Mateo left, and it was just Mack and me. I figured things were about to get awkward.

"I just got dizzy; I'm fine." I wasn't sure but thought he might have been concerned. I brushed his hand away and looked at him suspiciously. After all the snarky comments he made during training and the fact that he barely spoke to me outside of that, it seemed unlikely.

"So did you sneak in and take the books from Zoey's room after she gave you the one to hold?" Mack asked me accusingly.

"Am I that transparent?" It was unnerving how easily he could read me. He didn't respond to that, except with a curt nod.

"Let me see your eyes. Can you come up with some light?" His voice was softer, more compassionate.

I did a weak fire spell and held my hand up so he could see in my eyes. "Better?"

"That helps," he said, "But I don't see anything wrong. Let me check your stitches and make sure they're holding."

I let him turn my head and part my hair. He carefully moved my hand with the tiny orb of fire so he could get a better look. "The stitches look good. There should barely be a scar once it heals. You may have a bit of a magical concussion."

"Great. That will make the rest of this trip fun." I let the fire spell blink out. "Wait, didn't you say he hit me with something else?" I had almost forgotten that statement.

"Aye, lassie. He broke a chair over your head. You were lucky we found you when we did." Mack breathed.

He was still pretty close to my face. My heart jumped a little in my chest. Was I that unnerved by him?

He placed his hand on my cheek and muttered a few words under his breath. The headache eased a little more. "Thank you, that's a little better,"

"Good, now you should go rest. We need to move fast tomorrow, and we'll need you at your best."

He started to pull away from me, but I grabbed his wrist.

"I don't want to be alone right now. Please." I can't believe I just told him that. What was wrong with me?

He nodded and leaned toward me. Then he did something that surprised me. He leaned even closer, kissed me on the cheek, and said, "I'm glad you're not seriously hurt. I don't know what I'd do without you."

"Thanks. You know, I thought you were working with Gill until tonight. I wasn't sure which one of you to watch more closely." My face turned a shade of red, admitting this.

"It's no big deal, I understand. It would be hard not to suspect Kyro and myself since we were his best friends. Hell, I thought I knew him, and I had no clue."

I could see the sadness in his eyes, even though the moon was barely showing tonight. Something about the situation made me act entirely out of character. I grabbed him by the shoulders and pressed my lips to his. I wasn't sure why, but I didn't regret it.

When we broke contact, he looked at me, his eyes wide. "What was that?"

"I, um, well, I'm not sure why I did that. But it was nice." My cheeks turned pink with embarrassment, but I shrugged it away. I wasn't used to acting on my sexual impulses like this. I preferred to keep that part of my life separate from work. It was also generally done on a no-names basis.

That was all the encouragement he needed because he leaned back into me, pulling me toward him until our lips met again. This time it was impossible to deny the passion behind it. It was as though my soul was finding its other half. It was an all-consuming need to be close to him, and no matter how close we were, it wasn't enough.

I don't believe in soul mates, so kissing Mack was an eye-opening experience. I ended up pressed back against some crates that were stacked on the deck. I all but pulled Mack into my lap as the kiss deepened, becoming more passionate than anything I had ever experienced.

He fisted his hands in my hair, taking care to avoid my stitches. He continued delivering kisses down my cheek and finding just the right spot on my neck. He kissed and nibbled my neck; his hands began to roam over my shoulders and down my sides. I couldn't believe I was letting this happen, but I wanted it as much as he did. We continued kissing, taking turns pushing each other against the walls to get the upper hand. It was like a make-out session combined with a wrestling match, and we were both determined to win.

TWO

Chairman

I WAS ALERTED TO Gill's arrival by one of my guards. I was relieved to see he was on time, for once. I hated to be kept waiting. Now to summon him and see if he was able to obtain the book as requested.

"Bring him to me." I dismissed the guard and took a minute to ponder what getting the book could mean. How sweet would freedom taste? What would I do with all that power? Wouldn't it be amazing when my boss finally bowed to me for a change?

My thoughts were interrupted by the gangly-looking boy being dragged in by the guard. "Was it necessary to drag him? Was he not able to walk on his own?" The guard just hung his head. I was ruthless but not known for unnecessary violence. I had yet to determine if this was necessary or not. After scolding the guard, I turned to Gill.

"Well, hand it over. I've been waiting far too long." I had to give him credit; he didn't hesitate or shrink in front of me. He handed over the leather-bound journal, then stepped back.

I opened the book, and a map with notes appeared. "Is this where they were going?" The details in the notes astounded me. I had half expected it to be coded and require deciphering.

Gill nodded enthusiastically. "They kept saying it was all in the book," he said.

"Good. I'll let you know if there is anything further." I waved my hand to dismiss him. The guard stepped forward to escort him away.

He shrugged the guard's hand from his arm and impressed me by standing his ground. "You said if I got the book for you, you would let us go."

"I did say that. And I may. But not until this is finished. You may still be of use to me."

"Can I at least see him? It's been so long, and I was promised so much. Please, sir, I've done what you asked. Can I just join him in his cell?" This one was persistent.

Color me impressed at the backbone and the manners. At least Gill remembered to say please. "Take him to the dungeon, and put him in the cell with his mate," I said to the guard on my left, who was not the one responsible for dragging Gill in the room earlier. "There. Done. Happy?" With that, I turned and walked away.

I took the book and headed down to the catacombs. I kept a seer in the lower dungeons and wanted him to look at the book before I tried using its capabilities. If it contained traps, I needed to know. I desired its power, not to destroy it. My boss was planning to eradicate the book and everyone who'd stood in his way of obtaining it. My goal was to steal the book's power and overthrow the boss.

Jeremy's workshop was simple, with no decorations on the walls. He claimed there were fewer distractions for him that way. I didn't care, so long as he did what he was told. I suspected, however, that the lack of decoration was actually to prevent me from learning about his personal life. Recently, people were taking notice of the fact that I had been using their loved ones against them. He couldn't stop me, but he might be able to slow me down a bit.

I walked in without knocking. Jeremy was standing at his workbench, and it appeared he was working on a potion. Jeremy was average, both in height and build, with nothing memorable about him. He blended in with others perfectly, with his mud-brown hair and eyes and lightly tanned skin. His clothing was simple: beige shirt and brown slacks, designed to blend in with his workshop walls.

"Jeremy, I need you to take a look at this. I must be aware of any traps or triggers that would destroy the contents."

He jumped slightly at my voice but continued what he was doing without any other acknowledgment of my presence. Usually, I would be pissed about being ignored, but I had dealt with Jeremy long enough to know that he was focused on the potion. The quality of his work was worth the occasional lack of manners.

"Almost...and there. Done," Jeremy said as he turned to me. "My apologies, sir, this potion is extremely volatile, and I didn't want to blow us both up. You said you have something for me to check out?" He dipped his head slightly in a show of respect as he spoke. His words and actions showed respect, but his expression showed irritation at being interrupted.

I handed him the book. "I need to be able to extract the information from this book without destroying it. I want you to determine if there are any traps or triggers that would render it useless."

"I'll get right on it, sir. I should have answers for you within a day or two, depending on what I find." He ran his hands over the book gently, as though he was afraid it would explode. I wasn't convinced that it wouldn't.

"Take care of it as soon as possible. I do not wish to wait." I caught his eyes with mine and glared at him. He nodded in response and walked across the room to his desk, placing the book down gently. He began to gather supplies for this latest mission.

My face was a mask void of emotion as I walked away, while inside, I was anxious and concerned. I needed answers, and fast. I wanted to harness the power of the book before someone discovered I had it in my possession.

THREE

Gill

THE GUARD LED ME down to Trav's cell. It had been weeks since I had seen him, even before he'd been taken. The only exception was when I was astrally drawn into the dungeon and had to watch the goons torture him because I hadn't got the book yet. The Chairman had promised me that he would be kept safe, so long as I did what I was told. I didn't trust him, but I thought he would keep his word on this for some reason.

The dungeons were dark and damp. Prisoners grabbed at my arms through bars as I passed, begging for help. They wanted to escape the daily torture and slavery. Little did they know, I did too.

I hated that I had to help the Chairman, but I had to protect Trav. I had been captured as a part of the Resistance. For some reason, they had decided to lock me up instead of killing me on the spot. I had thought that was fortunate at the time. Once I found the real reason they kept me, I didn't feel so lucky. I had managed to keep my work with them a secret from Kyro and Mack. It made me sick to betray my dearest friends.

The only good thing about the whole arrangement was that I learned the ins and outs of The Order. I got access to their history and to be in the room for a couple of meetings. He had granted me access to only what I needed to fulfill my purpose. I still hadn't met the Chairman's boss, though he never admitted to having one. He wanted everyone to think he was in charge. I had overheard things, though, that made it sound like there was someone he had to answer to. It was just a matter of a little more spying to discover the identity of the mysterious boss.

We made it to the end of the hallway, turned left, and walked down three doors. This was my cell. At least they hadn't moved me again. Before being sent out on this mission, I was kept in this dungeon for weeks and moved around several times. This one was in a better-kept part of the jail, so hopefully, Trav would be kept away from the diseases down here.

The guard opened the door and shoved me inside. "Thank you," I said to him as he slammed the door. His look of surprise indicated that no one had ever thanked him for locking them up before. I was just glad to have the chance to see my husband again.

"Trav?" I didn't want to startle him, so I spoke softly.

"Gill, is that you?" He sounded hoarse.

"Yes, darling, it's me. Are you OK?" I hated that he was being kept down here. I understood why I'd been taken because I was the one who was friends with Kyro, but it didn't make sense to me why they had taken Trav. There should have been a better way.

"I'm much better now that you're here." He struggled to his feet and stumbled into my arms.

I held him tight for a moment, then took a good look at him. His green hair was longer than I remembered, almost to his shoulders now. He had lost weight, looking almost sickly. I was surprised he had the energy to keep the hair color spell in place with as weak as he appeared. His leg had been injured, causing difficulty standing up and walking. But his eyes were the same pale green I had fallen in love with when we met, only where once there was happiness, now they held pain.

"Here, sit. Let me take a look, and I'll see if I can heal your leg." He did as I asked, and I checked how nasty the wound was to see if a mild healing spell would help. It was a deep jagged cut and had started to become infected, but I was confident I had something that would halt the corruption.

"How did this happen?" I was confident I already knew the answer, but I couldn't stop myself from asking.

Those pale green eyes met mine, and Trav responded, "They tried to make me project to you, and I wouldn't let it happen. Once they realized I had powers, too, he made them torture me until I allowed myself to go to you in your dream. With these wounds, I wasn't strong enough to fight against the astral projection spell. I'm sorry." His eyes held so much pain and defeat. He covered his face with his hands.

I pulled his hands from his face and lifted his chin, so his eyes met mine. "Don't beat yourself up about it, dearest. There was no way you could have stopped him. But at least now I know why our connection was broken." I spoke softly as I worked on cleaning and healing his wounds. "There now, that's a little better."

I would see about getting some fresh water in the morning to clean it with and do another healing spell to take care of the cut. After all, I had done what I was asked. I brought the book to the Chairman, and now he owes me. Once the spell was complete, I gathered Trav in my arms again, refusing to let go. We laid down on the bed, still wrapped around each other, and that's how I fell asleep.

Upon waking in the morning, I went to the door and peered through the barred window. There was no one to be seen down the hall in either direction. I waited a while, standing there at the door, watching through the bars. I spotted a guard pushing a cart with trays of food on it. He was dropping off what passed for breakfast here to each cell. "Hey, can I have some water?"

He glared at me and kept working. I wasn't sure if he didn't understand me or if he was ignoring me. When he got closer to the door, I decided to try again. "Please, can I get some fresh water?"

He turned to face me, picked up a cup from the tray, and splashed the contents in my face through the bars of the door. From the smell, it was water, but not at all fresh.

Once the guard had delivered our meager breakfast and left, I began to search my memory for a way to create water. I needed to clean and treat Trav's wound before the infection entirely took hold.

"Do you remember that spell...it was one we used a few years ago when we were camping and ended up lost in the desert...it pulls the water from the air?" I figured asking Trav made the most sense.

He stared at the wall above my head for a minute or two before responding. "I'm not sure. It sounds familiar, but I just can't quite get the wording." He shook his head and scrunched his face in concentration. I knew from experience that he would sit like that, making that face, until he came up with the correct wording or remembered what book held the spell. All I could do now was wait.

Four

q

TAKING A BREAK FROM rolling around on the deck with Mack, I took a moment to pull myself together. "Why don't we continue this in my room?" I figured there was no way out of whatever was happening between us at this point. We might as well have a comfortable place to continue. Mack looked at me for a minute as though thinking over the ramifications of this particular action. I was sure my waist-length hair was a huge knotted mess and ran my fingers through it to tame it slightly.

"Are you sure you want to do this?" He asked hesitantly, fiddling with his rust-colored beard.

I looked at him and smirked. "Are you asking if I'm going to regret this in the morning? Because that's going to depend on how skilled you are." He interrupted me with a snort, then composed himself. "I'm not asking for promises, just one night, and then we take it from there. Deal?"

I wasn't sure exactly why, but I hoped he didn't turn me down. I wasn't sure if I just wanted the release or if something was pulling me toward him. I just knew that at this moment, I wanted to be with him more than I could remember ever wanting to be with anyone before.

He again seemed to be weighing his options. I wasn't sure if that was good or bad. "Aye, but don't be blaming me if you fall in love tonight. I'll not be held responsible."

With that, we headed back toward the stairs. "Wait, we can't go to your room; we'll have to go to mine."

"And why is that?" It seemed odd that he be hesitant to go to my room with me.

He looked a little sheepish, "Well, because Zoey put up a perimeter spell around your room to keep you safe while you were knocked out. So, they both probably know by now that we were out here and what we were up to a few minutes ago."

"Are you embarrassed? Because you know we're both adults, right? We can do what we want, with whom we want. We don't have to answer to anyone about it." I sounded kind of possessive with that statement, which was somewhat out of character for me. I wasn't one to let emotions tangle things up. "If you're worried about it, we'll just go to your room, then." I knew I had taken a somewhat defensive tone, as though knowing that we had been caught offended me somehow.

With that problem solved, he led the way back to his room. We may have seemed like an odd couple personality-wise, but I'm sure we looked even more so. Two different shades of red hair, an almost two-foot difference in height, and yet I'm sure he could have thrown me over his shoulder, and caveman carried me back to his room. Honestly, I half expected him to do just that and may have been a tiny bit disappointed when he didn't. He was so muscular and stout. His strength was a major turn-on, especially since his attitude toward me was so flippant most of the time.

We crept down the stairs toward Mack's room. He stopped me at the bottom and checked to see if the coast was clear. It was, so we proceeded, rushed but quiet, not saying a word until his door closed behind us. And then there weren't words, so much as gasps, groans, and feral mating sounds as we tore at each other's clothes, desperate to join together.

Five

Mack

I WASN'T SURE WHAT had happened on the deck, but suddenly Q couldn't keep her hands off me. I decided I preferred it that way. She was beautiful, but there was something about her. I wasn't sure how to explain it, but I had decided when we met that she was off-limits because she's broken. I could see it in her eyes. It was easier to be curt and slightly rude to her than to see that uncertainty and pain. If she was angry, she didn't look sad. I liked her better mad.

But this, well, this was even better. I decided I liked seeing Quinn's eyes clouded over with desire best of all. After spending the better part of an hour tumbling back and forth on the deck, we decided to take our little party of two back to my room for more privacy. I hated having to explain to her about us cleaning up her room and Zoey putting up that spell, but it had been for her protection. I hoped she understood that.

The second the door closed, we pounced on each other, and an almost feral mating ritual began. We were tugging at clothes, desperate to get them off. The more articles of clothing that hit the floor, the more desperate we got. I managed to steer her toward the bed. I wanted to give myself an advantage since she was markedly taller than me. That fact didn't seem to bother her. She stopped for a moment to take in the view of my almost naked body.

I didn't mind because it allowed me a chance to look at her as well. She was perfect. Her body was thin but muscular, her hair the color of the sunset, and her skin was as pale as the moonlight. I could spend eternity drinking her in, just as I was at that moment. But that would involve telling her that I'm a bit of a romantic, and that just wouldn't do for tonight. So I pushed her back onto the bed and climbed on top of her.

She grabbed my face and pulled me into another passionate kiss. It would be difficult not to lose my heart to this one. My thoughts turned to the future, and I was momentarily wistful. She used that moment to flip me over and climb on top of me, taking the upper hand away. That action brought me back into the moment, and we took turns taking the lead, guiding each other to ecstasy over and over, before we both collapsed from exhaustion.

She turned her face toward mine, planted one final kiss on my lips, and fell fast asleep in my bed beside me. I covered her up, then settled in next to her with my arm around her waist, holding her close. She purred with pleasure at being held, so I made sure we stayed that way for the rest of the night. I figured we'd deal with the details of what had happened between us in the morning.

I woke in the morning to an empty bed. I ran my hand over the sheets and found them cold. Quinn had to have left hours ago for the bed to have no trace of her. I wondered how she would react to me calling her by name instead of just Q. I chuckled and decided that I might just try it. I sat up and looked around the room. It didn't look too bad considering we'd made love on every possible surface last night, except for Gill's bed. I had imagined it would be completely trashed. I wondered if she had woken early to clean up before I had the chance.

After showering and getting dressed, I decided there was no point in delaying the inevitable. I needed to talk to Quinn and see where I stood. I wasn't one for casual, and I sensed that was what she was used to. There were moments last night when I felt such a deep connection to her that I believed if I had offered her my heart, she would have taken it. In the early morning light, I wasn't so sure.

I checked the galley for her first, but it was empty. I guessed that meant everyone was on deck since Kyro and Zoey always rose with the sun to start training. Zoey was determined to be ready for anything and trained harder than any of us.

As soon as I reached the deck, I knew something was wrong. I heard the commotion before I saw what was happening. Quinn was yelling obscenities at the uniformed guards who were boarding us. I ran over, and it didn't take long to find out what they were doing. I almost felt bad for the guy. He was a few inches shorter than Quinn, with jet black hair and a stocky frame. He looked like the type of guy who thought he was better than the rest of us.

"Ma'am, I told you. We're just here for the fugitive. Once we have her, we will leave, and you can be on your way. Screaming at us isn't going to make this any easier. Please calm down." Ouch, that guard must not have a lady in his life, or he would know that was the worst thing he could have said. You never tell a lady to calm down. Never.

Of course, this riled Quinn up again, but before she could start tearing into the guy, I stepped in between them and put a hand on her arm. "Aye, Love, what's all this?" She looked down at me, and her angry grimace relaxed a bit.

"These morons just decided they could board us without permission and search for some fugitive. I was just trying to explain to this one that we don't have any fugitives, and they needed to leave." Her tone was razor-sharp, but I knew that wasn't directed at me.

"It's all right, Love; let me see what I can do." I wondered if she even noticed what I called her, given how furious she was. I decided we'd deal with that later and turned my attention to the guard. He spoke before I had a chance to address him.

"Sir, I'm sorry for any inconvenience, but we need to search your boat for this fugitive. If you would allow me to explain, I can describe her and tell you about her crimes." His expression was pleading, and his eyes held a hint of fear. I imagined that fear wasn't of me.

I took Quinn's hand in my own, encouraging her to sit so she could indeed calm down. She obliged, though she didn't look thrilled about it. I turned my attention to the guard once again.

"All right, boy, I'm listening. Tell me why you've decided your fugitive is on our boat. Then I can explain that she isn't, and you can leave." I kept my voice harsh and stern, though I suspected what he would say next may change things.

He nodded. "We are looking for a Zyterran fugitive from the space station Calliope. She goes by Zoey, and we have reason to believe that she is on this boat with you. She is considered armed and dangerous, and we have orders to shoot to kill."

My jaw dropped. "Wait, Zoey? What is it you're accusing her of, boy? And mind you, choose your next words carefully, as they may be your last." I was beyond pissed that this cocky son-of-a-bitch had decided to smear sweet Zoey's name through the mud. My hand balled into a fist as though it had a mind of its own.

"Sir, you can't just threaten Patrol members. That's a serious offense. I'm going to let it slide because you are both upset. As for the fugitive, she killed the Head of Technology on Calliope before fleeing to Earth. The Director of the Planet Patrol sent us to bring her in to face her punishment."

With that, Q started in on him with the obscenities again. I turned to her. "Please, love, take a moment. I'll snap him in half if I need to. Just breathe." Then I once again turned my attention to the guard.

"Do ye see what my problem is? Ya keep saying things that make it sound like my friend has done something wrong when I know she hasn't. Now you've upset my best girl, and I won't be having that. You'll not be taking Zoey today, so you can load up your men and get off my boat." I know it's not my boat, but this guy doesn't.

Mr. Cocky seemed unmoved by my veiled threat. "We will vacate the boat as soon as we've searched it and are confident the fugitive isn't here. Now, if you don't mind..." With that, he turned and walked away.

I looked at Quinn. "Are you all right, Love? Where are Kyro and Zoey? This whole thing gives me a bad feeling."

She looked at me and smiled. "First of all, yes, I noticed you were calling me Love, and no, I don't mind it. I kinda like it. I'm fine. I just want to remove that guy's head from his shoulders. I haven't seen Kyro or Zoey at all this morning. I got up early to shower and try to clean up my room a little more, and then I heard these guys boarding, so I ran up here."

I kissed her on the cheek, and then she stood up. "Let's go see if we can find Kyro and hide Zoey before these goons find her." I held out my hand, and Quinn took it as we walked below deck.

SIX

Zoey

I WOKE WITH A jolt as though I was escaping a bad dream. I sat up and searched the room with my eyes as if I was looking for someone, or something, that wasn't there. After a moment of panic, I started to remember bits of what had happened. It was all a blur.

First, I was on a ship with Kyro, Mack, and Q. We were sailing somewhere to find clues to help Ian. I could remember the names and faces, but I couldn't remember which ones went together. At least now, I was sure Jack wasn't lying to me about leaving Calliope.

"Oh, no. Jack! Where are you? Where am I? What happened?" I spoke aloud to myself. I glanced around the room again, this time taking note of the sparse decorations and layout. It reminded me of the bedroom I had grown up in on Calliope before my parents left. The slate blue walls were devoid of decoration aside for one picture framed and hung on the wall across from the door. The floral scene seemed as sad as I was at being locked in this room. I sat there looking around and trying to remember the rest of what had happened.

"Jack used a transporter to bring me back to Calliope. I remember that much, but what happened after that?" I closed my eyes and leaned back on the bed, trying to focus on fading memories. *We were going to sleep. I was asleep, and something woke me. What was it? Why can I remember bits and pieces of everything else, but not how I got here?* Then it hit me...I'd been drugged!

"Elena! She must have drugged us...but why?" I got up and raced to the door. It didn't surprise me to find it locked. Once I remembered how I got here, I figured we were being held prisoner. I had to stop myself from panicking since I had no idea who Elena was working for.

I began to search the room for clues that would tell me where exactly I was. I needed to find Jack and get out of here. I wasn't sure exactly what I had been doing on Earth, but I got the feeling that it was urgent and I needed to get back to it.

After discovering the locked door and realizing there were no windows, I took a closer look around the room. I needed to find a way out. I couldn't find any secret panels, but I did locate what may have been a camera near a light fixture. I wasn't sure how to tell if I was being watched or not. I decided that maybe beating on the door would get a response from my captors.

I screamed until my throat was hoarse, and then I pounded on the door for what seemed like hours, with no response. My hands began to hurt, so I stopped beating on the door and sat down beside the bed on the floor. Just when I had given up on anyone coming, there was a click, and the door opened.

seven

Jack

I CAME BACK TO consciousness slowly, with a pounding head, as though I had drunk too much last night. I shook it off, wondering where the hangover had come from. I knew I was with Zoey the previous night, and we weren't drinking. With that thought, I bolted upright.

"Zoey!" I looked around the room and realized that something was wrong. This room wasn't the hideout, and Zoey was nowhere to be seen. I took a deep breath, releasing it as I scanned the room. I noticed the cameras right away. "Who are you? What do you want? Where's Zoey?" I spoke to the camera directly.

I knew it would be useless to attempt to escape since there were no windows, and the door was reinforced steel. The walls were a bland beige, and there was nothing else on them. Whoever had taken us had to have been paying attention to the camera since it was only a few minutes until I heard movement in the hallway.

I stayed where I was on the bed, waiting. I heard the soft click as the lock released and the creak as the door slowly swung open.

I had decided that if they were smart enough to kidnap me from the catacombs on Calliope, they'd be smart enough to expect me to fight. I was planning to take that off the table and be as cooperative as possible.

Once the door had opened all the way, Elena walked into the room. She was dressed in a Planet Patrol jumpsuit and was carrying a tablet. Her expression was pained, as though she was fighting to hide her anger or sadness. It was hard to tell until she spoke. There was venom in her words. "Come with me," she ordered as she turned and walked away without looking back.

I jogged down the hall to catch up to her. "What's going on here?" I waited for an answer, but she refused to even look at me. "Why are you wearing a Planet Patrol uniform?" Still no response. She just kept walking. I looked around as we walked. The walls here were just as commonplace as the ones in my room. The whole place was rather depressing. I wondered if that was why Elena was giving me the cold shoulder, though I was pretty sure it was something else, and she wasn't going to talk. I would have to figure it out on my own.

We turned left at the end of one hall, walked to the end of the next one, and turned right. After about five minutes of walking, we ended up outside a conference room. Elena tapped a button on the tablet. "He's here, ma'am."

The conference room door opened slowly, and Elena silently gestured for me to go inside. I was getting frustrated that she wouldn't talk to me, but I did what she requested. I took a seat at the end of the table and waited. Elena nodded at the camera, and then she left without another word.

A moment later, another door opened, and Mama Bear came into the room. I stood up to greet her, and she motioned for me to sit. "Jack. I trust your accommodations are comfortable," she asked casually.

"What's going on here, Mama Bear? Where's Zoey?" I was starting to worry about exactly who had taken us.

"It's all right, dear boy. We were able to sneak you both in without anyone knowing. Elena is very good at her job." She looked at me knowingly.

"Wait, Elena works for you? Or the Patrol?"

"Both, though her work for me is kept under wraps. I can't have people finding out about our secrets."

"You didn't answer me. Where's Zoey? Is she OK?" I had to take a couple of deep breaths to calm myself before I did something I would regret.

"She's safe, Jack. She's being held in a room much like the one you were in. I've managed to cut surveillance to her room, though that will only work temporarily. I'll have to get you both out of here before the scouts come back." Mama Bear gave me a sly smile.

I felt better knowing she intended to help us escape the Patrol. "So, you're getting us out? How?" I hated not having all the information about a plan.

She glanced at me thoughtfully. "We have a plan. But I want to see her first. I want to tell her part of what we've been doing. I can't tell her everything, but it's time there weren't so many secrets between us." I could have sworn there was a tear in her eye when she looked at me.

"What about the scouts? How did you get us off Calliope without the Patrol knowing?" That was the part that puzzled me. I thought the catacombs were my secret place, but obviously, other people knew of them too. I hated that I had put Zoey in danger. If Mama Bear knew, others probably did as well.

"I see the wheels turning over there. It's fine, Jack. You didn't put her in danger. Elena and I are the only ones who know about the secret passages. And I trust her with not only my life but yours and Zoey's as well."

I nodded. It didn't do any good to worry over it, especially since I may never see Calliope again anyway. "So, where will we go? Do you have a plan?"

"You'll be joining Zoey's quest. I'm going to return her to the boat and you along with her. By nightfall, you'll both be on your way. It's all right there in the encrypted files."

She handed me a tablet with instructions and maps. "That tablet is for you. That's our new way to communicate. Everything sent and received by it will be encrypted. The only way to decrypt the code will be with the partner tablet. Right now, Elena is the only one who has access to it."

I looked at the files on the tablet. "I'll be working with Elena?" I asked hopefully.

Mama Bear chuckled. "Yes, my boy, you'll be reporting to her instead of me. If she feels something warrants my involvement, she will let me know, and I will be in touch." She turned and walked out of the room, leaving me alone with my thoughts.

At least I knew Elena couldn't ignore me forever. There would come the point when she had to listen to what I needed to say.

EIGHT

Zoey

I SAT THERE ON the floor, staring as the door swung open. I waited to see who was there, mentally preparing to attack. The last person I expected to see was my mother.

"Zoey, it's good to see you. These aren't the circumstances I wanted for our reunion, but we don't always get to choose, do we?" She walked in and closed the door behind her.

"Mama? What are you doing here? Where are we? I have so many questions." I didn't even try to stop the tears as they ran down my cheeks. It had been so long since I had seen my parents. I didn't realize until now how much I had missed them.

Mama sat on the edge of the bed and extended a hand toward me. I took it and stood up to climb onto the bed next to her. She pulled me into her arms and held me for a while.

"I know you have questions, baby. I'll answer what I can. But you know my work is classified, so I can't tell you everything." She kissed the top of my head. It reminded me of when I got hurt as a child.

I turned to look at her. "Mama, where are we?"

She looked around the room. "We're in a safe house owned by the Patrol. But my bosses don't know that you're here. And you can't stay long. I've already explained it all to Jack."

My face lit up with surprise. "Oh, Jack! Where is he? Is he OK?"

She nodded and smiled. "He's fine. Jack works for me. He's wanted to tell you for a while, but I wouldn't let him. His job is to protect you and keep you safe while I'm away."

I couldn't believe what I was hearing. Jack works for Mama? That seemed so strange to me. "Where will we go? Will I be safe? Do they actually think I killed Race?"

Mama wiped a tear from her eye. "You'll go back to your friends who are helping you with your quest. They will keep you safe. Jack will be with you as well. I'm afraid some people think you may have killed him, but most of us know better." She stood up, hugged me again, and then walked to the door.

"I must go; I have work to do. I'll send Jack to get you when everything is ready. Just rest for now." And for the second time in my life, I watched my mother as she walked away for the sake of duty.

I waited in my room for hours before anyone came. When the door lock clicked, I expected Jack to be on the other side, but it was Elena. She brought me a tray of food. At least they weren't going to let me starve while they got our escape plan ready.

"Elena. It's good to see you. Thank you for helping us." I tried to make small talk, though I could tell she was upset about something.

She glared at me as she thrust the tray into my hands. "Zoey. Your mother made me bring your meal." She turned to walk away. I put the tray down on the bed and grabbed her arm.

"Elena, wait. What's wrong? Please talk to me." We had been friends on Calliope, or so I thought. I couldn't figure out what she was so upset about.

She paused with her back toward me. "What's there to talk about? You've won. It's obvious he's yours. You don't have to rub it in." The pain in her voice was hard to miss.

"I have no idea what you're talking about. Please, Elena, tell me what's bothering you." I begged her to share with me. I couldn't understand what had her so upset. I didn't let go of her arm.

Suddenly she whipped around to face me, jerking her arm out of my grasp. "You're going to pretend like you don't know what I'm talking about? I walked in on the two of you in bed together after he had just seduced me not even a week before! I thought you were better than that. I guess I was wrong." She turned to go, trying to leave before I had a chance to respond.

I stepped in front of the door and closed it. "Wait. Just wait." I held my hands out in front of me to stop her from coming any closer. "Do you think that Jack and I...that we?" I couldn't believe it. She thought Jack and I had been intimate, and she had walked in just after. It was unreal.

"I saw the two of you with my own eyes, Zoey. You can't lie your way out of it. You were sleeping together." She spat the words at me. If she had been gifted with lasers for eyes, I would have been fried on the spot.

I needed to defuse the situation and fast. "Well, yeah...but, no. Elena, I know what you think you saw. Please, let me explain. It wasn't what it looked like. Jack and I aren't an item. He told me he was falling for someone else and was concerned about sleeping in the bed with me because of it. I insisted that he sleep there instead of on the floor. I guess your reaction tells me who he was talking about."

"Wait, you were just sleeping? And he told you he was falling for me? You expect me to believe that?" She seemed reluctant to believe me, but her expression softened a bit.

"He refused to give me any info. He just said there was someone and that nothing could happen between us." I let my hands fall. "To be honest with you, I'm pretty sure I was or am seeing someone who is helping me with my quest. The transporter kind of wiped my memories, but things are coming back in flashes. And if I'm not seeing him, I'd like to be."

She seemed to accept my explanation, and her mood shifted a bit. "I'm sorry I jumped to conclusions and got jealous. It looked like that was what had happened. He had an arm wrapped around you, after all. I should have known to ask you about it first. I hope I can fix this."

I hugged her tightly, then let go. "He's a snuggler and has been since we were kids. I can assure you that is the most that happened. You just have to talk to him. Tell him what you thought had happened but that you talked to me and know that your assumptions aren't true. You can fix it, I'm sure. He's crazy about you."

"I'm sorry, Zoey, I have to go find Jack. I'll see you again before you leave." And she ran out the door, chasing after the potential of love. I crossed my arms over my chest and smiled to myself as I stood there with the door open, glancing down the hallway.

Nine

Jack

After Mama Bear left, I sat there reading through documents and maps on the tablet for a few minutes. I couldn't believe Elena was working with the Patrol. It shouldn't have been that big of a shock since I really didn't know her very well. As bad as I felt about lying to her, I had justified it by reminding myself about the mission. To find out that she was in on it the whole time was disturbing. I could have had someone to confide in, someone to help me figure things out. But because I didn't know, I made mistakes that drove her away. I sat there brooding for a while longer, then headed back to my room. I needed to get organized so I'd be ready when I met with Elena.

Once I was back in my room, I sat on the bed, figuring out what I could say to fix this with Elena. I struggled to come up with anything that didn't sound lame or like I was blaming her for not telling me who she was working for. I laid back on the bed in frustration. All I could do was be honest about my feelings and hope it was enough.

Just as I came to this realization, the door clicked and began to open. Since I knew where I was, I wasn't worried about whoever might be coming in. I didn't bother to sit up. I heard the door close, and suddenly Elena vaulted on top of me, pinning me to the bed. Before I could respond, her lips found mine in a crushing kiss. My arms wrapped around her as though they belonged there.

She leaned back to take a breath, planting her hands on my chest to hold me in place. "Does this mean you're done being mad at me?" I panted.

"Not exactly. You made a habit of hiding things from me, and you lied to me. I'm not going to get over that instantly. But at least now I know you weren't cheating on me with her." She leaned toward me again, pressing her lips to mine.

I gently pushed her back up. "What do you mean, 'cheating on me with her? Who are you talking about?" When she dipped her head, I cupped her chin and brought it back up so I could look her in the eyes. "Wait—did you think that Zoey and I...?"

She grinned. "I did. It's OK; I've already talked to her about the whole thing. And she assured me that she's interested in someone else. She even claimed that you made it clear to her that you weren't interested in her because of someone else."

I chuckled at the sly smile playing across her lips as she spoke. "Oh, yeah? She told you all that, huh?"

"Yeah, she did. She said you wouldn't tell her who you were talking about, but she figured it out pretty quickly."

"Hmm, I wonder who she was talking about. I don't recall telling her anything about being interested in someone." I tried to keep the smile from spreading across my face, but I failed.

"Well, I'll just have to convince you that you're interested, then." She winked at me, then moved back in to press her lips against mine. Her tongue teased my lips apart so it could dance with mine. I groaned in pleasure as she ran her hands down my chest.

We spent the next two hours exploring each other and making up for our little fight. Once we were both satisfied, I slumped on top of Elena on my bed, gasping for breath. "That...was...amazing," she sighed. "But I'm going to have to go. I have so much to do to get the arrangements done so you and Zoey can leave. Plus, I'm supposed to be working right now," she said, laughing.

I winked at her. "You have been working. I could call Mama Bear and tell her how hard you've been working the past couple of hours if you'd like."

Elena laughed again. It felt good to make her happy. "I appreciate that, but please don't. You know how she feels about 'inter-office relations.' She wouldn't exactly be thrilled to know her right-hand woman was giving it to her favorite lackey."

"Oh, I'm a lackey now, am I?" Our playful banter was as easy as breathing. I would miss this after Zoey and I went back to her mission.

She brushed my hair out of my face, and her hand rested on my right cheek for a moment. "I wish you didn't have to go. I understand why, and I know it's for the best. Zoey needs you right now. But I don't have to like it." Elena reached up and pressed a kiss to my other cheek.

"I know what you mean. I have to protect her. I gave my word years ago, and I won't break it. I wish I could take you with me. I want to see where this will go. I think we'll be perfect together." I wanted to promise her so many things, but I knew I might not be able to keep those promises, so it was better not to make them.

"I know you won't make promises you can't keep. So just promise me you'll stay as safe as possible. We can explore this after you're finished saving the world. I'm not going anywhere." Her words were like a salve for my soul. It made leaving a little easier knowing that she would miss me as much as I would be missing her.

I pressed my lips to hers gently, then rolled over so she could get up. We dressed quickly, knowing our time together was short. I was determined to make the most of whatever we got. Once all of this was over, I would come back for Elena and make all the promises I couldn't make now.

Before she left, Elena explained to me which room Zoey was in to talk to her. We needed a game plan for returning to the boat. I needed to see if she had regained any of her memories. I wasn't sure how we could complete the mission without Zoey remembering it.

I opted to shower and change before heading to Zoey's room. I had so much on my mind and needed some time to work through it all.

тen

Chairman

Knowing that something had removed Zoey's memories, it was apparent I would need to act fast to draw her to our side. After our conversation, I was hoping she would call out to me, but it wouldn't be a big deal if she decided not to join me since I already had the book.

I had Jeremy and another group of wizards working on potions that would control people and turn them into my minions. Once he perfected it, there would be no one to stand against me.

So far, the results of these potions had been mixed at best. Of course, we tested on prisoners, and a handful had died from ingesting the mixture. The latest batch had just been tried and failed miserably. I decided a pep talk of sorts was in order.

A few random threats later, they were back to work, convinced if they didn't get it right this time, their lives were in danger. As far as I knew, this kind of potion had never been perfected. The noted attempts at creating a mind control potion were less successful than what we'd had so far. It had been pointed out that the majority of subjects had died from ingesting them. I was confident we were on the right track.

If they could perfect the potion, I could find a way to slip it to Zoey and then have complete control of her. That would make usurping the boss a lot easier. Who knows, I may be able to control her friends, too. I had already witnessed what they were capable of and could use that kind of talent in my organization.

With the wizards focused on the mind control potion, I was able to raid their library and take the books I wanted without anyone knowing I had been the one to take them. Jeremy had gone through the magic journal carefully for the past few days and could not locate any traps or mechanisms that would cause it to self-destruct.

I just had to figure out how to harness its power. Perhaps that ability lies within the items Ian was sending Zoey to find. I would have to find resources to discover the power in those items once I finished my current research.

I was looking for a way to erase memories to more easily turn people into my minions. If they didn't remember they had initially worked for someone else, they would follow me more easily. I took the books to my chambers to read them in comfort, without being disturbed.

ELeven

Zoey

I HAD ALMOST MEMORIZED the spell for combating memory loss while we were still on Calliope. I could remember the ingredients I needed well enough to make a list in my head. As I ate my lunch, I realized Elena had put a comm device on the tray. I picked it up and inspected it to see if it was unlocked. It was pre-programmed with two numbers—Elena's and my mother's. I guessed it was for either Jack or me, so I figured it was OK to use it.

I dialed my mother's number and waited for her to answer.

"Hello?" She seemed uncertain of who was calling her.

"Mama? Is that you?" I asked hesitantly. Maybe this wasn't a good idea after all.

She responded, "Zoey, did you need something? Is everything all right?"

"I needed a few things and found the comm device with my lunch. I hope it was OK to call you."

"Of course. What do you need? I'll have someone bring it right over."

I gave her the list I had been going over in my head. If she realized it was a list of spell ingredients, she didn't say.

"Well, the notebook, purified water, ginseng, and ginkgo biloba will be fairly easy...I have some of that in my room and the supply room. The candles as well, I'm certain I have silver, black, and indigo. The lemon balm will take a few minutes to track down, as will the fresh rosemary."

"Will it take long to get the ones you don't have?" I wanted to get this spell done before Jack found out what I was doing. The book I got the magic from said it was risky, and I knew he wouldn't be OK with me doing something dangerous.

I could hear her tapping keys in the background before she answered. "Normally, I would send Elena to pick them up, but her comm device is turned off. That's strange."

I barely suppressed my giggle. I was sure I knew why Elena's comm device was turned off, which meant Jack was busy. I might have enough time to pull this off. "Isn't there someone else who could get the items?"

"I'll find someone to go after them. You'll have all the items on the list within half an hour. Was there anything else, dear? I have work I need to do, though I hate rushing you off."

I silently wiped a tear from my eye. "It's all right, Mama. I know you're busy. Thank you for helping me with this. I won't keep you."

She paused for a moment. "Thank you for that, child. And you know you can never tell anyone that you were here or that I'm your mother. Right?"

"Yes, Mama. I know."

Knowing that she wasn't one to share her emotions, I didn't bother telling her that I love her before disconnecting the call. Those words would just aggravate her, and I needed her to send someone for the spell ingredients.

Since that was taken care of as much as possible, I sat down and focused on remembering the spell's wording. The book had indicated that the terminology needed to be just right to allow the memories to come back. There wasn't anything specific in the book to help with it, either. It said that the spell had to be worded differently for each situation.

Mama was true to her word, and I had the complete list of items in my hands within thirty minutes. I double-checked the amount of each thing she sent and realized she had included extra of everything, which would help if I made a mistake. I laid the items out on the floor by the foot of the bed. Then I took the notebook and pen she had included and began to craft the spell's wording. I figured practicing wouldn't hurt as long as I didn't say the words out loud.

At this point, knowing how much was riding on the wording of this being perfect, I wished that I knew a witch or a wizard who was good at spell crafting. I wasn't confident enough in my intentions to just jot something down and go with it. After a few failed attempts to craft a spell that carried both the purpose I had and the questions I wanted to be answered, I came up with something I felt confident about.

I read over the spell I had written and rewritten to get just right. Then I reread it. I had to be sure it would do what I wanted it to, or it wasn't worth the risk in performing the spell. It was pretty risky performing the magic without the supervision of someone who had achieved such magic before. I took a few moments to rearrange the spell ingredients around the bowl I had saved from my lunch and had decided to use for mixing. It had been cleaned and dried, and it was currently the centerpiece of my first attempt at magic.

Or at least, I thought it was my first attempt. I couldn't remember the past six weeks, so to be fair, I could be an amazing witch and just not know it yet. I guess I'd find out soon enough. It was almost time to perform the spell.

I made sure everything was laid out in the order it was to be added to the bowl, then laid my new spellbook (that I had just created by writing this spell) next to the bowl. "Well, here goes nothing. Please work." I took a moment to ground and center myself, then began the ritual that would hopefully bring back my memories.

I set the candles up around the bowl, making a triangle with the bowl in the center. The silver candle was at the top, the black one went on my left, and the indigo one was set up to my right. I lit each one carefully, concentrating on thoughts of recovering my memories.

I poured a cup of purified water into the bowl, to which I added a teaspoon of ginseng, two teaspoons of ginkgo biloba, the needle-like leaves from a single stalk of rosemary, and three crushed up leaves of lemon balm. I stirred this mixture, making sure to crush up the rosemary and lemon balm more since I needed to ingest the concoction.

I spoke my crafted spell out loud.

"With these items, I combine,
sending myself through space and time,
memories lost but seeking to find,
answers to questions deep inside,
a forgotten quest, now remembered,
a group of friends, now returned,
all things forgotten, now remembered,
my thoughts and desires, now returned,
with these items, I combine,
sending myself through space and time,
memories lost but seeking to find,
answers to questions deep inside."

I finished speaking the spell's words; I drank the potion from the bowl and leaned back against the foot of the bed.

The next part of the ritual involved meditating to allow the answers to come to me. I leaned back and closed my eyes, carefully measuring my breaths and opening my mind to allow the answers to come. I'm not sure how long I sat like that, waiting, praying it was going to work. After a while, I decided that nothing was happening, and I should just clean up my mess and wait for Jack.

I opened my eyes and began to stand when it happened. The room went black, and I collapsed on the floor. As my vision cleared, I got flashes of memories from the past. *These are not the things I wanted to remember.*

The visions flew past me quickly. I saw my home planet, Zyterra, before it was destroyed, back in a time when my parents were together and lived with me. Next, I saw moments in time that couldn't have been my memories since they seemed to be from someone else's perspective.

I saw the way Jack had looked at me when we were doing our best to respect Race and just be friends. His pain was obvious; I have no idea how I missed it back then. I saw Race taking every opportunity to take other lovers while we were dating. Those realizations hurt but still weren't the memories I was searching for.

After seeing things involving Jack and Race, I saw my mother having a meeting with Jack in the cargo bay. That must have been when she recruited him. Wait, who was that meeting with Race the very next night in the cargo bay as well? The figure was obscured, but it looked like my father. If Race was working for the Chairman, there was no way that was right. Daddy would never work against Mama.

Just when I thought the visions were never going to answer any questions I had, they changed. I saw a dark dungeon, and a scene played out where I watched myself fight to escape. I didn't think I was strong enough to fight for anything, but this proved I could do it if I tried.

The next scene gave some clarity to who the people on the boat in my dream were. I witnessed my first meeting with Kyro and the sensation of hearing his thoughts and then tracking down Q and convincing her to come with us. Next was finding Gill, then Mack.

The visions showed me that Kyro and I were becoming an item, and there was a spark between Mack and Q that could bloom if nurtured. I would have to help with that one when we got back to the ship.

I saw our struggles with beasts and monsters and the hunt for the dodeca and pearls. It made me sad that we hadn't found any of the items yet, though Jack had given me the dodeca before we were brought here.

I wondered if Elena had brought it here as well, but I wasn't sure how much she knew about the quest. Then the visions showed me scenes of the book. At this point, I knew I was seeing things out of order and would have to put them together like a puzzle.

The final piece of this puzzle was the book. And Ian. He was the wizard who controlled the book and tracked me down for this quest. I saw the conversations Ian and I had about why he needed the dodeca and the pearls. Now I knew I needed to get back as soon as possible. I was sure it would take some time to piece everything back together in the correct order, but at least now I had the pieces.

The visions spun faster and faster, making it hard to see what they were trying to show me. It appeared that I may be getting flashes of the future now, but so rushed I couldn't understand it.

Once the visions stopped, I regained consciousness and began to write everything down in the notebook Mama had given me. I needed to make sure I didn't lose these details again. I wasn't sure I got everything, but it was more than I had before, and what I did get made me realize the true importance of the mission.

I was glad Mama had given me extra of each ingredient and that she had made sure they were packaged for easy travel. She had included a small knapsack to make carrying it all easier as well. I carefully packed the vials and bags into the knapsack, then tucked the notebook and pen inside, along with the comm device.

I was so glad to get rid of my old one to avoid being tracked that it surprised me how much I wanted to keep this one. Perhaps because it connected to my mother, and I had missed that dearly in the past few years. I wasn't able to talk to her or my father after they went away for work. All I knew was that their work was vital and very secret. I had heard from them sporadically over the years, but it wasn't the same as having them in my life every day.

Once my new bag was packed, I decided to shower and wait for Jack to show up. I had a lot to tell him, and I knew we'd end up fighting when he found out what I had done. But it didn't matter, because I was finally back. I knew what I was doing and where I was going.

TWELVE

Jack

I HAD A BETTER understanding of The Order of Orpheus after reading articles and documents on the tablet that Mama Bear had given me. It was a very structured organization and one that would be difficult to break into.

There was no way I would be able to infiltrate it, but someone like Elena might. I would never ask her to do that, and I would be distraught if she did. It wasn't a matter of trust; I would be worried about her safety. This thought scared me because it meant that she was more than a fling. That could be a problem in the future, giving someone leverage over me. But I would deal with that later.

I decided I would take the tablet with me when I saw Zoey to show her some of the things we would be up against in this mission. I wanted her to be prepared for anything. I had to keep her safe, no matter what.

I walked down the corridor, carefully following the directions Elena had given me. I hoped I would get to spend more time with her before Zoey and I had to leave. I located Zoey's room with no problems. I knocked, then opened the door slowly to avoid scaring her.

"Zo? Are you in here? It's Jack," I called out cautiously. The last time I had entered one of her rooms unannounced, I was attacked. I wanted to avoid that if possible.

"Jack? Is that you?" She responded excitedly.

"Yeah. I'm guessing you've talked to your mom, so you should know most of what's going on."

She walked over and threw her arms around me. "Thank you for protecting me. I had no idea you had made a promise to my mother all those years ago. But I do appreciate everything you've done."

I returned her hug, feeling relieved that our talk was going so well thus far. I had been worried she'd be mad about being left out of the decision to have me protect her. "We have things to discuss, Zo. We have to get ready to reunite with your friends and resume the mission. I'm coming with you this time."

Her face exploded in the biggest smile I had ever seen from her. "That's fantastic! Kyro is going to love you! It'll be so handy having you around to help Q with the engineering and tech stuff on the boat. She's smart, but she's not an engineer. And you'll have so much fun sparring with Mack." She was talking so fast; it was hard to keep up.

I scrunched my eyebrows in confusion. "Wait, you remember? How did you get your memories back?"

She gave me a sly smile. "I have my ways. And yes, I have most of my memories back, though they don't feel like memories, more like a movie I watched. But I do know the details of what I was doing and why."

"That's great. We should have less trouble getting the mission done if you know what we're doing. I still want to know how you did it, but I can't make you tell me." I didn't want to push too hard because I still needed her to trust me and share the mission details with me.

"So, what do we need to go over first?" Zoey seemed ready to get started.

"Well, I have intel on this tablet about The Order. I think it would be beneficial if you read it, so you know exactly what we're going up against." I held the tablet out to her, and she took it, dropping down on the bed to read the articles I had pulled up about The Order and what they were trying to do.

When she finished reading, I knew she'd have questions. I sat down beside her and waited. I wondered if she would realize just how much danger we were putting ourselves in by attempting this mission.

THIRTEEN

Zoey

AFTER READING THE ARTICLES Jack found for me about The Order, I felt like I had more questions than answers. We still had no idea who was in charge or even what they wanted beyond power. I knew there was a chance that was all they were after, but somehow it felt like part of the story was missing.

It explained that under the "Big Boss," who was never identified, three others, including the Chairman, were assigned zones. These zones were areas of the Earth that were split evenly. Any members of The Order within a zone would answer to the "boss" of that zone.

We didn't have the exact split of the zones or any of the zone bosses' identities. It seemed like every piece of info we got raised at least two more questions.

We did have a list of Lieutenants and Commanders and lower-level thugs who did odd jobs for The Order. It almost seemed like a cult instead of a crime organization.

From intel, it was clear that each zone was controlled based on the desires of its "boss," who ruled somehow right under the Patrol's noses without being detected. That was probably because it was so hard to pin down exactly who was in charge.

"So, it's a very ordered Order, huh? With Lieutenants and Commanders and the whole nine yards. But that doesn't tell us who the boss is or how to find them."

Jack nodded. "I wondered if you'd catch that. Do you realize just how dangerous this group is?"

"I'm beginning to see just that. But we can't give up now. We're so close to getting back to the others. We have the dodeca, which brings Ian that much closer to his goal of fixing all this."

The look on Jack's face told me he hadn't decided if Ian was trustworthy yet. "I get that you know nothing about this guy. But I've talked to him. I trust him. So please, if you trust me, help me." I knew I had to convince him to go with me, or there was no way I could pull this off.

"I already gave my word to your mother. I'm not about to back out now. But you're right; I don't trust this guy. I'm not sure I trust your crew, either. I know nothing about the entire mission." Jack was frustrated.

"Well, we can go over the intel on The Order, or we can go over the mission from Ian. I'm fine with discussing either. We just need to be on the same page. Otherwise, The Order will defeat us, and we'll never be able to fix what Ian and his friends broke."

I explained what Ian had told me about how The Change occurred and the part he and his friends had in it. Then I explained everything that had happened since I met up with Kyro. Well, almost everything. My love life was none of his business. When I was finished, Jack had questions of his own.

"Why do you think he insisted on Kyro? There has to be a reason, right? And what about the others? Gill was a poor choice since he screwed you all over. How do we know the others aren't going to do the same thing?" Jack was playing devil's advocate.

I understood his concerns, but I wasn't planning on giving up that easily. "I can only guess that Ian chose Kyro because of his power, which is related to Poseidon being his father. As for the others, we found a clue that led us to Q—who just happens to be Ed's descendant, and then Kyro decided he needed Gill and Mack to help. We're not sure why Gill is working for the Chairman, but it can't be of his own choice. He's not a bad person, I'm sure of it."

I didn't know what else I could say to Jack to convince him I knew what I was doing. If he couldn't trust me enough to back me up on this mission, I wasn't sure I could let him come with me. Even after laying it all out for him, he seemed hesitant to trust me. It hurt after all these years to realize that my word meant so little to him.

"You know what, Jack? Maybe it's better if I go back alone. I can talk to Mama and convince her that I don't need your help. I have the intel now. That will help us figure out what to do next. You can stay here with Elena. It's OK." I didn't wait for a response, and I left him standing in my room with his jaw hanging.

I immediately headed down the hall, searching for Mama's office. I knew she'd never let Jack out of his promise. I was hoping that he'd come after me and then tell me that he could trust me enough to go along with the plan. After a couple of minutes of walking, I was beginning to doubt my idea.

I heard footsteps behind me and turned, expecting to see Jack. I was surprised to see Elena coming down the hall toward me. I stopped and waited for her to catch up. "Come on, I'll take you to your mom," she offered, and we continued down the hall.

"How did you know where I was going?" I asked sheepishly.

She grinned at me. "I would say a little birdie told me, but we both know that's not true. There's nothing little about that birdie. He's not trying to be an ass; he's just worried about you and wants to make sure you're safe. It's not easy to earn his trust, especially where you're concerned. He cares for you more than he's willing to admit. That's why I jumped to the conclusion that I did."

My cheeks flushed. "But there's nothing between us like that. I don't understand why he can't trust me."

Elena laughed. "It's not you that he doesn't trust. It's the rest of the world. And as for there being nothing between the two of you, I disagree. At first, I thought it was romantic, but now I'm starting to see it's more familial. He wants to protect you like a brother taking care of his sister. Which means no man will ever be good enough."

My thoughts wandered back to Kyro. I missed him so much, and it had only been a couple of days. I wondered how things were going on the boat and how they had all reacted when they realized I was missing. I hoped they hadn't gone after the Chairman. I wondered if Jack was upset because of Kyro. I didn't think I had said anything to lead him to that conclusion, but I wasn't sure.

I turned to Elena quickly. "What if they went after the Chairman when they realized I was gone? What if they've all been captured? I just don't know what I'd do if something happened to them. They only got involved because I asked it of them."

I was almost in tears from being scared of what was going on in my absence. Elena slipped an arm around my shoulders and hugged me. "It's OK, Zoey. I'm sure they didn't go chasing after the Chairman. They were all still on the boat yesterday, and your mom has been monitoring their position all day. We would know if there was any danger. I promise. Nothing will happen to them. We'll get you back there safely, and you'll continue the mission."

Her words were comforting, but I still wasn't convinced. I wanted to get back to the boat as quickly as possible. That was the only way I would know that my new family was safe.

Fourteen

Kyro

I HAD SLEPT FITFULLY during the night, unable to chase away
the demons in my mind. There was something strange about these
dreams; I couldn't quite figure out what it was. I saw myself going on
a trip with Gill, Mack, a red-haired woman, and the most beautiful
girl with pale blue skin and hair the color of midnight.

It seemed odd to me that I couldn't remember her name. In my
dream, I saw us in an embrace. Our faces were just inches away from
each other, then we leaned in and shared the most passionate kiss
I've ever experienced.

I woke with a start, my hand instinctively reaching for the opposite side of the bed. It was as though I was trying to keep her here
though I had no idea who she was. There was something wrong,
something missing. I scanned the room, searching first with my eyes.
Then I got up and started rifling through my belongings. I had no
idea what I was looking for but figured I'd know it if I found it. I
started searching the bathroom, and when I found nothing out of
place there, I turned to the closet.

The only thing that seemed out of place was the pink backpack in the bottom of my closet. It looked as though someone had hidden it there. I carried it back to my bed and began to look through the bag.

It had to be magical because the pile of stuff I pulled from it should not have been able to fit. There were seven hard-bound books, three small notebooks, some hair ties, two pairs of pants, three tank tops, a couple of button-up shirts, two pairs of socks, and a couple of lingerie sets. There was also a leather-bound journal with pages that seemed to glow around the edges.

It was apparent this bag belonged to a woman, and not just because it was pink. I wondered if its owner had midnight blue curls that hung halfway down her back and eyes that could see right into your soul. I carefully returned each item to the bag. I knew she'd be aware of someone going through her belongings but hoped she would be able to trust me when I told her I didn't read her journal.

Just as I was pulling on my jeans, there was a pounding on my door. I thought I was alone on the boat and had been for weeks. Before I could get to the door, it swung open, and Mack walked in. Holding his hand was a tall red-haired woman. She looked familiar, but I couldn't quite place her.

"Mack, what's going on? What are you doing here?"

"Kyro, are you OK? Where's Zoey?"

We spoke at the same time, and neither of us understood the other's questions.

The tall woman held up her hands between us. "Hang on, guys. One at a time. Kyro, where's Zoey?"

I looked at her dumbfounded. "Do I know you? And who's Zoey?" I glanced between her face and Mack's, searching for answers that I didn't find.

They exchanged a concerned look, then turned back to me. "Ky, this is Q. You and Zoey went to Spain and got her before coming to get Gill and me. Zoey is the lovely young lass who we're helping with her quest. Do you not remember?"

"Mack, I have no idea what you're talking about. I'm sorry. Wait. Where's Gill? Didn't you say he's here too? Maybe he knows what happened or where Zoey went."

Another concerned look exchanged, and the woman Mack had called Q decided to try again. "OK, so I don't think you're faking it. But it's a long story, and there just isn't time right now to go into all of it. Gill isn't here. Can you help us look for Zoey, please? She's kind of in trouble, and we need to get to her before these goons do."

She looked around the room as if hoping to find a clue. "Oh, that's her bag! I'm guessing that's where the book is, right?"

At this point, I was beginning to think I was crazy. "So, the bag belongs to Zoey? Well, I guess that means she was here. She can't be too far away then, right? There are several books in it, but I didn't read any of them."

"I promise we will explain the whole thing to you. We just need to find her first." Q was trying to be reassuring, but her anxiousness bled through.

"I don't think it's a good idea to split up, but I do think you should put her bag in the vault until the Patrol leaves, just so we know it's safe," Mack suggested.

It was a pretty good idea since I had no clue why the Patrol had boarded my boat or what they wanted with Zoey. I locked the bag in the safe, and then we headed out to search for Zoey.

"Why are they looking for her?" I asked Mack and Q. It wasn't often that the Patrol went on a search. The crime had to be something big.

Q responded. "They think she killed someone. We're pretty sure she didn't, but even if she did, I've got her back. If she did it, and that's a big if, there was a damn good reason. Though I'd need her to tell me that she did it and how she managed it because she's the most gentle soul I've ever met."

Mack nodded in agreement. "It doesn't matter if she did or didn't; they can't take her. We'll not allow it." They seemed pretty protective of this mystery girl, and it made me wish I could remember her.

We spent a while searching rooms and found no hint at where she could be. On a positive note, that meant the Patrol couldn't find her either. Once they were satisfied that she had somehow escaped, they made a few thinly veiled threats about arresting us for harboring a criminal, and then they left.

It was all Mack could do to keep Q from blasting them with her fire powers. I hadn't even realized she was a mage until that moment. Though I probably knew, I just couldn't remember for whatever reason.

FIFTEEN

Trav

I THOUGHT I WAS dreaming when the guard let Gill into my cell. He'd been gone for weeks, and I had dreamed of him so many times. It seemed as though I would never see him again. I honestly thought I'd be dead before he came back.

The Chairman had punished me every day since he sent Gill out to steal that book. It was my fault because I refused to tell him what I knew. I was good at playing dumb. I'd been doing it for so long; I wasn't sure I knew how to do anything else.

I hated lying, but when it protected the planet and those I loved, I knew I had to do it. And I was pretty good at it. I had convinced Gill I had no family after all. As far as I was concerned, that was true, though. My family was the reason I hated lying and also the reason it was a skill of mine.

My parents were harsh. They favored my older sister and had no problem showing me I wasn't valued. Nothing I could do would ever be enough to surpass her. It didn't matter that she was cruel and bullied kids just for sport. They were proud of her, and she could do no wrong.

At some point, I accepted that I was born into the wrong family and would never be like them. They were anti-magic and homophobic, so basically, they hated me on a molecular level. I had no idea where my magic had come from, but I learned how to hide it from those I didn't trust at an early age.

Being gay was harder to hide. As a teen, I tried dating girls and had fun hanging out with them. I just wasn't attracted to any of them. After my parents had beat me half to death because I told them I preferred men, I ran away. I survived on my own for six months while I practiced my magic to heal and protect myself.

Then I met Gill. I knew in an instant he was the one. I also knew he was so far in the closet; I'd have to build a back door to get him out. He was so kind to me and so protective. He offered me a friendship that blossomed into love. And I had lied to him. I continued to lie to him.

I wasn't sure I knew how to tell him the truth. I wasn't sure I even wanted to. I liked our relationship the way it was. Just the two of us, with no family to cause issues. I had convinced myself that telling him would do no good anyway since my family would never accept him.

I knew there was no way out of the dungeon we were being kept in. Gill kept telling me he would figure it out, and he would find a way for us to be free. But I knew better. He still didn't know the full extent of my powers. I wasn't even sure I did. Honestly, as long as I could stay off of the Chairman's radar, I thought we'd be all right.

I spent my days half-assing my attempts to remember a water spell that I could have figured out in ten minutes. I spent my nights building up the wards in my mind to astral project and see if I could find help. It was draining, and as much as I hated lying, I knew I couldn't tell Gill.

If the Chairman suspected anything, he would torture me until Gill talked. And Gill would. He hated to see me in pain. So, I lied. I convinced myself it was OK because I was doing it to protect us. But in my heart, I knew it would be the end of me if the truth got out.

There were nights when Gill had nightmares about betraying his friends. He thought I didn't know, but I had watched him sleep long enough that I could tell when he had a bad dream. The first time he had this particular nightmare, I astrally projected into it without realizing that's what I was doing, as I was asleep at the time.

It only took a moment to realize what had happened. Fortunately, I had practiced cloaking enough that I was able to hide where I could watch what was happening without Gill knowing I was there.

I was pretty sure the Chairman created this nightmare. In it, Gill replayed his betrayal of his friends. There was an added part, though. The Chairman had Gill kill his friends and burn the boat they were on to make sure no one came after The Order. Once I had seen enough, I pulled my consciousness back into my own body and woke up. I watched him sleeping fitfully, then pretended to be asleep.

I knew he wouldn't tell me about the violent images he had seen. There would be no discussion, no explanation, no way for me to make him feel better. Because to do so, I would have to give away one of my secrets. And I couldn't do that.

Instead, I worked on my shielding abilities. I perfected my shields, then moved on, projecting a barrier over Gill while he slept. It was exhausting, but I prevented the Chairman from sending nightmares to mess with my husband's head. I was reasonably confident I had managed to do it in such a way that I wouldn't get caught.

sixteen

q

"So, you don't remember me at all?" I questioned Kyro.

"Not even a bit. I mean, you look familiar, like I've seen you before, but I have no idea where or how we met." He was adamant about having lost his memories.

I was still skeptical because I already suspected him of working for The Order with his mother. And since I had been right about Gill, I couldn't rule this out as a trick. It did seem odd to me that he wasn't more upset that Zoey was missing.

As close as they were yesterday, he should have been going crazy, wanting to search for her. So maybe there was some truth to his claims. I guess I would just have to wait and see.

"What's the last thing you remember?" I probed, hoping to trip him up somehow.

His eyebrows knitted together thoughtfully. "Well, I had just come back to the boat after meeting with my father. We had words about his desire for me to stay in the ocean with him and train as his replacement. Nothing out of the ordinary in that."

"Was that when Ari told you about Zoey and the quest?" Mack asked cautiously.

"There may have been mention of a quest coming my way. How did you know that?" It was hard to hold onto doubts when Kyro made confused faces like the one he had now.

"You told us. We've been trying to explain it to you. That quest is why we're all here, and it's why those guys were looking for Zoey. We need to tell Ian that she's gone and see if he knows anything." I had to convince him this was the best thing to do since I had no idea where the book was or how to use it.

"Who is this Ian you keep talking about? This is all just too much to take in at once." Kyro growled. This needed to be settled now before he went off half-cocked again, like when I questioned him about his mother.

I held up my hands defensively. "Ian is the wizard who communicates with Zoey through the book she has. It looks like a leather-bound journal. She said the pages glow. Mack and I haven't seen it up close because Ian warned Zoey of a spy who was trying to take the book, and they were trying to figure out who it was."

I sighed deeply at that statement. It hurt not to be trusted, even though I completely understood why Zoey was on guard. Every one of us was keeping something from her and each other. We just had to find a way around it so we could finish what we had started.

"You seem awfully interested in that book. Care to explain why? And why didn't Zoey want you to have it?" Now it was Kyro's turn to be skeptical. Great, at this rate, we'd never get to talk to Ian about Zoey's disappearance.

I looked down at Mack, who seemed amused watching this exchange. "Could ya help me out here?" I jabbed at him with my elbow.

He jumped at the contact. "Hey, watch it." He started to get after me, then seemed to change his mind. "Ky, I agree with her. We need to talk to Ian. At the very least, we need to tell him Zoey's missing and see if he has any ideas where to look for her. As for the book, it's magical."

Mack paused before continuing. "Of course, we're curious. But we all agreed it was safer kept between you and Zoey. We're not asking you to give it up. We're asking you to let us be in the room when you use it to talk to Ian."

It seemed as though Mack was getting through to Kyro. I held my breath waiting for his response.

"Well, Mack, you're my oldest friend. If I can't trust you, I can't trust myself. If you think we should use this book of Zoey's to talk to the wizard, then I guess that's what we should do."

"Great, let's get started," I jumped in.

Kyro held a hand up to stop me. "I'm not giving either of you the book. I'm not saying I don't trust you, but it's not my book to give away. I'll let you both talk to the wizard guy, but if the book belongs to Zoey, it'll stay with me until she comes back. I may not remember her, but it seems like she trusted me with it."

Mack and I spoke at the same time. "Agreed," was my response, and "No problem" was his.

Satisfied with our answers, Kyro walked back toward his room. We followed close behind.

Once we were gathered around the small table in the corner of his room, he pulled the book out of Zoey's bag and set it on the table. Mack made sure the door was secure, just in case the Patrol came back. When everything was ready, Kyro opened the book. He looked at me and asked, "So how does this thing work?"

It was handy that Ian responded since I had no idea.

Kyro, I sense something is wrong. Is that why you've contacted me? Where's Zoey?

"Ian, we have a problem," I said. "Kyro has lost his memories and Zoey's missing. She was here last night and gone this morning. The Planet Patrol searched the boat for her, and they couldn't find her either. Of course, we're glad they didn't find her since they wanted to arrest her for murder. But that's not the important part. Do you have any idea where she could be? Where do we start looking for her?" I probably shouldn't have jumped in, but it was easier to explain it all this way, and Kyro seemed relieved I had taken over this part.

seventeen

Ian

WHAT DO YOU MEAN, she's gone? Gone where? She couldn't have just disappeared. That's not possible. You'll have to go looking for her.

"That's why we came to you. You can tell us where to start looking." Q took the lead on talking.

What makes you so sure I know where she went? You should be looking for her, not questioning me. How long has she been gone?

"We never said that, you know. We figured you'd have an idea of who could have taken Zoey and made Kyro lose his memories. Just point us in the right direction. Near as I can tell, she's only been gone a few hours." Mack was pissed about the whole situation.

Wait—Kyro? You don't remember anything? How much time is missing?

"Well, sir, I'm not sure. Mack and his friend both keep telling me that I know the girl they're asking you about, but I have no memories of her. I don't even know how Q got here, or Mack, for that matter. The last I remembered, Mack and Gill were in Africa."

Mack piped in, "It seems as if he's lost about six weeks."

That's no good. We'll never find the pearls or dodecahedron without Zoey. But even if she was here, we need Kyro's memories as well.

"What pearls? Could someone please tell me exactly what we're looking for and why my memories are so important?" Kyro yelled. Mack and Q shrugged, indicating they had no idea what Ian was talking about.

Well, I had hoped you'd realize it on your own, but as it seems that just isn't possible right now, I'll tell you. At some point in the past few years, you came into possession of one of the pearls. It would be about palm-sized and one of three colors. One is white, one is red, and one is purple. I have no idea which one you had, and I have no indication that you still have it, but I had hoped you would remember what had become of it. I also held out hope that you would be willing to help Zoey find it. My sources may have been wrong, though.

Kyro's face stilled. "You want the pearl? That's the whole reason all of this is happening? Why should I give it to you? I don't even know what it does. What reason do I have to trust you? You just admitted that you held information back from us at the very least, and at most, you lied directly to us. For what? What do you hope to gain by gathering these pearls and whatever that another thing was?" His voice kept rising as he spoke. It was one of the few times I was glad I was on the other end of this book.

So, you do still have it? That's fantastic. Which one do you have? I have leads on the other two but nothing concrete on the dodecahedron. Now we just need to find Zoey and get the plan back on track.

Seeing how upset Kyro was becoming, Mack stepped in to defuse the situation. "Would you just explain to him—and the rest of us—exactly what you want with the pearls and dodecahedron? And tell the whole truth this time. Then we can talk about which pearls we need to search for once we find Zoey." It was apparent Mack wasn't going to let Kyro tell me which pearl he had or where he had it stored.

Fine. I'll tell you what I can. I trust Zoey has filled you in on what happened to cause magic to run rampant?

Q stepped in this time. "She said it was something you and your friends had done and that you are trying to undo it."

Good. That's exactly right. We made a mistake, and I need the pearls and dodeca to correct it. The power contained in those items will allow me to close the rift I accidentally opened. This rift led to the creation of The Order of Orpheus and eventually to Earth's near destruction. A ritual uses these magical items to close the rift and take the magic from those who weren't born with it. That would solve the most significant problems. After that, we may have to work a little harder to make this world a better place.

"That's all well and good, Ian, but lying to people isn't going to get you what you want. We're not going to help you until we're convinced you're not lying about any of what you've told us. And I'm not sure how to tell right now." With that, Kyro walked out of the room.

Wait. Where is he going? We need to find Zoey. She must continue her mission. You don't understand how important this is. Without her, I can't fix this. Please. What if whatever happened to him also happened to her? What if she's lost somewhere without her memories?

"We'll talk to him. But you need to tell us if you have any ideas or thoughts or sources to help us find her. We're worried about her, too." Q was showing a softer side today. I wondered what had changed her.

She turned and whispered something to Mack, and then he left the room. Her attention then turned back to me and the book.

"You can either tell me what I need to know, or I will set this book on fire, and we'll just forget your little mission." She sounded serious. And with her being Ed's descendant, she had the firepower to back it up, as well as the volatile temper to match.

It's probably The Order that has her. But you already knew that. There is nothing I can do to help you find her. If I were physically there, it would be different. My magic barely reaches far enough to talk to you. I can't perform spells through the book. Tell me what you want me to do, and I'll try my best. Please don't abandon the quest. I need this.

"Then you'd better start sharing info."

A moment later, Mack came back, handed a book to Q, and she left.

EIGHTEEN

Mack

AFTER WATCHING THAT EXCHANGE with Ian about Zoey being gone, I was torn between being proud of the way Quinn stood up to the wizard and terrified that she might just set us all on fire and walk away. I was hopeful that we shared feelings, but I didn't know her well enough yet to say for sure. And that was one thing that terrified me about our relationship.

Once Ian had agreed to tell us everything he had told Zoey, Quinn left Kyro and myself with the book and went up on deck. She claimed she needed to clear her head. I had stepped out for a moment earlier and brought her a book on scrying magic I kept in my room. We needed to be ready for any method that might help us find Zoey. I was struggling to pay attention to what Ian was telling us.

"So, there are three pearls and a dodecahedron, and you need all four items to craft the spell to bring magic back under control? Is that what you're telling us?" Kyro wanted it spelled out in black and white.

Precisely. Once magic is under control again, there will be no need for The Order or the Patrol to chase after enchanted items. And as I will be completing the spell in your past, that means neither organization will be created. Once the spell is complete, the only people who will possess magic will be those born with it.

That idea sounded pretty good to me. That meant I would lose what little magic I had learned, but I had dealt with plenty of magic-wielders who weren't born with it and had instead found a way to take someone else's magic as their own. Most of them were power-hungry and immoral.

As soon as we finished with Ian, Kyro placed the book back in the backpack and turned to me. "Do you think we can find her? And should we be helping this guy? We don't really know much about him." It would be fairly easy to latch onto Kyro's doubts and just abandon the mission. It wasn't our mission in the first place.

"If you want to look for her, we will. I'd like to know that she's safe. But as for completing Ian's mission without her, I understand your hesitation. I'm not sure we can trust him either."

He stood up and began to walk toward the door. "We have no idea where to even begin looking for her. I would love to find her, but I can't see racing all over with nothing to tell us if we're going the right way."

Suddenly, something hit me. Kyro knew how to scry. Maybe Quinn wouldn't need that book after all. "What about a scrying spell? Could you find her with that?"

"It's possible. But without memories of her, I'm not sure I could make it work. I need my memories back. Maybe Ari or Isa can help." And he took off toward the deck. I imagined that I could hear the splash as he dove off the boat and swam down to his father's kingdom to ask the girls for help.

With Kyro gone, it was just me and Quinn. Gods help us. This could get rough. It seemed to me that neither of us was sure how to feel about what had happened between us. And I still hadn't found a good way to bring it up with her.

I paced back and forth in the galley, trying to work out exactly what I was feeling. I had seen this woman at her best, but I feared I hadn't come close to seeing her worst. I wasn't entirely sure I could handle it.

NINETEEN

q

I COULDN'T SIT THERE and watch Ian manipulate us any longer. I needed to call in to base and discover if it really was The Order who had Zoey. But I couldn't do that with Mack or Kyro hanging around. Even though I didn't trust the wizard, I knew he was right. We needed to find her, and fast.

I chose my moment and stormed off in a huff. I wasn't nearly as upset as I made it look. I just needed to make sure neither of them followed me. Once the door closed behind me, I made a beeline for the upper deck. The moment the wind hit my face, I pulled out my comm device, looking around as I dialed.

"Q, is everything OK?" The voice on the other end sounded slightly strained.

"Not exactly, James. I have a problem, and I need some answers." James cleared his throat. "How can I help?"

"Zoey is missing. I need to know if The Order has her, or if the Patrol got to her first. Can you do some research for me?"

"Absolutely. Just tell me what you need. I'm on it." James was always the most helpful of my coworkers. He never complained about my moods and would defend me to the end.

After explaining to James what I needed, I disconnected the call. He'd find the answers I was looking for and get back with me soon. With any luck, I'd find out today who had Zoey.

I stood there staring out at the sea, letting my mind wander. It seemed as though my thoughts were planning to settle on Mack for the foreseeable future. I didn't mind, but I wasn't sure anything real would come of it. There were moments when I wished I could be just a regular person, but at the same time, I couldn't give up my career. *Career, ha! That's a good one. More like obsession.*

To be fair, capturing the Chairman *had* become an obsession for me. I can't even count the number of times it almost got me killed. We were close this time, I could feel it. A part of me couldn't help but wonder what would happen if I did find him. What if we actually caught him? Would I just go off and live my life as though this whole thing had never happened? Or would it be nearly impossible to move on?

I tried to avoid thinking about Mack and my emerging feelings for him. There was no way a real relationship would work between us. We were two totally different people. He was sweet and kind, and I was, well, a bitch. He deserved so much better. I would have to make him see that at some point. *But it couldn't hurt to enjoy his company for a few more days, could it?* I tried to convince myself that it couldn't hurt, but I knew better. I was convinced I didn't deserve to be happy, so I would find a way to screw it up before it got too serious anyway.

I couldn't stop myself from going back and forth on the situation. I was a very decisive person, so for this to bother me as much as it did, I knew it was a big choice. Maybe I would just let it be and see what happens. I'll leave it up to the universe, even though I would call someone else stupid for that very thing. I didn't believe in fate. I made my own choices.

I was just aggravating myself more and more. I walked from the bow of the boat to the stern, where we had our mats set up for training. There were makeshift training dummies as well, and I decided to take some frustration out on one.

I kicked the dummy in the head, then punched it in the gut. I practiced tactical maneuvers like rolling out of the way of strikes. Then I just unloaded on the poor inanimate thing. I punched until my knuckles bled, and there was almost nothing left of the dummy. By the time I was finished, I didn't have the strength to fight the tears anymore. I sat down next to the destroyed practice dummy and cried until there were no more tears.

I knew there was no way I could explain to Kyro and Mack why I am the way I am. I wasn't even sure I could explain it to myself. I felt different with Zoey gone and Kyro's memories missing as well. It was like a part of me was missing. I didn't know how to fill that void, so I took it out on people.

I knew I could have been nicer to Kyro, and there was a tiny voice in my head scolding me every time I snapped at him. But the bitchy voice took over, and I didn't give myself time to think about it. That voice kept me from feeling the pain of my actions over the years, and I was grateful for it.

Acting hateful had always been my way of dealing with things I didn't want to face. It was part of the reason I ended up in the Resistance. That and the fact I was good at keeping secrets. I was learning more and more that it was hard to earn trust when there were so many secrets around.

Maybe it was time to try a different approach. Maybe I should be nice and helpful. *Yeah, and maybe I should just walk the plank now and get it over with.* There was no way my friends wouldn't be suspicious if I suddenly started acting completely different than I had for the past few weeks.

I would have to find another way. I was starting to get tired of always manipulating people into doing what I needed them to do. But that was the story of my life so far. The transition from being the person who was manipulated to being the one doing the manipulation was a large part of what shaped me into who I am today. It was so hard for me to not be selfish. I'd been on my own for so long.

I knew I wouldn't be here if I hadn't figured out how to turn it around and use what I had learned against everyone around me.

That ability was hard-learned in the camp where I grew up. I had told Zoey and Kyro that I knew my family, but that had mostly been a lie. I knew for a fact that my ancestor Ed had passed from old age, but only because I had researched my family tree.

My childhood was difficult, growing up in the magic camp that had been set up by The Order. I wasn't sure if my new friends were aware that those places even existed. I wasn't planning to be the one to tell them. Thinking about it now, my childhood may be the reason I have so much trouble trusting people, and why I keep suspecting my new friends of working with the enemy.

Maybe I secretly suspected myself of being a sleeper agent. Perhaps I was terrified that I could end up doing to my friends all the horrific things that were done to me as a child. I knew in my heart that I would never let that happen. I'd die first.

TWENTY

Trav

I SAW FLASHES, MEMORIES that weren't mine, things that would happen in the future, and things that had happened in the past. I wasn't sure where this power had come from, but a name kept coming up in my mind. Ian.

I needed to find this guy and ask him what all of this was about, but I had no idea how to do that while I was stuck in this cell. I would have to find a way for Gill and me to get out of here. Perhaps the Chairman would find another mission for Gill, and I would be able to convince him that I was needed for the mission to succeed. But that was risky, so it would take quite a bit of planning.

"Gilly? Are you awake?" I didn't want to bother him, but I needed to do some spell work, and it was easier if he was sleeping. I couldn't block his energy as well if he was awake.

He grunted in response, then rolled over and started to snore lightly. I chuckled and whispered the words to a spell that would open his airways and stop the snoring. I could have used a sleep spell on him, but he was a skilled enough sorcerer that he would know someone had done it, and then he'd start asking questions again.

Now that I was convinced he was sleeping soundly and wouldn't be waking up to interrupt my spellcasting, I could get started. I laid back on the bed beside him and meditated until I was relaxed and could easily send my soul out to search for this Ian who kept coming up in my dreams. Astral projection had always come easy to me. Controlling where I ended up was the hard part.

This time, I found myself on a boat in the middle of the ocean. The crew was sparse and in the middle of a heated argument about someone who was missing. One of them said they should ask Ian. That caught my attention. It couldn't be a coincidence that they had just said the name that had been following me.

I stepped closer to hear more clearly. There were three of them, two men and a woman. One of the men had dark curls and tanned skin, the other was slightly less tanned with hair the color of flames. The woman was tall, with crimson hair that hung almost to her knees. The debate appeared to be getting more heated.

I wasn't sure if this was happening currently, or if I was seeing the past or future. It was difficult to discern between time periods of the visions when it was close to the present. If it had been hundreds or thousands of years in either direction, I would at least know by the clothing that it wasn't the present.

The argument seemed to be settled, and the three of them went below deck. As I didn't have to worry about doors, I followed. I watched as the dark-haired guy pulled a book out of a pink haversack, placed it on the table and turned to the woman. They exchanged a glance, then began to talk to the book.

I was momentarily confused, then I realized they were calling the book Ian. Either Ian was tech disguised to look like a book, or he was a sorcerer trapped inside one. I'm sure there were other possibilities, but those were the two I came up with off the top of my head.

I needed to get more information about these people and this book. If I knew where they were, or who they were, I might have a chance to figure out why the name Ian kept coming up in my dreams. I wasn't sure if I was supposed to help him or defeat him.

Suddenly, my soul shivered. I knew this meant Gill was awake and shaking me. If I didn't go back, he would start to worry, and then he would start trying healing spells. It was sweet, but unnecessary. My heart ached to leave without the answers I needed. I didn't have a choice, though. I had to go back to protect Gill.

Just as I suspected, Gill was gently shaking me when I woke up. "I'm up. What's wrong?" I tried to keep the irritation I was feeling out of my voice. He didn't seem to notice.

"I thought you were having a bad dream. Then you didn't wake up right away. I was starting to worry that something was wrong." He was so sweet.

Another pang of guilt smacked me in the face for continuing to lie to this man. As much as I wanted to avoid it, I knew at some point the truth would come out. I didn't want it to happen here, though. If there was a chance Gill would hate me forever, I wanted him to be able to get away from me if he chose.

"I'm fine. It was just a dream. It's gone now. And I'm safe because you're here. Will you hold me for a while?" It may have been unfair to distract him with snuggling, but I had done worse in the past to avoid a conversation about my powers.

twenty-one

Kyro

AFTER MAKING SURE THE book was secured, I took off to clear my head. I was planning to talk to Ari, and maybe Isa. Mostly, I just needed a few minutes to process what we had just been told. I ran up on the deck and, just as quickly, jumped off into the water. I planned to swim for a bit, then call to Ari.

I made it about twenty feet from the boat before I noticed the storm clouds roll in. This didn't appear to be a regular storm, though. It seemed the clouds were laced with magic. I had watched my father do this trick once or twice to frighten an enemy away from a treasured item or a person in harm's way.

There hadn't been any storms I could remember in a while. Of course, with the memory loss, I may have just not known. I turned my back on my boat once more and swam a few feet further. When I turned again, it appeared as though my boat was gone. The storm had taken over that area, and the rain was like an opaque sheet falling from the sky.

I didn't see the haze settling over me until it was too late. I had already inhaled the fumes before I realized it was part of the storm.

I woke up in a tank, onboard a boat. This vessel was similar to mine, but where we had a training area, this one had tanks. Each tank had a different creature in it. One contained a giant sea turtle. Another had trapped an enormous electric eel. I was in the third one, and there was a fourth that appeared to be empty, though I could sense its occupant. That octopus was really good at camouflage; it blended in perfectly with the boards on the deck below the tank.

I had no doubt this was a smuggling vessel. If I could get out of the tank, I would change back to my human form. I could only imagine the confused looks that would get from whoever had captured me. This boat didn't look familiar and we were currently in waters I know—I couldn't rule out the possibility I had been captured by The Order.

I knew better than to go off half-cocked when I was upset, but I did it anyway. Now I'm stuck in this tank alongside these other poor creatures who have no chance of escaping. I wondered if I could send a message to Ari from here.

I remembered her instructions on how to cast the message spell. I just needed to clear my mind and concentrate on her. Then she should be able to astrally project into my thoughts. I took deep breaths as I closed my eyes.

Once I had cleared my mind, I thought of Ari and my desire to talk to her. In just a few moments, she appeared in my mind as though she was standing in front of me. "Ari! This is an amazing spell. You can hear me, right?"

"Yes, Kyro, of course, I can. I came as soon as you called. What's wrong?" Ari seemed worried, which could be good or bad, depending on what she had on her mind.

"Well, I'm stuck in a tank on a boat. I'm not sure who caught me, but they used a magic fog to do it. Is there anything you can do to help?"

"Oh, no! That's not good at all! I feel like there's more you're not telling me though."

"OK, you got me. Zoey is missing, and I honestly can't remember her. I've had vague flashes, but I don't know who she is. Mack and his friend are set on finding her, but I just don't understand why it's so important."

Ari looked defeated. "I was worried about this. I had a vision of something happening. In this vision, you abandoned the quest because your memories were gone. It didn't end well for anyone."

"Wow, you don't usually tell anyone about your visions of the future. What's the big deal?" I needed to understand why this mission was so important.

"I shouldn't have said that. It has to be your choice. Anything I tell you could take that choice away from you, and that would be worse than the alternative." Ari wasn't giving up anything. I hated it, but I understood.

"Well, I can't do anything from here. I'm trapped, so unless you have an idea of how to help me escape, I'm not going to be much help on Zoey's quest." I knew there had to be a way out of this tank, but I had no idea what I would encounter once I was free.

Ari's brow knitted in thought. "Have you tried anything yet?"

I shook my head. "No, I just called you. I didn't try anything else."

"Well, surely you can think of something. I may be able to alert the others, but I can't come up with anything else useful. I'm sorry. I'll let you know if I think of anything that might work." And with that, Ari's image disappeared.

TWENTY-TWO

Zoey

IT SEEMED LIKE IT took forever for Mama and Elena to get everything ready for me and Jack to leave. Apparently, there was some concern that we would give away the location of their secret island base if we just left. I felt like the whole thing was ridiculous, but Jack seemed to understand the concern. I was anxious to get back to the quest, and if I was being honest, to Kyro.

Jack and Elena spent a few more hours together while Mama ironed out details with Al, who would be driving the boat to take us back to Kyro's boat. Al appeared to be in his thirties and had shaggy looking dark hair. He was shorter than me and was husky for a human.

This left me with time to wait, and I was more nervous by the minute. By the time everything was set for us to leave, I was practically jumping out of my skin.

"Remember, you can only contact me if it's an emergency. I can't be connected to your escape from the Patrol at all. It will jeopardize the entire mission." Mama was adamant that I give the comm device to Jack, because she didn't trust me with the no contact restriction.

"I know, Mama, I gave Jack the comm. I promise, we're not going to do anything to hurt the mission."

Once her fears were acknowledged and settled, we climbed into the boat. It was white with red accents. It appeared to be styled after an ancient fishing trawler. The boat was about a hundred and twenty-five feet long. The bedrooms were small, but the common area was large enough for Jack and me to hang out if we wanted.

Jack and I would have to stay below deck for most of the trip, so we couldn't figure out where the secret island was. It didn't matter to me, but it seemed important to Mama, so I didn't argue. I didn't want to jeopardize her job. Soon enough, I would be free to stand on deck while sailing across the ocean. I could handle hiding for a bit, knowing I was heading for my freedom.

It was late afternoon when the boat finally left the island. There was nothing for us to do except wait for Al to locate Kyro's boat and plot an interception course. Jack went off to make use of the gym equipment that was just up the hall from the galley.

I settled in on a couch in the common room with the tablet Mama had given to Jack. I had decided to read through everything about The Order of Orpheus again and see if I could figure out any new information from the articles. I must have dozed off from the rocking of the boat, because I woke to an alarm blaring.

"Jack? Why's that alarm going off? What's happening?" I groggily pulled myself off the couch and secured the tablet in my knapsack. Jack wasn't in the common room, and the alarm sounded like it was getting louder. I pulled my arms through the straps on the knapsack and walked down the hall to look for him. I knew I couldn't afford to panic, but I was on the brink. When Jack wasn't in the gym, I jogged back to the galley. He wasn't there either.

I knew we were supposed to stay below deck, but with that alarm going off, I needed to find Jack and see what was happening. I quickly climbed the stairs and opened the door that led to the deck. That was when I realized why the alarm was going off.

Above the boat was a dark gray storm cloud, and the rain was coming down in sheets. There was very little visibility, and it didn't look like anyone was on deck. I fought my way to the wheelhouse, looking for Al. When I made it across the deck to the bridge, Al was fighting to keep the boat upright. The storm seemed determined to flip us.

"Al! Have you seen Jack? I couldn't find him below." I had to yell for him to hear me.

He nodded. "He's trying to secure some of the equipment so we don't lose everything to the storm. He told me to keep you here if you came up."

The storm raged on, tossing the boat back and forth on the biggest waves I had ever seen. Luckily for me, there were reinforced steel bars attached to the wall for just such an occasion. I held onto that bar tighter than I thought possible, as the boat pitched and tossed. I was terrified that Jack had been lost to the storm, but there was no way I could go back out there. The storm had grown more ferocious since I made it to the bridge.

It was so dark, and with the waves and rain, I couldn't see anything out the windows. I kept searching for any sign that Jack was alive, but I couldn't find anything.

Suddenly there was a crash of water against the glass separating the bridge from the elements outside. I threw my arm over my face to shield it from the fragments of glass and the rush of water as the window burst. I held the steel bar with my other hand and prayed I wouldn't get swept away.

When I lowered my arm from my face, I saw Jack on the other side of the window, holding onto the railing just a few feet away from where I was. He was fighting to hold on the same as me. It was a relief to see he was OK.

I saw a movement to my left and turned in time to see Al get bitten in half by a massive great white shark that had been ushered onto the now sinking boat by the wave that had ripped half the bridge off. A scream tore through the air, and after a moment, I realized it was coming from me. I held my breath as another wave crashed through the bridge, taking the shark and Al's body with it as it receded.

I tried to calm myself, but I was in a panic. I looked back to where Jack had been just before the last wave came through. The railing was still there, but Jack wasn't. "I can't do this by myself. Jack! Jack!" I started yelling for him, even though I knew he couldn't hear me over the storm. Another wave crashed over the boat, and it was clear we were sinking. I needed to move, but wasn't sure where to go, or how to get there without being washed away. I turned my head back and forth looking for Jack, while I got lashed by the sheets of rain.

Just before the next wave crashed over me, Jack grabbed my arm. He had popped up behind me, although I had no idea how he got there.

"Zoey, we have to go. I got the life raft set up, but we have to go now. The boat's going down, and if we don't leave now, we'll be dragged under with it."

"Can we make it to the raft from here?" I was terrified to let go of the bar that I was gripping.

Jack took my free hand, and I looked at him. "We have to. Your quest is too important not to make it. Do you trust me?"

"Of course, I do, Jack. Let's do this."

Still holding Jack's hand, I let go of the bar. Another wave crashed over us, tossing us toward the back of the trawler. Luckily, that's where the life raft was tethered. Unfortunately, that's the part of the boat that was going underwater first. The railing Jack had tied the raft to was sinking fast.

"OK, Zoey, I need you to get in the raft and hold on tight to the rope. Don't let go, no matter what. I'm going to untie the raft, and then I'll get in."

I did as he asked and watched him dive below the surface to untie the rope tethering the raft to the boat. I knew what he was risking by going below the surface. My heart raced as I waited for him to return. The rain and waves beat down on me, and I worried the raft would go under too.

Just as the raft started to dip and my fears seemed destined to emerge as reality, Jack's hand broke the surface and grabbed the edge to pull himself in. Once he was in the raft, he unstrapped the oars from the side and handed me one. We rowed as if our lives depended on it...because they did.

I had no idea how long we had been rowing, but we managed to put enough distance between our raft and the boat to not be pulled under as it sank. The storm fizzled out, and we took a break from rowing.

TWENTY-THREE

Jack

Zoey leaned back against the edge of the raft, dropping her oar into the middle of the tiny boat. I could tell she was exhausted physically and emotionally from what we had just been through. And now that we had lost everything with the trawler sinking, I wasn't sure how we would manage to find Kyro and get Zoey back to her quest. I refused to admit defeat. I would find a way to get us where she needed to be.

"Just relax for a while, Zo. I'm wiped, too. We can regroup after. I hate that I didn't have more warning. I could have salvaged at least part of our belongings."

She smirked. "Well, I did grab my knapsack. so we do have a few things. Not really anything that will help us here." She pulled the bag off her back and opened it to judge the contents. I didn't know what most of it was, but she had little bags and jars of what looked like herbs and oils. Then she pulled out the one thing I had forgotten about—the comm device Mama Bear had given us.

Seeing the look of shock on my face, she handed the comm device to me. "Zo, this is amazing. This could get us saved." I turned it on and checked for signal. "The storm must have knocked some towers out. I can't get signal. You don't have the tablet in there, do you?"

Zoey laughed as she pulled the tablet out of her bag. "What can I say? After I snuck the comm device out of your jacket, I figured I'd keep that and the tablet in my bag just in case." She handed it to me in trade for the comm, which she secured in her bag.

"This is fantastic! This has sailing charts and maps. We should be able to figure out where they are and find them. I don't know how long it will take, but hopefully we'll get signal on the comm soon and be able to call." The sinking feeling I'd been carrying in my chest since the boat went down finally eased. We really could make it.

That spark of hope was all I needed. And with the tablet, I had just enough signal to send a message. We may not be able to call, but I'd be able to at least let Elena know we were alive. I checked the charts, noting that Kyro's last known position was marked. Now I just had to figure out where we were.

"I don't suppose you have any idea how to read these charts? Or how to figure out where we are?" I asked.

"Oh, Jack. Do you really think I spent all that time in the library and didn't learn how to read sailing charts? It's a good thing I read almost every book in there and have a pretty good memory." I couldn't tell if she was kidding with me or if she really had read that many books. "Let me see the tablet. I may remember how to figure it out after I see them."

I handed the tablet over to her and watched her face as she examined the charts. "Well?" I tried to hide my anxiety, but I was sure I failed.

She looked up at me and made a face. I couldn't tell what she was thinking. "Zoey, please, just tell me. Can you figure it out?"

She looked around us for a moment, then turned back to me. She was still making that face I couldn't read. It was going to make me crazy. She looked back down at the tablet and tapped a couple of on-screen buttons. Then she looked at me again.

"Sorry, Jack, I'm really not trying to drive you crazy. I know this does, though. I think I can figure it out, but not until the sun sets. I need to see which direction we're heading, then I need to see where the stars are in relation to that. Once it starts to get dark, we're going to be closer to an answer."

It wasn't what I wanted to hear, but it was better than giving up. Just knowing that I had managed to keep her safe meant the world to me. I couldn't take it if anything happened to her. I'd spent half my life looking after her. I wouldn't change a moment of it, except maybe the moment I told her we couldn't be together because of Race. I might have sometimes wished that moment never happened. But now she had Kyro, and I had Elena. As long as she was happy, I knew we'd be OK.

Becoming uncomfortable with my train of thought, I tried to maneuver my thoughts to the present. I looked around us to see if I could figure out how long we had until sunset. Now that the storm was over, the sun was almost directly overhead. I thought it was a safe assumption that it was around midday. "Well, we have a while until sunset. We should probably try to rest for a while."

Zoey nodded and tucked the tablet back in the safety of her bag. Luckily, we had both worn long sleeves today, so we didn't have to worry too much about sunburn. Of course, with my genetic makeup, it would take days for me to burn, but I didn't expect Zoey to remember that little fact from when we were kids. I would have happily given her my shirt to keep her from dealing with a sunburn.

She rested her arms on the edge of the raft, then laid her head on them. Within five minutes, she was snoring softly. I kept an eye out for any indication that we were getting close to land or another boat. I didn't think I could sleep. There was too much running through my head. There were too many ways that something bad could happen to her if I fell asleep too. I watched her sleep for a bit, then decided that was a little bit creepy, so I turned in a way that I could still see her, but I also could watch the water rise and fall with the waves.

I saw the fog in the distance, in the direction we were headed. It didn't occur to me that it could be a problem. The raft was solid, and I could see well enough in difficult atmospheres. As we got closer, I realized the fog was different than any I'd ever seen. Once it was almost on top of us, I could see through it ten feet or so, and I realized it wasn't fog at all. It was a smokescreen to hide the boat.

It looked to be a fishing boat, somewhat bigger than the trawler we had been on this morning. As we got even closer, I could make out cages on the deck of the boat. That didn't look good. I'd heard that poaching seemed to be making a comeback down here on Earth. I had also turned down several of the guys I worked with on Calliope who had offered to take me on "fishing" expeditions. I knew what they were really doing and wanted no part of it. I wondered what poor creatures had managed to get themselves captured by the ones operating this ship. If our current course kept up, we'd be finding out soon.

"Zoey, wake up. We've got company." I nudged her gently as I spoke in a hushed tone.

She jumped at my touch, then settled when her eyes met mine. I couldn't be sure if she had been having a nightmare or if I just surprised her that much by waking her up. I pointed at the boat next to us.

"I think it's a poaching ship. Do you think we should try to board and see if there are any innocent creatures we can free while these people take us to your boy's boat?" I said as I cocked an eyebrow and gave her a sheepish grin.

She gave the boat a once over, then returned her eyes to mine. "Do you think they'll let us board?"

"Let's find out." I dug a flare out of the emergency kit on the raft and shot it out above the boat. Sure enough, two heads popped up over the railing on the side of the boat to see where the flare had come from.

One of them called out to us. "Are you all right? Do you need help?"

I waved at them and called back. "Our boat was sunk in a storm this morning. We could use a ride, if you have room."

The two heads disappeared for a moment. I assumed they would have to talk about letting alien beings on board. Who knows if they had ever seen anything like the two of us? One of them came back to the edge. "We'll throw a ladder down for you. Climb up, and we'll see if we can help you out."

Zoey and I exchanged a look. I shrugged, and she put her knapsack back on after securing it closed. I helped her get situated on the rope ladder our new hosts had rolled out for us, then followed her up. Once we were on the deck of the boat, I looked around to see what they had in the cages. We were still too far away to tell, but I could see that they were actually tanks with water in them.

We found ourselves in the presence of our new hosts, a man and a woman. They rolled the ladder back up, then introduced themselves. He was tall and thin, with brown hair that was thinning on top. She was shorter and a bit heavier, with blond hair that was pulled back in a ponytail.

I'm Chris, and this is Katie," he said as he gestured to her.

"Welcome to our boat. What happened to y'all? Why were you out here on that raft?" Katie had a lot of questions and probably would have kept asking if Chris hadn't nudged her in the ribs.

"Katie, honey, let's give them a minute to breathe before we start the inquisition." Chris chuckled, as though trying to make his statement seem less threatening.

I decided I'd better offer them some kind of explanation before I asked to use their comm system. I was planning to turn them in for poaching, then rough them up if they tried to fight me.

"It's fine, Chris. We have nothing to hide. I'm Jay, and this is my girl, Zee. We were taking a boat trip to visit some friends when we hit a storm. The Captain and crew were lost, and the boat sank. It was pure luck that we managed to get to the lifeboat." I looked at Zoey to make sure she understood why I had embellished the truth. She smiled up at me, and I knew she would go along with my story.

"I was so scared that we'd be in that raft all day and not find anyone or land, and we'd have to spend the night in it. Thank you for saving us." Zoey really laid it on thick, but our hosts didn't seem to notice. She went above and beyond by insisting to hug Chris and Katie to show her gratitude.

Katie smiled at her. "It's no problem. I'm glad we found you. These waters aren't safe. There are so many monsters out here."

Chris grabbed her arm and she stopped talking. "Now, honey, we don't want to scare them. Why don't you go see about some food for our guests?"

Then he turned back to us. "It's safe here, she just gets a little dramatic. You don't have to worry about it anymore."

Zoey gave him a relieved smile that said she was happy to be here. I shook his hand and thanked them again for letting us come aboard.

"Is there someone you need to call? Or can we drop you off somewhere?" Chris seemed helpful, but maybe a little too helpful.

I nodded. "Actually, it'd be great if we could let Zee's mom know we're safe. She probably heard about the boat by now, and I'd bet she's worried sick. Do you have a radio or comm system on board?"

He nodded and gestured for us to follow him. I knew I would have to be slick to get privacy for the call. I hoped Zoey would cooperate. Once we were on the bridge, Chris showed me to the radio.

I turned to Zoey and prayed this would work. "Are you feeling alright, babe? You look a little sick."

Right on cue, she put her hand over her face. "Oh, the room is spinning. I don't feel so good. I might throw up." She took it even further by making herself gag. It was pretty convincing, even though I knew she was faking it.

"Chris, would you take her to get some fresh air? She seems to get seasick when she's inside. It usually gets better out in the breeze. I can manage the radio. Thanks, man."

He took the bait and gently grabbed Zoey's arm. "Come on, dear, I'll help you outside." She made sure to keep the act up until they were out on the deck. I could see them through the window on the door to the bridge. He seemed concerned that she might get sick.

I took advantage of the moment of privacy and called Mama Bear. I knew it was a risk, but I had the feeling we were in trouble. I got through to her and made sure she knew I couldn't wait for responses.

I told her in code about our situation, making sure she knew that the little blue package was still with me and had not been delivered yet. I barely had time to disconnect the call and wipe the history before Chris came back inside.

"Did you get it taken care of?" He asked me, and I wondered if he was suspicious. I had hoped to be completely done by the time he came back.

I nodded and tried my best to look confused. "I'm not good with all this tech stuff. I think I deleted something when I disconnected.

Is it messed up?" I stepped back to let him check it out. I looked out the window and saw Zoey walking toward the tanks we had seen earlier. It was my turn to be the distraction.

"Oh, it looks like you just wiped the call log. That's not a big deal. You should have told me you didn't know how to use this model. I could have had Katie come up and take care of Zee while I helped you call." He seemed sincere, but I still didn't trust him.

"It's fine. I figured out how to call. I just wasn't sure how to disconnect and ended up clearing the log. I'm sorry. I hope that doesn't inconvenience you any more than we already have."

"Nah, man, you're fine. Those logs didn't have anything important on them. Don't worry about it. Let's go down and get dinner. I'm sure Katie has it done by now. Do you think Zee will be able to eat?"

"I hope so. She hasn't had anything all day, with the storm and all. Thanks again for helping us. We really appreciate it." My stalling wasn't going to work for much longer. Chris was set on heading down to the galley for dinner. I couldn't blame him. We honestly hadn't eaten anything all day because of the storm and trying to survive.

Zoey wasn't where he had left her, so I asked more questions about the boat to distract him while giving her time to get back. He didn't seem suspicious and answered my questions. He seemed like he enjoyed showing off his boat.

TWENTY-FOUR

q

I WAS JUST STEPPING out of the shower when I got the call. I grabbed my towel and dove for the comm device, not knowing if Mack was in the room or not. I knew it had to be headquarters or James, and I didn't really want to explain either right now.

I glanced around the room as I picked up the device and silenced its ring. I was alone, so I quickly wrapped the towel around myself and answered the call. "What is it?"

"Wow, am I interrupting something? You said to call as soon as I knew anything about what may have happened to Zoey. I can call back later if you're busy." James tried to sound sincere, but I knew him well enough to detect a hint of sarcasm. He knew I needed that intel.

I rolled my eyes and laughed. "I'm not busy, just got out of the shower. What have you got?"

"I figured you'd want to know...I just intercepted a transmission from a fishing boat to the Patrol."

"What does that have to do with Zoey?" I huffed my irritation at James. "Well?"

"Geez, boss, give a guy a second to create a dramatic pause, would ya?" James quipped back.

"OK, OK. Drama achieved. Now please tell me, before I find a way to come through this comm device and kick your ass."

He laughed at the empty threat. "You and I both know you love me too much to do that. Anyway, back to what I was telling you. I intercepted a call from that fishing boat to the Patrol. But it was a coded call—the caller used Resistance code to tell whoever answered that they are stuck on a fishing boat. They requested a pick-up."

At this point, I was convinced he was speaking a foreign language. I had no idea what he was trying to tell me. "Would you please just spit it out? I have no idea where you're going with this."

"It's Zoey. Someone else is with her, but I'm sure it's her. The two of them went through a storm, and their boat was sunk. The fishing boat picked them up. With the code the guy was using, he's Resistance, and the person he talked to was called Mama Bear."

I'd started getting dressed as we talked. The mention of Mama Bear stopped me in the middle of fastening my bra.

"Oh, shit. That's huge. She doesn't get involved for minor stuff. And to call her at the Patrol? But that doesn't tell me what makes you think it's Zoey. I'm gonna need more than that to go chasing after a fishing boat."

"Well, his code name was Gecko, and he said he got sidetracked by the storm and wasn't able to deliver the blue package. He asked if they could retrieve it from him and deliver it. I don't know exactly what it was that caught my attention, but I'm sure it's her. If you're not going to go after her, I will." James was getting irritated at me now. I had never questioned his instincts like this before, and I wasn't sure what had me doing it now.

"Hold on, Tex, don't get your panties in a wad. If you think it's her, then it's her. Send me the coordinates, and we'll go get her. I'm sorry I doubted you."

James disconnected the call and sent me the coordinates for the fishing boat. It was closer than I expected. We should be able to get there in a couple of hours. I quickly threw on my jeans and a three-quarter sleeve Henley shirt, and then I ran to find Mack. We needed to get moving.

I knew the name Gecko, and if the stories were true, Zoey was in very capable hands. He was one of the best operatives the Resistance had. I hadn't met him, or Mama Bear for that matter. But I was fairly sure they had heard of me as well. Our group was hidden, but the rumors spread like wildfire.

TWENTY-FIVE

Zoey

ONCE CHRIS WENT BACK inside to check on Jack, I knew this was probably my only chance to check out the tanks and see exactly what we were dealing with. I had to act quickly without drawing attention to where I was going. I risked a glance over my shoulder to make sure Jack saw me. We made eye contact, and I knew he understood what I was doing. He would buy me as much time as he could.

I jogged to the other end of the boat, keeping an eye out for Katie to show up. I relaxed a little when I made it to the tanks without being seen. There were four large tanks, roughly in the same spot as our training area on Kyro's boat. It was strange how the memories came back randomly, and some felt like they were mine while others felt like I was watching someone else.

I was pondering this when I came face to face with the occupants of these tanks. I stifled a scream when the electric eel brushed up against the glass and tried to zap me. I turned around and bumped into the cage next to it. I didn't see anything in this one, but when I looked closer, there was a hint of movement. I guessed it was a giant octopus, because they are the best at camouflage.

I turned and saw an enormous sea turtle in the third tank. It was beautiful, and so sad. I placed my hand on the tank, and the turtle laid its head against my palm through the glass. I wanted nothing more than to free these amazing creatures and force these people to stop trapping them. I would have to talk to Jack about how we could do that.

I shifted slightly and saw movement in the fourth tank. I have no idea how I could have missed the occupant when I first came to the tanks. He was incredible. And the moment his eyes met mine, I knew exactly who he was. I don't know how he got here, but I was staring Kyro in the face. He was looking at me strangely, like he recognized me but didn't know who I was.

I ran to the tank and put my hand on the glass. "Oh, Kyro! I thought I'd never see you again! How did you get here? Where are Mack and Q? What happened?"

He looked at me with confusion in his chocolate eyes. "I'm sorry. Who are you? Can you help me get out of here? You look really familiar. Do I know you?"

My heart shattered at his words. I couldn't respond. I shook my head and turned away as my eyes filled with tears. Either the transporter had caused him to lose his memories too, or these people had done something to him. It didn't matter why—it still hurt that he didn't remember me. I had to get him out of here. I searched for a way to open the tank but couldn't find one. I turned back to Kyro.

"I understand that you don't remember me, and even though I don't know why, I promise we'll fix this. We'll get you out of here, then I'll explain everything. Just stay calm, and I'll be back as soon as I can." He seemed confused but nodded and didn't call out to me when I started to leave.

I turned back to him, unable to leave things the way they were. "I just wanted to tell you that seeing you in this tank hurts me in a way I never knew possible. Even if you never remember me, I want you to know I remember you." I dashed off.

I knew I had been exploring for too long. I had to get back to Jack and our hosts before they suspected anything. I quickly walked around the opposite side of the boat and planned to lie if anyone asked me about seeing the tanks.

I saw Jack and Chris leaving the bridge, and I ducked behind a crate. Jack started asking questions about the boat, and Chris took his time showing Jack different parts of the equipment they used and explaining what it all did. I forced my anger down and quietly crept around to come up behind them.

Jack turned around first. "Oh, there you are, dear."

I hugged him tightly. "Sorry, I took a little walk around the bridge. The fresh air was nice. I saw dolphins playing and followed them for a bit. I hope that's alright." I directed the last statement to Chris, and he nodded. From the look on his face, he wasn't concerned with the tanks or if I had seen them. My guess was that he would expect a reaction from me if I had found his secret.

"Of course. I'm glad you're feeling better. We were just about to head down to the galley for dinner. You up for it?" He seemed relieved I wasn't feeling sick anymore. I guess I was a better actress than I thought.

I gave him a bright smile. "That sounds lovely. I don't think we've eaten all day! I didn't even realize it until just now. Thank you."

We followed him down to the galley. Jack made sure to keep my hand in his, thinking it would sell the idea we were together. Or he was as uncomfortable as I was and wanted to feel close to someone who cared. I really couldn't be sure.

Chris motioned to a table, and Jack held a chair out for me. When Chris walked away to find Katie, Jack leaned close so I could whisper to him.

"What is it? I can tell you found something."

"Kyro is here. He's in one of those tanks. We have to get him out. They have sea creatures trapped too. I just don't know how we'll manage it."

Jack kissed my cheek to keep up appearances. "It's OK, Zo, we'll figure it out. I've called for backup, so we just have to wait. Your mom will send someone to get us." I nodded, though I wasn't sure how I felt about that.

I wished I had that much faith in my mom. I knew it wasn't her fault. This situation was because of that storm. And it led us to Kyro, who needs our help. It had to be fate, right? Besides, I had faith in Jack. If he believed my mom would save us, maybe she would. All we could do was play our parts and wait.

TWENTY-SIX

Mack

QUINN ALMOST RAN OVER me as she sprinted across the deck at the same moment I was walking around the corner from the training area, heading across the deck. I had been working with Mateo. He wanted to be a part of what we were doing. I suspected he was worried that Kyro hadn't come back yet and didn't know what else to do. I couldn't blame him. The workout was a nice distraction.

"Woah, love, slow down. You almost ran me down. What's the problem?" I knew it had to be something big, because other than in combat, she didn't move this quickly.

She stopped, took a deep breath, and then started talking so fast it was hard to keep up.

"Fishing boat...Zoey...some guy...called for help..." She panted once the words stopped.

"OK, love." I rubbed my hand down her back and encouraged her to sit beside me on a crate. "Let's take a minute to collect thoughts and try that again. I didn't understand any of it." I smiled at her as she started to relax.

She nodded. "Sorry, I got excited. James just called me. He intercepted a call from someone to the Patrol. The guy called himself Gecko and said he had the little blue package. There was something about a shipwreck and being picked up by a fishing boat. James got the impression they were in danger. He thinks we can trust the Gecko guy."

She sat there taking deep breaths while I rubbed my hand across her back in large circles. I took a moment to consider what she had just told me.

"All right, so what do you think? Do you agree with James? And how do we find them? Did he have coordinates?" Now I had to stop and take a breath. I was starting to get worked up too.

Quinn chuckled. "I trust James with my life. If he thinks Zoey is there and the other guy can be trusted, I'd stake my life on it. He gave me the coordinates. From the charts, it looks like they're only a couple hours away from here."

"Good, we'll change course and go pick them up. Maybe we'll find Kyro in the process. Mateo is starting to worry about him." I didn't have to say I was too. I knew even after this short time together, she could read me like a book.

"Yeah, I'm starting to worry about him too. Hopefully we'll have our little family back together soon." She slipped her arms around me and pulled me to her for a hug, then kissed me tenderly before letting go.

We changed course to meet with the fishing boat Zoey and her friend were on. Once the boat was on course and Mateo had volunteered to man the helm, Q and I started cleaning up the mess that was left by the Patrol.

By the time Mateo yelled that he could see the fishing boat, we had finished putting everything back where it belonged. At least now when Kyro came back, he wouldn't have to deal with it.

"Mack, I see it. Do you want to call them on the radio?" Mateo called to us as we came on deck. I nodded as we walked over to the comm system Kyro had installed next to the wheel.

Q grabbed the radio and dialed into the usual channel for fishing vessels. Strangely, there was no response. We didn't see anything on deck, but we couldn't just board their boat without cause. That would be a great way to have the Patrol come after us as well as Zoey.

We changed course and decided to try again in a few hours. We might be waiting a day or so. It would probably be a good idea to watch the boat from a safe distance for a time, just to be sure. If our lead was wrong, we didn't want to chance getting locked up. We would just sail back in a while and try to talk to the sailors on the boat. Hopefully they would have some answers.

TWENTY-seven

Jack

As we sat down to eat, I realized something was off with our hosts. They didn't act like a typical couple, but that could be from years on this boat away from society. I knew not all of the inhabitants of Earth had grown up with aliens like myself and Zoey. Because of that, some people were naturally curious, and some even went so far as to stare at us.

I wasn't prepared for the line of questioning that began when we took the offered seats.

"So, what planet are you from? It's obvious you both are aliens. Tell us about your home." Katie started the conversation as if it was perfectly normal.

At least Chris had the decency to look moderately embarrassed by her question, but he didn't bother to comment. He looked as though he had wanted to ask the same thing.

"Well, I'm a Garlax, and Zee is Zyterran. But we both grew up on the space station. Neither of us really knows our home planets." I hoped they would drop that topic and move on.

"I don't understand. How did you come to grow up on the space station? They allow aliens to live there?" Obviously, this conversation wasn't going anywhere. It seemed as though our hosts may have been a little bit racist. This should be fun.

Zoey looked at me, and I subtly shook my head. I didn't want her to feel like she had to defend herself to these people. I would take care of it.

I cleared my throat and gave Chris a look that told him he needed to get his woman under control. Then I turned to Katie. "Yes, aliens can live on the space station. We hold positions there as well. I'm the Head of Engineering, graduated top of my class. You have a problem with that?"

She shrank a little from the harshness of my tone. "Well, I, I mean, I didn't mean anything by it. I just didn't know how things worked up there." Sure, play dumb. I was fairly certain Chris had put her up to the line of questioning anyway, so I didn't hold it against her.

"It's fine. I understand that education here on Earth isn't the same as it is on the space station. It's not surprising you wouldn't understand how things were done up there. Just like I'm sure I don't understand how things are done here." I probably had a better idea than she realized, since half my studies had been completed here, but I wasn't letting that bit of information out.

At this point, I was beginning to wonder why they had rescued us if they were just going to insult us. Then it hit me. They weren't rescuing us; they were trying to capture us. Before I could figure out a way to warn Zoey, she was face down on the table.

"What did you do to her?" I turned to Chris, who was smirking at me.

He shrugged. "I don't know what you mean. I didn't do anything. Did you really think we wouldn't know she was snooping earlier? Faking motion sickness to get a look at our cargo was pretty slick, but we're not going to let you steal it from us."

I balked at him. "We aren't pirates. We were on a boat heading to meet friends, and the boat sank. We told you the truth. What's this all about?"

He pulled a gun out of his coat and waved it back and forth between Zoey and me, as if he was trying to figure out which would keep me in place more easily. He decided it was her and trained the gun on her head. I had to admit, it was smart. There was no way I would fight when it meant anything would happen to Zoey.

"OK, you've got us. Now what? Did you poison her?" I hoped it was just a drug to put Zoey to sleep, but I couldn't be sure what they were thinking.

Chris scoffed at me as though I had hurt his feelings. "I'm not planning to kill either of you. I'm planning to sell you both, along with my cargo that your girlfriend spied on earlier. Altogether, you should bring us quite a profit."

Well, at least I knew he wasn't planning to kill us. Unless he was a psycho and just lied to my face. It was possible, but over the years I had become pretty good at reading people. I felt like he was actually telling the truth.

"All right, what do you want me to do now? And who are you planning to sell us to?" I hoped I could get information from him, but I didn't want to push too far. I didn't want to give him any reason to hurt Zoey. I had to get her back to her mission. That was the most important thing right now.

Chris seemed to ponder for a moment before he answered. "Well, I have some regular connections who buy whatever I catch. But I think I may have to go black market auction to get my money's worth out of you. The hassle will be worth it in the end."

He kept the gun trained on Zoey as Katie picked her up and walked out of the room with her limp body.

I stood up. "Where is she taking Zee?"

"Sit." Chris pointed the gun at me now, and I did as commanded. It grated on me to be ordered around like this, but I had to think about Zoey.

TWENTY-EIGHT

Jack

KATIE YELLED FOR CHRIS once she got Zoey wherever she took her. He pointed the gun at me and motioned to the door. I stood and went with him. There had to be a way to protect her from these crazy people.

I watched in horror as Chris trained the gun at Zoey to keep me in check while Katie implanted a device at the base of Zoey's spine, just below her hairline. I wasn't sure what I'd be able to do once the twin device was implanted in me. But fighting now would make him kill Zoey, and there was nothing that would hurt me more. I hoped there was something in our alien DNA that would block the effect of the devices, but I didn't have much knowledge on that subject.

"Why are you doing this?" I knew it was pointless to ask, but I couldn't resist.

Chris responded without taking his eyes from Zoey or moving the gun. "To control you, of course. We'll use you both as slaves until we find a buyer. Then we'll sell you to whoever offers the most. Don't take it personally, it's just what we do."

"Who are you planning to sell us to? If you need the money, I can get you money." I wondered if I could distract him with an offer of cash.

He raised an eyebrow as if my offer had piqued his interest. "I'll keep that in mind. But for now, I'll be satisfied using you both as slaves. If I change my mind, or can't find buyers, I'll have Katie remove the device, and we'll negotiate."

It pissed me off that he wouldn't listen to me, even more so that I couldn't protect Zoey. I had no idea how this device worked or if we would even know our actions weren't our own.

I watched as Katie pinned Zoey's hair up off her neck. She cleaned the area with medical soaps and alcohol. Then she picked up a scalpel and began to make a three-inch incision at the edge of Zoey's hairline. Katie didn't falter as she implanted the mind control chip into Zoey, then stitched the incision closed and taped a bandage over it.

Once she was done, I knew it was my turn. My heart raced as I held tightly to the hope that the chip wouldn't work. Katie pulled out a syringe to sedate me as Chris gathered Zoey and took her out of the room.

"Can you just do it without drugging me? I can take the pain." I looked at her, pleading with my eyes in an attempt to change her mind.

She scrunched her eyebrows. "I've never implanted one in some-one who was awake. I guess it would tell me how long the device takes to fully integrate itself. Sure, I'll try it. But just know that one wrong move will cause you to be paralyzed or worse."

Since she agreed to my request, I laid on the table and positioned myself face down for the procedure. She pinned my long hair up just as she had done for Zoey, then prepped the back of my neck in the exact same manner. I didn't flinch when I felt the scalpel begin the three-inch incision, but Katie's hands didn't feel as steady as they had looked during Zoey's operation. She implanted the chip, then stitched and bandaged my neck the same as she had done for Zoey.

"Like I said before, I've never done this with someone who was awake. I have no idea what you'll feel. I'm going to monitor your vitals and see if I can tell when the device attaches fully to your nervous system. You can turn over and we'll put the head of the bed up so you can sit up."

I did as she asked without thinking about it. I wasn't sure if it was her suggestion or my own decision to comply. I realized I didn't have much choice, especially with this device in my head.

Before she left, Katie told me to stay put until she returned. I waited until she left, then found myself unable to move from the bed I was sitting on. I took that to mean that the procedure was a success, much to my chagrin. I was hoping to be able to fight it off and keep it from connecting somehow by not letting her knock me out for the operation.

I wasn't sure how I would get us out of this, but I remembered I had called in a distress extraction to Mama Bear. They would have to come get us at some point. I just wasn't sure how she would do it without the Patrol taking Zoey.

In that moment, I remembered Zoey was still somewhere on this boat, suffering from the same problem I was having. I was fairly certain it would be worse for her, since she would have no idea what had happened.

After a few minutes, I found myself hoping Katie would be back soon, so I could leave this room and at least know that Zoey was alright. I had so many more questions I wanted to ask about this procedure. I doubted I would get the chance, but I wouldn't know for sure until she came back.

TWENTY-NINE

Zoey

I WOKE WITH A mild headache and pain at the base of my neck. I tried to bring my hand up to inspect the area, but I couldn't move. Panic engulfed me for a moment. What had happened to paralyze me? The only thing I remembered was being in the galley with Jack, Chris, and Katie. Oh, no. Something had happened, but I had no idea what.

The room I was in was not familiar to me at all. It looked almost like the doctor's suite on Calliope, though I was certain it wasn't. I turned my head to look toward the door. Well, that was something at least. I had control of my mind and my head. Now if I could just get my body to cooperate.

I laid there, concentrating on the tips of my fingers on my left hand until I could feel them twitch. Once I could flex my left hand, I started on my right. Fear crept in that someone would catch me, and I stopped moving every time I heard a noise. I waited a few minutes, then started again. I kept my left hand moving while I worked on my right.

After I had managed to get both hands moving, I decided to start moving toward my shoulders. If I could manage to sit, I would have a better idea of how to get out of here. It was a slow process, and I had to pause a few more times because of noises outside the door. Eventually, I was able to pull myself into a sitting position. Instantly my hands came up to inspect the sore spot behind my head.

I found a small line of stitches. I couldn't stop the twinge of panic at what could have happened to me. I felt normal, other than the obvious incision and stitches. I had an aching urge to find Jack and get out of here. Now that my top half was working, I just had to get my bottom half going again.

Sitting there, staring at the door and willing my feet to move was even more terrifying than when my whole body was immobile. I knew that Chris and Katie must have been the ones to do this to me. I was scared that if I lay back down, I'd never get up again.

I struggled with my feet, then my legs. It felt like I had been in this room forever by the time I was able to stand again. I expected to find the door locked when I finally made my way over. To my surprise, the knob turned and the door opened without any resistance.

I walked out the door and headed down the hall toward the stairs. I climbed the stairs to the deck, my heart pounding more with every step. Freedom was so close I could taste it. I knew I couldn't leave without Jack, but maybe I could at least figure out an exit strategy.

I couldn't help but feel antsy about the whole thing, given the situation. The moment I stepped onto the deck; I knew something was wrong. Something was more than wrong. It was like a force had taken over my body. I couldn't move toward the life rafts or the bridge. I couldn't even make my legs move toward the tanks where Kyro was being held.

I was relieved that I still had my thoughts, but I was terrified that my body would no longer listen to my commands. I tried to run, but my legs didn't respond. I stood there for a while, testing what I was able to do. I had the ability to walk but not in certain directions.

Well, if I can't escape, I might as well look for Jack and see if he's having the same problem. I found out quickly that my legs would work to head back downstairs. I made my way to the galley and looked around. It was empty. I wasn't sure where to head next. We hadn't really been given a tour of the boat, and I hadn't been on one laid out like this before.

I grabbed a drink out of the fridge and sat down. I needed a plan. If I couldn't even walk to the edge of the boat, I wasn't sure how I would escape. And if I couldn't even walk over to the tanks, I had no idea how I would be able to keep my promise to Kyro. I had to save him.

After a few minutes of sitting there, pondering my next move, Katie walked in. "There you are! I've been hunting all over for you. Don't run off like that again!"

I found myself nodding automatically at her demand not to run off. I opened my mouth to ask her what she had done to me, and no words came out. She must have noticed the frustration on my face.

"I know you don't understand what's going on yet, but you belong to us now. Don't try to fight it; you'll just get hurt if you do. Your friend didn't fight us, and he's recovering nicely. He'll be up and around soon."

"Come with me. I'll show you where you'll be staying." Katie's words shot through me, and I stood to follow her. It was as if I had no choice but to do what she told me to. I tried to respond, but again no words came out.

Katie looked at me and laughed. "You'll get used to the chip. It will just keep us in control of your emotions and actions. You won't be able to fight against us or say anything against us. It's best if you stop trying. I meant it when I said it would hurt. That tiny chip packs quite a punch, electrically speaking. Now follow me." She turned and walked away, not looking to see if I agreed to follow.

Of course not, she knew I had no choice. What had she been talking about? Had she implanted a chip in my head to control me? That would explain why I couldn't move toward the lifeboats. It didn't explain why I couldn't go to the tanks, though. There had to be more to this chip than she told me. If only I could find a way to ask her. I needed more information so I could find a way to remove the chip or disrupt its signal. I took comfort in the fact she couldn't see what I was thinking, even if I couldn't talk.

I pondered this question as I followed her to the room she said was mine. She ordered me to stay in the room until she or Chris came back for me. I figured I'd have plenty of time to consider my next move if I was trapped in here until they decided to let me out.

THIRTY

KYRO

I HAD WATCHED THE crew for the past few days. It seemed like something had changed, especially with the new people. The pretty blue girl who claimed to be Zoey didn't even seem to notice me anymore, and the joy that had been in her eyes the night she promised to save me seemed to be gone.

I guessed that the big green guy had come with her, as they seemed to have an easy friendship. The fact that I had never seen him before also helped with that assumption as well. He appeared nice enough, but something was off about him too. Of course, being stuck in this tank kept me from spying on them very much.

It had been a few days since I had seen my boat. I knew Mack and Q were searching for me. I wasn't sure why they had left without coming aboard and saving me. I heard the wind hitting the sails but couldn't see my boat until it was sailing away. I tried yelling and splashing around, but it did no good.

I tried yelling for Zoey, but she didn't respond. It was almost like I had gone invisible. At this point, I still hadn't even seen my captors.

After a few hours of trying desperately to get someone's attention, I gave up. I allowed myself to wallow for a moment in the thought that I would never escape whatever crazy fate I was on my way to meet.

Over the next few days, I was certain I had seen Zoey looking at me from a few feet away. I was guessing my captors had said something to her to make her afraid of me. It just didn't make sense. She promised to save me, then just pretended I didn't exist. I couldn't figure it out.

Of course, I really didn't remember her, so maybe that was it. Maybe we had a strained relationship, or maybe I had done something to upset her. She seemed to remember me. I wished I could talk to her. It was impossible as long as I was in this tank.

I had tried everything to escape the confines of the tank, all to no avail. I couldn't break it. I couldn't open it. I had tried drawing every rune combination I could think of and nothing worked. I wondered if Ari had been able to talk to Mack or Q.

I tried a few times to astral project to her, but I couldn't seem to do that now either. I knew if she didn't intervene, it was because she had seen what was fated to happen and couldn't stop it.

Just when I had all but given up hope of rescue, Ari came to me in my dreams. She looked scared.

"Ari? What's wrong?" I focused on her face, willing her to tell me.

Tears filled her eyes. "Kyro, I'm so sorry. I tried to reach your friends, but I haven't been able to. And I tried to talk your dad into a rescue mission, but you know how he is."

The tears were streaming down her cheeks. It broke my heart to see her cry.

"It's all right, Ari. Don't worry. Zoey is here, and she's brought help. But I think something is wrong."

Her face lit up at the mention of Zoey. "She's here? And she brought help? That's fantastic! Why are you still in this tank?"

I scrunched my brows up. "That's the problem. I think something happened to them. Can you investigate? You know Zoey. The guy with her is obviously alien, but I've never seen anyone like him before. He's huge and green, kind of reminds me of a lizard."

Ari looked confused. "So, what's the problem?"

"Well, neither of them has talked to me since the first day they came to the boat. And sometimes it seems like Zoey wants to come talk to me, but she can't. They aren't shackled, so I'm not sure what's keeping her away."

"I can try. I'm just not sure it will work. But I do have some good news. I may have found a spell that will bring your memories back." She reached out a hand and placed it on my head as she muttered words I didn't understand.

When she was done, she pulled me into a hug, and though it wasn't real, it was the best thing that had happened to me since I got captured.

"When will I know if the spell worked?" I asked.

She shrugged. "I'm not sure. Just give it time. I'll be back when I can." With that, she disappeared.

After talking to Ari and watching my captors, along with Zoey and her friend, avoid me the rest of the day, I decided to try something crazy. Worst case scenario, it wouldn't work. Best case, I'd get some answers.

Once I figured everyone was settled in for the night, I relaxed into a meditative state and prepared to astrally project. I was going to try to talk to Zoey while she slept. I thought maybe she would be able to tell me what was happening. Then we could plan our escape.

It seemed as though the spell Ari had done was either slow working or didn't work at all. The only memories I had of Zoey were the dreams I'd had after she disappeared. And we still weren't sure what had happened there.

I still wanted to help her, so I continued my plan to try and talk to her. I sent my soul out searching for her and slipped into her dream as easily as Ari had come into mine. She was standing on the deck of my boat, looking out over the water.

"Zoey?" I wasn't sure how much she knew about magic or what I could do, so I figured I'd move slowly.

As she turned to face me, I watched a smile spread across her features. She ran to me and threw herself into my arms. I wasn't sure how to feel about it, but it felt right. In that moment I wanted to kiss her so badly, but it felt like it was too soon for that. She must have sensed my hesitation, because she leaned back and pulled out of my embrace.

"Kyro? You're really here. How? I had no idea you could astrally project. And I can talk to you. This is fantastic!" She gushed.

I was glad she knew it was actually me but confused about the rest of what she had said. "What do you mean, you can talk to me? Please tell me what's going on. It's been a while since you came onto the fishing boat, and you haven't talked to me in days."

"I've tried every day to go to you. These people. They planted a chip in mine and Jack's heads. We can't do anything they don't want us to, and we can't talk unless they let us. Even if we do, we can't say anything against them. I can't figure out how to get the chip out. And I can't talk to Jack about it. The whole thing has been terrifying."

I pulled her back into my arms and held her. "We'll figure it out. I have no idea how, but we will. We have to. You have a quest to complete."

She looked up at me with a curious grin. "Did you get your memories back?"

I thought about that question for a moment and realized that I did remember her. I wasn't sure if I remembered everything, but I knew her. And I knew I wanted to be with her.

"I'm not sure. I think I remember you, though. And I know we need to get off this boat. We'll figure out the rest once we're home."

THIRTY-ONE

Zoey

IT WAS A HUGE surprise to see Kyro in my dream. Even more so to realize it wasn't just a dream, but he was really there. It was thrilling to know I was still me inside my mind. At least they couldn't take that away from me. Now we just had to figure out how to fix this.

"So, what can we do?" I asked Kyro, who still had his arms around me.

He pressed a kiss to my forehead. "I'm not sure. I can try to astrally project to Mack and get him to come back, but I'm not sure if it will work. I had Ari try when I first got captured, but she couldn't get through. There could be other reasons for that, but it doesn't matter now."

"You should try that. Maybe you can reach him, since you know him so well. Or I could try. I want to try. I haven't been able to do anything I want since they implanted this stupid chip. Will you let me try?" I looked at him hopefully.

"I couldn't refuse you if I tried. But I think maybe we should try together. I feel like we're stronger together. What do you think?"

My heart sang at his words. He really seemed to believe in me. I loved that he felt stronger when he was with me. And I felt the same.

"Together. I like that. Do you want to go now?"

"The sooner the better, I think. Hold my hand and focus on Mack. We'll see if we can do this." His arms released me, and I put my hand in his.

I focused on Mack, concentrating as hard as I could. I needed this to work. I was getting more desperate with each moment Kyro and I spent together.

My consciousness shifted, and I was on Kyro's boat again. He was still holding my hand, but we were in the same spot we had just been standing in. I looked at him curiously. His face said exactly what I was thinking. It didn't work.

I felt the tears welling up and turned away so he wouldn't see them. Then I heard something.

"Kyro, is that really you? And Zoey? How is this possible? Where are you?" I turned back to see Mack jogging toward us.

"I thought it didn't work," I whispered to Kyro.

He nodded. "Me too."

Mack almost tackled us in a hug as he made it over to where we were standing. "Where are we? This isn't my dream. I was somewhere else, then suddenly I showed up here."

Kyro and I shared a surprised glance. I had never heard of someone being pulled out of their own body and into someone else's, except for when the Chairman had done it to me. I thought it was something he had come up with.

"How did we manage this?" I wondered out loud.

Kyro shrugged. "Mack, we're in Zoey's dream. We need your help. You sailed past a fishing boat a few days ago. I need you to go back and free us. I'm in a tank on the deck, and Zoey is there too, along with her friend, Jack."

I jumped in. "Jack and I have had mind-control chips implanted by Chris and Katie, who own the boat. We can't fight them or even speak if they tell us otherwise. What if they tell us to fight you all?"

I knew it was a valid concern but wasn't sure how to deal with that possibility. There had to be something we could do.

"What if we drug you both to knock you out? Then Q, Kyro and I can carry you off the boat with no fighting. And once you're safely on our boat, we can figure out how to remove the chips." Mack was quick to come up with an idea.

"But how will you drug us? It's not like we'll have the ability to just drink something. We won't even be able to cooperate. I hate this so much." It may be the best plan we had, but I wasn't convinced it would work.

"Q can make an injector, and we'll do it that way. If we do it right, you won't even know it happened until it's all over with. But I'll need to know how big this other guy is, so I can get the dose correct." Mack was confident in his idea.

It seemed like his confidence was contagious. Kyro was smiling at us as we went over details to make sure everything was set.

THIRTY-TWO

Chairman

I HAD BEEN PUSHING Jeremy to figure out the mind control spell for weeks now. It was even more urgent since I hadn't been able to astrally project myself into Zoey's dreams. I needed another way to get to her. I was going to have to find another wizard if he couldn't deliver.

I knew there was tech that would do what I wanted, but I didn't trust it. You could hack tech. You couldn't hack a spell. A spell was created with finesse and was immensely personal. It would create an unbreakable connection between us, and she would be mine forever. I would be able to take her powers for my own and leave her as an empty shell.

The thought of using her for my own pleasure and then draining her power from her got me so excited. I tracked down Shannon. I knew she'd be up for some extra-curricular activities, especially if she thought it would get her closer to powers of her own. I could promise her anything. She'd never know I was lying.

I took her back to the room I used for carnal pleasures. She was ready and willing to do anything to please me. It was so easy to manipulate the weak. I knew Zoey would be more of a challenge to break.

"On your knees, worthless scum." I didn't have to be an ass to get what I wanted, but I found that I enjoyed it more if I made her beg.

Shannon was attractive, but not my type. She had dark, loose curls that hung just past her shoulders and her skin was a sun-kissed copper color. From what I'd seen, her coloring was passed on to her son. He didn't look much like his father at all. But that was another subject.

She dropped to her knees and pressed her face to the floor. We'd done this enough for her to know any resistance would result in punishment. It was hard to find someone who could please me. I'd been told my tastes were somewhat...eclectic.

As much as I enjoyed the punishments, I wasn't in the mood to be defied today. I wanted someone who would pleasure me while I imagined it was Zoey after I had finally convinced her to join me.

I liked what I liked, and I wanted what I wanted. If someone couldn't keep up, they suffered. There were moments where I preferred to torture prior to my release and others where I only wanted to dominate. Before Shannon had come to me, there were a few "accidents" that had to be covered up. It wasn't like I had killed those people for fun. Things got a little out of hand, that's all.

My boss did not take well to my tastes, and I wasn't willing to give my life up for them. So I kept things pretty quiet. What he didn't know wouldn't hurt me, after all, and I knew Shannon would take whatever I threw at her. Tonight, that would be milder than usual. I wanted the release more than her screams from the torture.

I spent half an hour or so beating her with a riding crop while she begged for more. It wasn't as satisfying as if I had used my tools to burn or cut her, but it would do to vent my frustration at Jeremy.

Then I had my way with her, forcing her to please me sexually while I enjoyed my daydreams. I imagined breaking Zoey to the point I had Shannon. It would be a most enjoyable process, and I was anxious to begin.

Once I had finished, I threw Shannon off me and told her to go. I knew she hadn't enjoyed our time together, because I made sure to never let her get off. But she still thanked me and begged me to allow her to please me again. It was pathetic, but it worked.

After she left, I set to planning how I would break Zoey once I had her in my grasp.

THIRTY-THREE

Mack

WHEN I WOKE IN the morning, I briefly wondered if that dream had been just my imagination, or if Kyro and Zoey had actually managed to pull me out of myself. I rolled over to tell Quinn about it, but she was up already. She had been getting up earlier for the past few weeks since Zoey disappeared.

I checked the galley for her first, then her room. Though she spent her nights in my room, sometimes she needed privacy, so she kept her own room as well. I wasn't possessive or jealous enough to be upset by it. Everyone needs alone time. When I didn't find her in either place, I headed to the deck.

I found her sparring with Mateo, who had basically joined our crew since Kyro went missing right after Zoey did. He was adamant that we find them both. Needless to say, he was instantly welcomed aboard as family.

"I need to talk to you both. Something happened last night, and I'm not sure what to think about it," I said as I walked over to the training area on our deck.

They stopped sparring and both turned toward me. Quinn spoke first. "What happened? What's wrong?"

Mateo grabbed two small towels and handed one to Quinn. "Please, tell us what's going on."

"Honestly, I think I'm going crazy. But I hope it was real. I just don't know enough about magic yet to know for sure. Anyway, I think that Kyro and Zoey pulled me out of my body last night." I waited for a response before continuing my story.

Quinn's jaw dropped, and Mateo broke into a huge grin. "Astral projection. I know it's possible, but it's more difficult to pull someone in than to project yourself out." He laughed as he spoke.

"So, you believe me? Just like that?" I was still struggling with the whole thing.

Mateo stopped laughing. "Of course, Mack. Kyro is really powerful, and so is Zoey. It wouldn't surprise me for them to be able to do that."

"What did they say?" Quinn interjected.

"That they're trapped on that fishing boat we passed the other day, just like James told you. Kyro is in a tank, and Zoey has a mind control chip in her head. Oh, and her friend Jack does too."

"So, what you're saying is we need to board this fishing boat undetected, release Kyro from the tank, somehow get Zoey and Jack to come with us, and get back to our boat without anyone knowing?"

"Yeah, Mateo, that pretty much sums it up. Any ideas?" I looked from him to Quinn, and they were both staring at me intently.

It still sounded crazy to me, but I felt better that they believed me. Now we just had to formulate a rescue plan.

Since we finished our plan, Quinn was working on the knock-out drug for Zoey and Jack. She had to get it just right, or we could end up killing our friends instead of helping them. Mateo was working on ideas for distractions in case we came close to getting caught. And I was working to make sure Jack couldn't get out of the manacles I created to make sure he couldn't fight back.

We waited until night, then sailed to the fishing boat. We'd been tracking it since we sailed past it the first time, we just couldn't come up with a good reason to intervene until now. We silently pulled beside it, tied our boat off to one of the railings, and climbed on board. Mateo would wait on our boat and jump in if he was needed. Otherwise, he would protect the boat and be ready to sail when we returned.

Quinn and I followed Kyro's directions exactly to the location of the tanks. We had decided that stealth was our best chance to obtain our goal.

It was horrifying the conditions these beasts and Kyro were being kept in. Quinn started looking over the tank with the giant turtle first. She quickly found the lock and went to work picking it. If we were rescuing, we were rescuing them all.

I turned to the tank that looked empty. Kyro had already explained that it housed an enormous octopus. I climbed on top and started picking the lock. I heard a noise to our left and stopped suddenly.

As I turned my head, I realized it was just Quinn releasing the lock on the turtle's tank. We would need Kyro's magic to get these animals out of the tanks, so our plan was to just unlock all of them and let him take care of the rest.

She moved onto the next tank, the one with the electric eel in it. By the time I had the octopus tank unlocked, she had the electric eel tank done. We moved to Kyro's tank together. It took longer to manage his lock, as it was slightly more complicated than the others had been. I breathed a sigh of relief when the tumblers finally clicked, and Quinn removed it.

We lifted the lid from the tank, and Kyro used his magic to vault from the tank onto the deck. Neither of us had ever watched him transform before. It was mesmerizing to watch his tail glow then split into legs. I had no idea how the magic worked, but from the look on Kyro's face, it hurt. He stood and hugged us both.

Then he turned to the other three tanks. He used his water magic to swirl the contents of the tanks gently, then lift the lids and return the creatures to the water. Once that was complete, we headed off silently in search of Zoey and Jack.

This is where Zoey's intel became important. She had been watching their captors' schedules and knew when it was safe for us to head downstairs. Quinn had already set up the jammers and turned them on. We had five minutes to get both of them and get back to the boat.

We stopped at Zoey's room first. She had left it unlocked. That was helpful at least. I turned the knob and we quietly entered the room. Kyro and I stood near the door, and Quinn crept slowly toward the bed. Zoey must have heard us, because she sat straight up in bed, her face terrified. Quinn used that moment to inject the knock-out drug, and Zoey slumped forward.

Kyro picked her up and took off toward our boat. Quinn and I headed toward Jack's room. The door was unlocked there as well, but he wasn't sleeping. I turned the knob and we crept inside. Jack was sitting on the bed, facing the wall opposite where we were. Quinn did a ninja roll across the floor and injected him with the drug.

His head turned as the injection happened. His eyes grew wide, and for a moment I thought we were going to die. He stood up and started toward me, ignoring Quinn completely. Three steps into crossing the room, he fell over. It had just taken longer for the drug to work on him. I released the breath I hadn't known I was holding, and Quinn sighed.

Our relief was short-lived though, as we realized he had made quite a thud on the floor. We needed to get him out of here before anyone came to see what the commotion was about.

He was heavier than we expected, but I still thought we could manage. We got him off the floor, up the stairs, and onto the deck. There was a noise behind us, but we didn't stop. By the time we got halfway across the deck, I heard gunshots. We kept running. Quinn shifted momentarily to let a fireball loose, but she never let go of Jack or stopped running. We tumbled onto our boat, a mess of tangled limbs. I pulled out a dagger and cut the rope attaching the two boats.

The gunshots were getting closer, but we still couldn't see the shooter. I signaled to Mateo to get us out of here, and the boat took off. I was fairly sure Kyro had used his magic to give us a boost. It felt good to have the family back home again.

THIrTY-FOur

q

THE GUNSHOTS DIDN'T STOP once we were back on our boat. Kyro and Mateo got the boat moving away from the fishing vessel but not quickly enough. They were actually chasing us!

"Mack, they're coming after us. What do you want to do?" I was debating between a fireball and a javelin. I wasn't sure which one would do better.

"Let's just see if we can put some water between us. If it comes to a fight, we'll fight, but let's try to avoid it." It was strange that Mack didn't want to fight, but there had to be a reason.

"All right. I'll go check on Zoey and Jack. Maybe we can figure out how to get those chips out of them." I headed down to the sickbay, where we had Zoey and Jack restrained and knocked out.

I knew something was wrong when I opened the door. Jack's cot was empty. I quickly shut and locked the door. I hoped he was still in the room with me. I knew I'd have to fight if he was, and I needed to do it without hurting him.

I turned at a sound on my right. Just then, Jack swung an instrument tray at my head. I ducked and punched him in the gut. He was solid. I may have just broken my hand.

"Jack, I need you to listen. My name is Q. I'm Zoey's friend. We're here to help. She asked us to get you off that boat. We're going to get the chips out of your head. But I can't do that if you make me kill you." I wasn't sure if words would even get through, much less have any effect on him in that moment.

He looked at me, confused and maybe a little scared. "The chip isn't working now. I didn't know who had us. I woke up strapped to that cot and didn't know if they'd done something else to us. I'm sorry. I didn't mean to attack you. I'm just trying to protect Zoey."

"That's great! It means there's a range on the chips. We should be able to get them out without too much trouble. Do you want to help me with Zoey, then I can knock you out and do yours?" I figured he'd be good with that.

"No. Take mine out first, but don't knock me out. Katie didn't when she put it in, and it wasn't that bad. Let's just get it over with." Jack looked at me pleadingly.

"OK, if you can handle the pain. Help me get the instruments together for both operations, since doing yours first will keep you from helping with Zoey's. I totally understand, I'd want that thing out of me too." I started gathering the tools I would need to remove the chip, and Jack helped me set everything up next to each of their cots for the operations.

I almost forgot we were locked in this room, then there was a knock at the door. "Is everything all right in there, love? We heard something. Why is this door locked?" Mack sounded worried.

"Everything is fine, babe. We're going to extract the chips. They have a limited range, and we're outside it now. Jack's gonna help me. I'll unlock the door when we're done." I hated making him worry, but I had this under control.

I heard him huff at the door, then walk away. I turned back to the cots. Jack had already positioned himself for me to remove the chip. The surgical tools were lined up and prepped. All I had to do was follow through and get this done.

I washed my hands, trying desperately to control the shaking as I dried them. I guess I wasn't as confident in my abilities as I had led Jack and Mack to believe. I took a deep breath and turned to where Jack was lying so still, I would have thought he was knocked out if I hadn't known better.

"Are you ready?" I asked, not sure if it was directed to myself or Jack.

"You don't have to be nervous. It's a fairly easy procedure. I can talk you through it if you want." Jack seemed like a nice guy. I hoped I didn't kill him so we got a chance to talk.

"OK, that might help. I'd never admit this to anyone, but I guess I'm nervous. Don't you dare tell anyone, or I'll call you a liar and make you miserable."

He chuckled softly. "Your secret is safe with me. Now let's get this done."

Jack explained to me how to clean the area, making sure to disinfect a perimeter around the original incision. I had to snip and remove the existing stitches. I took a deep breath as I reopened the incision with a scalpel, and Jack gritted his teeth.

"Are you OK? Do I need to stop?"

"It's fine. I can take the pain. Just get this thing out of my head."

Once the incision was open, I could see the chip. Jack had told me I'd have to cut it out, severing the nerves that were attached to it. After I did that, I used tweezers to pull the chip from him. I placed it in a bowl of water and clamped a lid on it. I needed to examine the tech but didn't want to take any chances of it escaping. We didn't know this thing's capabilities. I carefully stitched the incision closed, cleaned the area again, and bandaged it.

"You should probably rest now. Do you want to go somewhere and sleep on an actual bed?" I figured as big as he was, these cots couldn't be comfortable.

"Nah, I'm gonna stay here with Zoey. I'll go wherever she goes for now. It's not that I don't trust you, it's just that I'm responsible for keeping her safe. If that's OK with you, that is." I had a feeling he'd fight me if I tried to push the issue.

I nodded. "I get it. You don't know us. It's OK. You can stay here with her. I just need you to rest. There's no reason you can't watch the procedure and talk to me if you want."

Zoey's procedure took half as long as Jack's had, because I knew what I was doing this time. When I had finished, I got Kyro and Mack to come help me move them both into Zoey's old room, where they could get some rest.

THIrTY-FIVe

Jack

I LAID ON THE cot next to Zoey while Q removed the chip from her head. I could tell Q was nervous, although I wasn't sure exactly why. It was a fairly easy procedure. Then we moved to Zoey's room with a little help from Kyro and Mack. I wondered how long it would be before one of them approached me about my relationship with Zoey.

I could tell they were both pretty protective of her. That would make my job easier. As I lay there on the bed watching Zoey sleep, I wondered if anyone had grabbed her haversack from her quarters on the fishing boat. Chris and Katie had gone through our things, but didn't see any reason to take any of it away from us since we had no ability to say anything against them. And the comm device would appear to be broken until the passcode was typed in, so it didn't really matter either way.

I started to get restless. I wanted to talk to Elena. I wished she could have come with us. I felt like things would have gone a lot differently if she had. But we both had a job to do, and that involved us being in separate places for the moment.

I got out of the bed, tucked Zoey in, then decided to take a walk and check out this boat. It was well constructed in an ancient sailboat meets technology kind of way. I decided I already liked these people, even if I didn't fully trust them. I checked out all the other rooms that weren't locked, finding bedrooms, the galley, and a common area. Everyone must have been up on deck, since there was no sign of anyone down here. Because Zoey was safe in her current situation, I decided to head up and join them.

I walked out on the deck and looked around. I didn't see any sign of Chris and Katie's boat, so I relaxed a bit. I could hear something that sounded like a struggle coming from an area to my left. I followed the noise and found out where everyone had gone.

Kyro and a male dwarf were sparring, while Q and a blonde guy watched and talked about ways they could defeat the others in combat. Zoey had told me about the training sessions. I guessed the dwarf was Mack, but she never mentioned the other guy. I wondered if she even knew him.

As I got closer, I cleared my throat, wondering if it would be strange to just sit down and watch them fight. Or did manners dictate that I announce my presence? I was really bad at social stuff. Things were obviously different here than they were on Calliope.

Suddenly everyone turned and stared at me. I've never been self-conscious, but I may have understood that feeling a little better now.

"Hi. I just wanted to say thanks for saving us from those crazies back there. Things got a little out of control." There ya go, Jack, make things even more awkward. Kyro scowled at my statement.

"Oh, hey, Jack. It's no problem. We had to go get Kyro and Zoey anyway." Mack laughed as he spoke. Q walked over and slugged him in the shoulder.

"Be nice. This guy could come in handy," she said to him with a grin before turning to me. "Don't worry about it. We're a family here. It's what we do."

Kyro looked over at me but didn't move. The blond guy walked over with a hand outstretched. "I'm Mateo. I've known Kyro all his life. I help out around here sometimes." I took the offered hand and shook it, relieved that at least this guy seemed normal.

"Thanks. It's nice to meet you." I looked at Kyro, who seemed to be trying his best to avoid eye contact. It didn't go unnoticed.

Q turned to Mack and Mateo. "Maybe we should go start dinner. I'll need both of you to help tonight. Come on." And the three of them walked away.

I knew it had been an excuse to leave me alone with Kyro. I suspected he had some concerns about me, and I knew I had some about him. I had to make sure he was good enough for Zoey.

I'd never admit it to her, or him for that matter, but I was still in love with her. I knew she had moved on from our almost relationship from high school and didn't want to stand in the way of her happiness. But I wasn't about to let her get hurt. Not if I could prevent it. Besides, I was with Elena now. And I definitely wanted to see where that was going to end up. It was a complicated mess, but that was the story of my life for as long as I could remember.

Once the other three were out of earshot, I turned to Kyro. "You look like you have something to say."

He looked me up and down, crossed his arms over his chest, and nodded. "I think we should talk." He gestured toward the chairs Q and Mateo had been sitting in when I walked up. I took the suggestion and sat.

"So, I'm guessing you've been thinking about what you wanted to say to me since your friends got us back to the boat? Or since you saw me with Zoey on the other boat?" I wasn't planning to be an ass, but I wasn't going to roll over and let him think he was in control either.

He laughed. "You're probably right. I've been thinking about it since I saw you with her on the other boat. And that was before I could even remember I knew her."

"I understand. She has that effect on people. The more you're around her, the more you want to be around her." I might have just shown him my hand. So much for the bluff I'd been hanging onto for the last twenty years.

"I thought so. There was something about the way you were with her that made me think you love her. It's nice to know I wasn't imagining it. So what do you intend to do about it?"

Wait, were we trying to have the same conversation with each other? This just got even more awkward.

"I was actually going to ask you the same question. I'm not planning on doing anything except being her friend. It's my job to protect her for one thing, and for another, I have a girlfriend. So you have nothing to worry about with me."

He scoffed at my declaration. "I hope that's true. I remember enough to know she wouldn't want to be fought over, so that won't happen. But if you're interested, I need to know so I can back off. It's not fair to put her in the middle of something like that."

It was my turn to laugh. "I agree. But even if I wanted to, I couldn't pursue her. It's a long story, and I won't go into it. Trust me, it's not a possibility."

"You don't seem too happy about that." Kyro acted like he wanted to be angry, but couldn't quite get there.

"I'm honestly not sure how I feel about it. But that doesn't matter, because you were all she could talk about from the moment she got her memories back. And if I'm being honest, she mentioned you a few times before she got her memories back. But that's not my story to tell." I eyed him curiously and watched his expressions change as I spoke.

"How?" He started to ask, but I cut him off.

"Look, I'm here to help. I'm gonna stick around until this thing is done, because I made a promise, and I don't break those. Trust me when I tell you that she wants you, and drop the whole thing. You have nothing to worry about from me." I knew that I meant every word, and at the same time if it hadn't been for the promise I made when I was still a kid, every word I'd just spoken to him would have been a lie.

He stared at me for a few minutes, not speaking. He seemed to be considering everything I had told him. It looked like he was leaning toward believing me.

"I need YOU to promise ME something, though." I hoped this part wouldn't be too difficult.

He cocked an eyebrow at me curiously. "What's that?"

I held my hand out for him to shake. "Promise me you won't tell Zoey any of what we just talked about. It'll just make her mad, and neither of us needs that."

He waited a minute, then shook my hand and nodded. "It'll be like it never happened. Are we good?"

It was amusing to me that he was the one asking if we were good, when he was the one who had a problem with me in the first place.

"Yeah, man, we're good. But if you hurt her, I'll break you in half." I couldn't help myself.

"I expect no less," Kyro responded before walking away. I sat there watching the ocean and hoping I could keep my word this time.

THIRTY-SIX

Zoey

I woke in a haze, realizing pain in my neck was worse. Ugh, had Katie done another procedure? I looked around the room and caught myself before I screamed. They had done it. I was on Kyro's boat.

It seemed odd to me that I was in my old room, since Kyro and I had been staying together before Jack transported me back to Calliope. But on the other hand, it made sense. Even with memories restored, it was better to take things slow.

That didn't do much to stop the sting of rejection. I wondered how long I'd been asleep. And where was Jack? I got out of bed slowly, as my head was still somewhat spinning, and headed to the bathroom. I checked the closet on my way, and all my clothes were still there. I grabbed what I needed for a shower and spent the next half hour standing under the hot spray, trying to ease the nausea that accompanied the spinning.

I dressed and stopped at the galley to get something to eat before heading up on deck. I had no idea what time it was but figured someone would be up. I found fresh rolls and peaches, so I grabbed one of each and headed up the stairs. I stepped out onto the deck to find the midday sun directly overhead. The sails were rolled to keep the boat from moving too much overnight. It was strange for them to be that way this late in the day.

I didn't have time to ponder the reasoning behind the sails, as another wave of dizziness hit me. I stumbled and blacked out. I felt the warm, hard wood as I hit the deck with a thud.

I woke in Kyro's arms, with Mack's face inches from mine. "Woah, there, pal. I don't do that on the first date." I tried to make a joke, but couldn't lift my head, and blacked out again as soon as the words were out.

The second time I came to, I was on a cot in the sickbay, with Kyro pacing as Mack checked for a concussion. "Ky, our girl's awake again. Hopefully for more than a moment this time."

Mack stepped back to let Kyro see me. "Zoey, are you alright? What happened?" The concern in his eyes made me tear up.

"I'm not sure. I was dizzy and queasy when I woke up but felt better after my shower. I didn't even get to eat my breakfast before I blacked out." I pouted about that, as if I wouldn't be able to have another roll or peach. It was silly, and I knew it.

"Quinn brought you a tray of food when she realized you'd be back in sickbay at lunchtime. She'll be in to visit after chores." Mack slid a small table with a tray on it to sit next to the cot.

"Oh, it's Quinn now, is it? Did I miss something?" I tried to keep things lighthearted, though I was worried about what could be the cause of my sudden illness.

"Well, she is to me. Though I'm not sure she'd like hearing you ruffians call her that." Mack tried to sound stern but laughed when he called us ruffians.

"So how bad off am I, doc?" I really didn't want to be confined to this cot. I wanted the fresh air, the sea, Kyro. I wanted freedom.

"I don't think it's anything serious, though we'll all be keeping an eye on you to make sure it's not an infection from the operation. I think you just weren't getting enough to eat while you were away. You look too thin." Mack didn't have a problem being blunt. I laughed at his assessment.

"I'm fine with everyone keeping an eye on me. I just don't want to stay in this cot. I want to go up on deck and enjoy the sun and the air." I sounded a bit like a spoiled child, and I didn't even care.

Mack and Kyro exchanged a glance. "I think that can be arranged. So long as you eat your lunch and you promise to rest while you're up on deck. And someone has to stay with you." Kyro seemed to be volunteering for nurse duty.

"Agreed, so long as you stay with me." I'd make sure he was the one, since I was dying to spend some time with him.

"Deal." He responded, and I began to eat lunch. I cleaned the tray, then giggled as Kyro picked me up to carry me up the stairs to a chair that had been placed on deck for me.

"I feel like I got duped here," I said suspiciously.

Kyro smirked. "I have no idea what you mean." He gently sat me down in the chair.

I smiled at him. "How is this chair magically here in my favorite spot on the deck? Did you plan this babysitting trip?" I teased.

He started to laugh. "Maybe? I've been sworn to secrecy, and I'll never tell." He winked as he sat down next to me.

THIRTY-SEVEN

Jack

WHERE IS IT? WHAT did I do with it? I knew Zoey and I had brought the dodeca with us when we left the Patrol's hideout. Why couldn't I find it? It was in Zoey's haversack--Oh, no! We left it on the fishing boat. Shit! We had to have the dodeca for Ian's plan to work. I hung my head as I walked out on deck to find Zoey.

"I can't find it." I cringed as I waited for her response.

"What did you lose, Jack?" Oh, wow, I'm stupid. Of course, she has no idea what I'm talking about.

"I can't find the dodeca. We had it when we left the base, but it's not here."

Zoey scrunched her brows in thought. "It's in the haversack that Mama gave me. But that's not here, either, is it?" Her question ended on a whisper, as though she already knew the answer.

"The haversack must still be on Chris and Katie's boat. We'll have to track them down again and get it back."

Zoey's eyes widened. She started to shake. "I can't go back there. I won't let them control me again. Jack, we can't win against them. How will we be able to get the bag back?"

I pulled her into my arms and stroked my hand down her back. "It's OK, Zo. I won't let them take you again. I promise. And I'm pretty sure we won't be going alone. Let's talk to the others and see if we can come up with a plan. I'm not even sure we can track them now."

Zoey laughed as she pulled away from me. It was nice to see that light in her eyes again. "Don't worry about tracking. I know someone who's a whiz with tech. May even be better than you."

"Oh, yeah? Better than me, you say? I'd love to meet this guy."

Zoey doubled over laughing and held her sides. "Yeah, Jack. But you've already met her. She's pretty impressive. I'm sure she'll be able to locate the boat again."

"You mean Q? I didn't realize she knew tech. I just thought she was the muscle around here. Let's go talk to her."

Zoey led the way to the room Q and Mack shared. "This doesn't mean I agree with this plan, but I know Ian needs the dodeca, so I'm going to let you talk to everyone about it." She knocked on the door.

Mack answered. "What's going on?"

Zoey cut me off before I could respond. "I need to talk to everyone in the galley in five minutes. It's important." Then she turned and walked off, not waiting for me to follow.

I watched her turn toward Kyro's room and knock. When he answered, she went inside. Mack and I looked at each other. "I guess we'd better get to the galley, then. I'll get Quinn, and we'll be right there," he said to me before closing the door in my face.

THIRTY-EIGHT

Zoey

AFTER KYRO INVITED ME to his room, I wasn't sure how to act. Clearly, I had managed to recover more of my memories than he had. It made things somewhat awkward. I wasn't sure if it was OK to hug him or try to hold his hand. I knew we needed to talk about it, but this just wasn't the time.

"I need to talk to everyone in the galley. I've asked the others to come and told them I'd be there in five minutes. Will you join us? It's important." I hoped that Ian would talk to us and that we could figure out what to do about the dodeca.

Kyro smiled. "Of course. I'll go wherever you need me to." It was cute how his cheeks turned pink when he tried to flirt with me. He was so different without those memories. I didn't mind, but I was really looking forward to picking up where we left off.

"Good. I'm also gonna need my backpack, please. I know I left it in here, but I don't see it." I didn't want to go digging through his closet. This situation just kept getting more awkward.

"Oh, sure, I'll get it for you." He stepped into the closet and came back out with my pink backpack in hand. Our fingers touched as he handed it to me. I could have sworn there were sparks the instant his skin touched mine. He stepped closer and whispered to me. "I think we should talk about this. I know right now isn't the best time, so I can wait, but soon. OK?"

He had angled his head so that our faces were a breath apart. My heart pounded at the thought of our lips touching. "OK," I responded weakly. I knew it had probably sounded lame, but it was all I could say.

He stepped back to give me room to walk out. I held my chin up and walked past him toward the galley. I wasn't going to beg him to kiss me. At least not yet.

I walked in the galley, and everyone but Kyro was already there, sitting around a table waiting for us. Kyro walked in after me and joined the others. For whatever reason, they were letting me take charge. Normally, they would all look to Kyro for guidance. To be fair, I was the one who called everyone together.

"We have a problem, and we're here to find a solution. Each of us will have a part to play, and we'll have to depend on each other. Does anyone have a problem with that?"

I knew it was a little harsh and probably more forceful than I'd been in the past, but I felt like they didn't respect me before. There was something about watching your memories play out like a movie to give you some insight.

No one spoke, and everyone shook their heads to indicate they had no problem with what I'd said.

"Good. Now let's get started. We all know Ian is the wizard who communicates with us—usually me—through this book." I held the book up for emphasis. They all nodded.

"We also know Ian has requested that we find certain items so he can fix whatever it was that broke in the past. His plan is to make our present—his future—a better place."

"What does this have to do with this meeting? Do you have a lead on the items he wants?" Q was blunt as usual, and I respected that.

"In a way. One of the items Ian needs is a dodecahedron. It's a long story, but the short version is...Jack had the dodeca and was holding it until I needed it. No, I didn't know he had it, but he did give it to me before we left Calliope."

Kyro's face lit up. "That's great news! Now we have two of the items Ian needs."

"Not exactly—wait. Did you say two? We have one of the pearls? You guys found one while I was gone? Why didn't anyone tell me?" I was hurt but impressed that they had gone on without me. The mission may have been mine, but it was way more important that it be completed than who did it.

"Well, Kyro has one of the pearls, but we didn't find it while you were gone. Apparently, he had it before we met you, and he hadn't decided if he could trust Ian or not. That's why you didn't know. None of us did, until you went missing and we talked to Ian about that and Kyro's memories being gone." Mack filled in the blanks.

"Oh. Well, it's good that we have one of the pearls. That will definitely help." I turned to Kyro. "I assume that's part of what you wanted to talk to me about later?"

He nodded, his cheeks pink from being called out in front of everyone.

"OK, you two can talk about that later. Please get to the important part, Zoey. We can't afford to lose any more time." Jack was insistent that we needed to move quickly, and I agreed.

Everyone looked from Jack to me. I could see the suspicion on their faces and almost hear their thoughts. *Great, more secrets, just what we need.*

"Thank you, Jack, for keeping me in line. Yes, back to the important part. I don't have the dodeca. I had it when we left Calliope, and I had it when we boarded Chris and Katie's boat, but I don't have it now. With any luck, they don't even know I left my haversack there. We need to find them, sneak onto the boat, and retrieve it. This is the part where we're all gonna have to work together. Thoughts?"

I stopped talking and just watched everyone's faces as they processed what had just been a huge info dump. To be fair, it would take me a bit to process that Kyro had hidden one of the pearls from me. I didn't know if I could pretend like that hadn't happened. And to think, just ten minutes ago, I had been wishing things were back to the way they were before I'd lost my memories. All it took to ruin that was one tiny little lie.

They all started discussing options for tracking the fishing boat, then options for sneaking on board and finding my bag. I was too distracted to listen. I couldn't get over the fact Kyro had lied to me. It hurt. And I knew I couldn't afford to get caught up on that right now, but I was. It seemed to me like we'd be having a talk all right, just not the one I had hoped. I guess it was a good thing I hadn't moved back into his room after all.

At this point, Jack had all but taken over the planning phase, so I quietly excused myself and went back to my room. I figured I could talk to Ian; then try to process everything we had just talked about. I walked into my room, closed and locked the door behind me, and sat down on the floor. I pulled Ian's book out and sat it in my lap.

"I think it's time we had a talk," I said as I opened the leather-bound journal.

THIRTY-NINE

Ian

ZOEY? IS THAT REALLY you? Are you all right? You seem upset. I take it you found out about Kyro hiding the pearl.

"It's not surprising that you know that, but it is a bit unnerving. Yeah, I know he lied. That's not important right now. I'm back, but we have a problem."

What is it? You still have the book and the pearl, so the quest is going pretty well.

"Well, I had the dodeca, but I've managed to leave it someplace that's not really safe. So now the others are planning to go after it. And to be honest, I'm terrified."

What aren't you telling me? I can't see everything, you know.

"My friend Jack built a transporter and pulled me back to Calliope. Kyro and I apparently lost our memories because of it. Jack had the dodeca and gave it to me. Then we were taken by my mom, and when we left there, we ended up captives of a couple who run a smuggling and poaching ring. It's an exhausting story, but the dodeca is in my bag on their boat."

That's not all of it, though. What else?

"This couple, they planted chips in Jack's and my head. Mind control chips. We couldn't fight back, couldn't run, couldn't even speak if they didn't let us. I'm terrified that will happen again if I go back to their boat."

Zoey, that was a horrible thing that happened to you, but you're safe now. Your friends will make sure that you're not in harm's way. You do trust them, don't you?

"Honestly, I don't know. I did before I lost my memories. But now that I have my memories back, I'm not sure who I can trust. I have no idea what to do." She started to cry softly, and the tears hit the pages of the journal.

Please don't cry. I understand that you're upset. It is difficult to trust someone who has lied to you, but we need Kyro to help us. And I understand it's probably not just him that you're having trouble trusting, but the biggest problem is with him, isn't it?

Zoey sniffed and nodded. "Yes. How can I just pretend he didn't lie to me for those weeks we spent chasing the pearls? Especially when he had one the whole time! I'm hurt, and I'm angry. I know I have to let it go and complete the quest, but I'm not sure how to do that. I had to leave the meeting I called because I couldn't stop myself from thinking about it. I left all of them to figure out how to get the dodeca back because I couldn't stand to sit there and look at him after he lied to me."

I understand. It's not going to be easy. And I'm not saying you have to trust him. What about the others? Can you trust any of them?

"I've known Jack my entire life. I'm sure I can trust him. But the others have all done shady stuff, too. I don't know if I can trust any of them. And to be honest, Jack has hidden stuff from me, too. Just not anything as important as the pearls we've been searching for."

Why do you feel like you can still trust Jack if he's hidden things from you, but you don't think you can trust Kyro anymore? Do you think you can track down the rest of the pearls without them? My visions have been pretty clear about all of you being involved. I wasn't sure who Jack was until recently, but I saw his part as well.

"You're right. I can't just go off by myself. I need all of them to help. I'm not sure how I'll deal with Kyro, but I'll figure it out. At least things hadn't gotten too serious with him before the memory wipe. Everything is just awkward now. Is there anything you can do to help with that? I have my memories back, but I don't have the supplies or the spell that I used on myself to use on him. Maybe if he could remember why he lied to me, I'd be able to find a way to forgive him."

I'll look into it and get back with you. A memory spell isn't an easy thing to come up with. Where did you get the one you used?

"I made it up. I researched herbs and candle colors that would help, and I wrote a spell. It worked a lot better than I expected. I just can't remember the exact ingredients or wording now."

That's fantastic. I've never heard of someone with that much raw power. I haven't even been able to write my own spells. I knew you were the right person for this mission. You amaze me, Zoey. And the way your powers keep growing is incredible. I wish I was physically there so I could study the rate and adaptations of your powers.

"As crazy as that sounds, Ian, I wish you were here too. I think I would feel better having you study me. Then maybe I would know what to expect from my powers. I never know how or even if they're going to work. It's frustrating."

I know, child. I promise it will get easier. You'll gain control of them and at some point, when they're all finished evolving. That will be an amazing sight. I have had visions of your powers in their final state, and it's really something to see. I can't give you any more than that. I'm sorry. Just know I'm here for you whenever you're feeling alone. All you have to do is open the book and talk to me. I'm going to go research that memory spell now. You need to get back to your friends and figure out how to get the dodeca back. Please keep me updated.

FORTY

Zoey

I FELT A LITTLE better after talking to Ian, but I was still hurt and mad. I knew it wasn't fair to bail on the people who were helping me, even if I didn't think I could trust any of them. I put the book away and hid my bag in the bottom of my closet. I was pretty sure no one on the boat would bother it, but I wasn't taking any chances.

I went back to the galley to see if they were all still there planning the retrieval of my haversack. When I walked in, I noticed Kyro and Jack weren't there. Mack and Q stopped talking and stared at me.

"What? Why are you staring at me?" I felt really self-conscious all of a sudden.

Q looked at Mack and subtly jerked her head toward the door. He obviously understood the signal, because he stood up and politely excused himself. I stared after him for a moment before turning back to her.

"Are you going to tell me why you were looking at me like I'd grown another head?"

She laughed. "Mack and I are worried about you. You're under a lot of stress with this quest. Not to mention the personal issues. We thought maybe you needed someone to talk to about it. I lost, so you're stuck with me."

"Let's not mention it. Yes, I am under a lot of pressure to find the pearls and to get the dodeca back. Maybe I'd be under less stress if people weren't lying to me constantly. Or if I had any idea why they were lying to me. It would be way less stressful if I had people around me who I could trust, instead of a bunch of selfish jerks who keep secrets and lie about important stuff."

I turned to walk away. I'd had enough of "helpful" Q. I liked her better when she was being a bitch. At least then I felt like she was being genuine. Right now, it seemed like she was being condescending.

I made it to the door before she grabbed my arm and swung me around to face her. She looked pissed.

"Every one of us has secrets. You're right about that. But not every one of us is a liar. That's where you're wrong. I don't know Jack, so I can't speak for him. And I can't really defend Kyro because I have no idea why he lied to you. But Mack is the nicest guy you'll ever meet, and I don't even think he knows how to lie. So, say what you will about me, but don't you dare talk that way about him."

Her words were like a slap in the face. It stung. But this was my Q. This was her being honest with me and not trying to talk down to me or sugar coat things.

"Thank you. I feel like that's the most honest thing you've said to me today. That's all I want. And yeah, Jack has lied too. But his lies didn't keep me from obtaining what I need for this quest. I know it's the same thing, but it's really not. And you're right, I have no idea why Kyro lied. I'm not sure I want to." At this point, I was blinking back tears, because I had decided that I wasn't about to cry over him.

Q threw her arms around me and pulled me in for a hug. "I'm sorry. I'm not good at people stuff. I don't know what to say to make you feel better."

"It's OK. You're better at it than you think. I'm just so conflicted about the whole thing. I don't even know if I want to stay here. I'm not sure I want to continue on this quest. I don't think I can do it."

Her eyes widened. "You can't give up. Not now. We just planned out how we're going to get your bag with the dodeca in it back from that boat. We can't do this without you."

I shook my head. "You really can. Probably easier than you can with me. I'm not going back to Chris and Katie's boat. I'm not going to promise that I'll stay, but I will be here when you get back. Then I'll go from there. That's the best I can do."

I didn't wait for her response, instead walking away and locking myself in my room once more. I wanted to hunt Jack down and yell at him until I felt better, but this wasn't junior high, and I couldn't do that. This mess wasn't his fault. It was mine, and the sooner I owned up to that, the better.

I spent some time meditating, trying to clear my mind. I had to decide what I was going to do. I didn't have many choices left. I could turn myself in to the Patrol and see how that turned out. Or I could go somewhere else and start over, where nobody knows me. Or I could stay here and pretend nothing happened. I was so conflicted; I couldn't decide what to do.

Forty-one

Jack

After Zoey snuck out of the meeting she had called, we planned how we would track down the boat. Then we planned how we would get on board, find the haversack, and get back to Kyro's boat without being caught. I thought it would just be easier to blow the boat up with Chris and Katie on it, but I got outvoted.

I wasn't really that anxious to kill them, I just wanted to make sure they couldn't keep trafficking people and sea creatures. Once the planning was complete, Kyro excused himself. I waited a minute and followed him. I had to make sure he wasn't going to try to bother Zoey. Her face had made it clear she wasn't interested in talking to him right now.

I followed him up on deck, where he stared at the water for a while. I walked over to him, intent on finding out exactly why he had lied. He didn't look up when I stopped next to him, but he did tense, as though he was preparing for a fight.

"We need to talk."

"You want to know why I kept the pearl hidden from everyone. It's an understandable question."

"Well?" I waited for his response.

"I keep asking myself that same question. At first, I thought it was because I didn't trust Ian. Now, I'm not so sure. Maybe I just wanted to keep it for myself. Maybe I wanted to surprise her with it when we failed to find it anywhere else. I mean, who wouldn't want to be her hero?" His voice was tinged with sadness. I guess he realized how this could change his relationship with Zoey.

"Why don't you tell her that? She'll forgive you." I hoped that was true. He seemed like a nice enough guy, and she had been absolutely crazy about him until it came out he had hidden this from her. Sometimes all it took was a seed of doubt to unravel everything.

"I don't think she will. I saw her face. She hates me now. Who am I kidding? I hate me now. I have no idea how to make her trust me again."

I didn't like this self-doubt turn our conversation was taking. It was starting to irritate me.

"Either way, you need to talk to her. Every one of us has a job to do. We need to be able to work together to do it." I didn't give him a chance to respond, instead turning and walking away.

I didn't stop until I was outside Zoey's door. I raised my hand to knock but heard Q's voice before I had a chance.

"Don't bother. She's really upset. Not talking to anyone. Says she's not going with us. I'm hoping she doesn't try to take off while we're getting the dodeca back." There was something in her voice, but I didn't know her well enough to tell what it was exactly.

"She told you all that?" I couldn't say I was surprised, because it sounded exactly like Zoey. She was stubborn and could hold a grudge for a long time.

Q nodded. "I just talked to Mack about it, and he thinks we should just let her be for a while. I tried to get her to talk to Kyro, but she won't. I think she's mad at you too. I have no idea why, but it's really none of my business. I'm looking for Kyro now to put the last-minute touches on our plan, since Zoey removed herself from it."

"He's up on deck, and he's just as stubborn as she is. I tried to get him to talk to her, but he won't. What a pair! As for why she's mad at me, I'd guess the same reason she has for being mad at him. I know I deserve it, even though my lies protected her. I make no apologies for it, and I told her I'd do it again if I had to. If she needs to be mad at me, so be it."

Q stood there and stared at me, as if she was trying to figure out how to respond.

"This is bigger than all of us, and we need to remember that. We've got to get it together, or this mission will fail. I don't know about you, but I don't want to have to pick up the pieces when it does. Because that girl in there will be a mess if she lets any of us, herself included, give up. So go get Kyro and Mack, and let's get the dodeca back. Then we can work on Zoey."

I turned on my heels and walked away. I wasn't sure where I was headed this time, but I needed some air. I went back on deck and made sure I headed to the opposite end of the boat from Kyro. I didn't want to talk to any of them right now. I found myself wondering if Zoey had the right idea. Maybe it would be better to just sit this out and let the others figure out how to fix it.

FORTY-TWO

Mack

QUINN CAME BACK TO our room, obviously upset. She headed straight for the bathroom and locked the door. That wasn't like her. I had to figure out what was going on here.

"Love? What's wrong? Please tell me what's happened." I pleaded with her through the door.

"I just need a few minutes. I'll be fine. I just got a gut check from Zoey, then another from Jack. I need a little time to process it, that's all. Can you go get Kyro so we can move on this plan?"

I hated to leave her but knew we needed to get moving. "I can do that. I'll be back in a few minutes."

I walked up on deck to find Kyro, half expecting him to be in the water by now. He was standing by the railing, looking out at the ocean.

"You wanna talk about it?" I asked as I approached him.

He shook his head. "Not really. I think I just got reamed by Jack. I feel horrible for hiding the pearl from Zoey. I've never felt so unwanted on my own boat before." His voice held a sadness I had only heard from him once before. That was the night we thought his mother had died.

"Ky, it's all gonna work out. She just needs time. And don't worry about Jack. Apparently, he's in a mood. He jumped all over Quinn a while ago too. We need to get ready to go after the dodeca. Zoey wants to sit this one out, so it's up to the rest of us to get it back for her. She deserves that, right?'

I knew it wasn't fair to guilt him into it, but I wasn't above using whatever method would get results.

"You're right. She deserves that and more. Let's get stuff ready." He seemed to snap out of the mood and into his usual self.

"That's better. Come on. Quinn wanted me to get you. We'll iron out the last of the details." I turned to walk back to my room.

"You should probably get him too." Kyro gestured toward where Jack was staring at the ocean on the opposite side of the boat.

"OK. You head down to my room, and I'll get Jack. We'll be down in just a minute." I walked over to Jack without waiting for a response from Kyro.

"Jack, we've gotta finish our plan so we can get the dodeca back. You coming?"

He turned and looked at me. For a minute, I thought I saw a flash of pain in his eyes. "Yeah, I'm coming. Let's get this over with."

FORTY-THREE

KYRO

WE GATHERED IN MACK'S room and finished the plan to recover the dodeca. I got the impression that with Zoey excusing herself from this mission, most of us were just going through the motions. It was hard to be all in when you realize the person you were all in for just took themselves out.

I couldn't help but kick myself for hiding the pearl from her. I tried to justify it because I didn't know Ian and couldn't be sure exactly what he wanted. Even so, that made it look like I didn't trust Zoey. And I trusted her. With everything I have. I honestly wasn't even sure why I trusted her so much, since I still felt like there were chunks of my memory that were gone.

I decided to wait and talk to her after we recovered the dodeca. I knew she was mad and hurt, and she had every right to be. But I couldn't let her bail on the quest. If she wouldn't or couldn't work with me anymore, I'd give Mack my boat and let him bring it back to me when they were done with it. I'd take myself out of the equation. Maybe I should do that anyway.

I'd decide on that after I talked to her. Right now, I had to focus. We needed to pack supplies and get moving to find that boat and the dodeca. We split up to take care of our individual parts, and I watched Jack knock on Zoey's door and get no response. I took that as a definitive answer she wasn't talking to any of us.

Q located the fishing boat easily enough, and we had caught up with them just before midnight. The boat was dark, and it didn't look like anyone was awake. We would still have to sneak aboard, but we would have to be even more quiet, so we didn't wake anyone.

Once we were on Chris and Katie's boat, we tied our boat to the side just like Mack and Q had done when they rescued Jack, Zoey and myself. We got Mateo to stay on deck and keep watch. At the first sign of trouble, he knew we expected him to cut the rope and get Zoey out of here.

Q cast a cloaking spell on us that was supposed to make us virtually invisible. I knew it was possible but wasn't sure this one had worked. I didn't have as much experience with spells as Ari or Isa, so I just took Q's word for it.

Jack led us to where Zoey's room on this boat was. I stood outside and kept watch while he went in with Q and looked for the haversack. Mack stood by the stairs and watched in the opposite direction. When Jack stepped out the door with the bag in his hand and gave a thumbs up, I thought we were home free. He handed the bag to Q, who strapped it on her back. I assumed they had checked for the dodeca and that it was there.

We hurried back up the stairs and across the deck to my boat. Before we could climb aboard, there was a loud noise from behind us. The four of us stopped in our tracks. I turned to see a gun aimed at my friends and myself. While I was trying to calculate how fast I could move water compared to how fast a bullet traveled, Q hurled two fireballs at Chris.

One of the fireballs hit his leg, and the gun went off. The other one hit his arm just after he shot. Out of instinct, I hit the deck and rolled away. I heard a grunt, which I was sure meant one of my friends had taken the bullet. I rolled over to see Jack lying on the deck, holding his gut. There was a growing puddle of blood underneath him. This was bad. I needed to get him back to my boat and into the sickbay so we could help him.

Just as I stood up to drag Jack onto my boat, Chris fired the gun again. I threw a spray of water at him, but it didn't stop the bullet from hitting me in the shoulder. It stung, then burned. I could feel the blood pouring from my arm like it was from Jack's stomach.

Q hit Chris with another fireball, while making sure she and Mack stayed behind some crates. This time the fireball hit him in the face, and he dropped the gun and fell to the deck. His anguished scream would haunt my nightmares for years. I was concerned that we hadn't seen Katie yet, but didn't have time to worry about that. We needed to get Jack to the sickbay and get the bullet out of him.

I crept carefully over to him and tried to pick him up. He wasn't able to help me, and I realized I couldn't do it one-armed. I whistled to get Mack's attention. He ran over and helped me pick Jack up. Together, we dragged him onto the boat, and Mateo took him down to the sickbay.

"Kyro, you have to go down too. Let Mateo start on your shoulder after he gets Jack settled. Quinn and I can handle this."

"I'm fine, Mack. I can help."

"Kyro, look at your arm. Go. We've got this."

I tried to argue with him, but my arm was covered in blood from shoulder to fingertip. I nodded and started to follow Mateo down. I turned toward the noise when I heard gunshots again. I ran in the direction Mack and Q had gone. I stopped for a moment when I heard gunfire again.

I felt a sting in my chest. I touched it with my uninjured hand and pulled it back covered with blood. I broke out in a cold sweat. I tried to turn and run, but I fell face down on the deck and couldn't manage to get up. As the world went dark, I thought about how I would have given anything to have that talk with Zoey before I went to the afterlife.

Forty-Four

Zoey

I HEARD THE COMMOTION and what sounded like gunshots. As much as I didn't want to be involved right now, I couldn't stand back and let someone get killed because Jack and I had been mind controlled and I didn't get to grab my bag. I ran out of my room and almost knocked Mateo over. He was carrying Jack to the sickbay, leaving a trail of blood behind them.

"What happened?" I asked, though I already knew the answer.

"Jack and Kyro got shot. I'm going to get Jack settled and stabilized. I heard Mack tell Kyro to come down too. I'm not sure Mack and Q can handle this."

I nodded. "Take care of him. I'll be back as soon as I can." I raced up on deck to assess the situation.

Kyro was lying on the deck. It didn't look like he was breathing. I rolled him over to find two bullet wounds, one in his shoulder and one in his chest. It was a shock to see him like this. I saw Mack behind some crates a few feet away.

"Mack! Kyro's down. I can't get him by myself. Can you take him to Mateo?" I called out to him.

Mack raced over. "I'll get him. Help Q. She got Chris down, but then Katie showed up with another gun. We're not exactly sure where she's shooting from. Be careful."

He picked Kyro up and headed below deck. I knew what I had to do, and I wasn't happy about it. First, I had to find Q and get her back on our boat. My eyes scanned the area Mack had come from. I spotted the flame-red hair before I saw the woman it was attached to. I crouched down and headed over to her.

"Q, we've gotta get out of here. Did you get the bag? Is the dodeca in it?"

She nodded twice. "Yeah, I've got the bag, and Jack checked to make sure everything was in it before he handed it to me. I can't find her. I can't stop her if I can't find her."

"Come on, we have to go. I can stop her. But we can't be on this boat when I do. Let's go."

Q gave me a strange look but followed me back to our boat. She quickly untied our boat from Chris and Katie's. Then she pointed out the spot where Chris had fallen. He wasn't there. But there was a trail of blood leading back to the bridge of the boat.

"It's fine. We need to move. Can you get our boat moving away from theirs? I'll take care of them if they come back out."

She looked at me quizzically, as though she wondered how I would take care of it. I really didn't blame her, as I had no weapon, and my training hadn't been going very well before my disappearance.

"Do you trust me?" It was all I could come up with to convince her.

She nodded and ran over to raise the sails. It seemed pointless with no wind, but I would take care of that in a minute. I had a boat to sink first.

I knew I had magic, and the visions I'd had when my memories came back had shown me just how powerful I truly was. I wasn't sure I could control my powers, but I had seen each element bending to my will, so I thought it was worth a try.

I glanced behind me to see Q finish raising the sails just as Mack came back to check on her. "Get below, both of you. I've got this." I called as I felt the wind swirling around me.

I could feel the power building inside me, begging to be released. I forced it to wait until my friends were below deck. Then I formed a whirlpool on the other side of Chris and Katie's boat. I pushed air into our sails and moved the boat away from theirs to keep us from getting caught in the whirlpool.

That should have been enough for me, but it wasn't. These people had taken my freedom and silenced me. If it hadn't been for my friends, I'd still be their slave. That anger took over, and suddenly it was pouring rain, and a storm was overhead. The lightning flashed across the sky before slamming into their boat. Just as the lightning hit, I blasted the boat with air from both ends, crushing the hull of the boat. It was certain to sink now. Lightning struck it again, and something caught fire.

The flames grew as the boat started to sink while being pulled into the whirlpool. I managed to use air to keep our boat just out of reach of the whirlpool, but close enough I could hear Chris and Katie's screams as the fire reached them. A dark grin crossed my face as I watched the boat sink slowly, the flames steady and strong, even in the downpour and whirlpool.

I gave one more push of air into the sails to move us further away. One moment, I felt amazing, like I was strong and full of power. The next moment, I felt the world spinning and hit the deck as I blacked out.

Forty-five

Mack

I carried Kyro's unconscious body down to the sickbay and placed him on a cot next to Jack, who was in almost as bad a condition. Mateo's back was turned toward me.

"How is he?" I asked, noticing he was covered in blood to his elbows.

"I think I've managed to stop the bleeding, but he's going to need the bullet removed." At that moment, Mateo turned to see what had brought me down.

"What happened?" He looked terrified.

"Two shots, one to the shoulder, another to the chest. I think it missed his heart, but it looks like it may have gone through his lung. And there's no exit wound on that one. At least that bullet went straight through his shoulder."

"We're going to have to do surgery on both of them?" Mateo sounded concerned.

"It looks that way. But I need to check on the girls. Is he stable enough that you can work on Ky?"

Mateo nodded and walked over to the cot I had put Kyro on.

I headed back up on deck just in time to find Quinn raising the sails. "What's going on?" I asked her.

"Zoey said she's got this. I have no idea what she has planned, but she told me to raise the sails and asked if I trust her."

At that moment, Zoey turned and looked at us. She yelled for us to get below. Quinn grabbed my hand and pulled me toward the steps I had just climbed.

"We can't just leave her out there alone. That storm will knock her overboard." I tried to get Quinn to go back up with me.

She just looked at me and laughed. "She's the one making the storm, Mack. It's OK. She can handle it. We need to help the others. I know it's bad. Can we save them?"

"I hope so. I'm not sure which one is hurt worse. We'll have to operate. It would be better if we could do both at the same time, but I don't think that's possible. I'll check their vitals, and we'll see what we need to do."

I headed off to the sickbay with Quinn following close behind. I knew she was worried about losing our friends, but I was worried about Zoey, too.

FOrTY-SIX

q

MACK DECIDED JACK HAD lost more blood than Kyro. Mateo helped Mack prep Jack for surgery. I got the internal repair equipment prepped for them. I couldn't stay to watch. I knew I'd break down if I did. It hit too close to home. I planned to stay close just in case they needed my help.

Once they started the surgery, I checked on Kyro. He was pale, but the bleeding had been stopped. Mack had hooked him up to a machine to help him breathe, since it looked like he'd been hit in the lung with one of the bullets. After I made sure he was stable, I figured I'd give in to Mack and check on Zoey.

I walked up on deck and looked around. Chris and Katie's boat was gone. There were pieces of it in the water, but I didn't see how anyone could have survived the wreckage. The storm had dissipated, which made sense when I saw Zoey unconscious on the deck.

I ran over to her and checked to see if she was breathing. I released the breath I hadn't realized I was holding when I saw her chest rise and fall. Her pulse was strong, and after a moment I saw her breathing was normal. I tried to wake her by gently shaking her and tapping my hand on her cheek. There was no response.

I knew Mack would be tied up the rest of the night between Jack and Kyro's surgeries. I would have to take care of Zoey myself. I wasn't very skilled at healing magic, but I was pretty sure I could get her tucked in and keep an eye on her. I hated that Mack was right about something bad happening if we left her alone.

I picked her up and carried her down to her room. I knew there were issues between her and Kyro when she didn't move right back into his room. I hoped they could work it out. Who knows, it could be over for good, especially if he doesn't pull through.

When I had her settled in, I sat on the edge of her bed and just watched her. She looked like she was sleeping, but I couldn't wake her. I was scared she'd be like this forever. I had no idea what had happened to cause it. Well, she wasn't going anywhere. I wanted to know how Kyro and Jack were faring.

I reluctantly walked out of Zoey's room, closing the door behind me quietly. I walked back to the sickbay and entered without making a sound. Mateo nodded at me, but Mack had his back toward the door. Jack was lying on a cot, with tubes and wires attaching him to machines. They were working on Kyro at the moment.

"Jack will make a full recovery. Kyro is hurt worse than we realized. His lung was fully collapsed. I'm doing a graft to repair it, but I haven't done this before, so I'm not sure it'll work." Mack spoke to me without turning around.

"Well, I don't want to distract you from what you're doing, but I have news." I wasn't sure it was bad, but I knew it wasn't good.

"What is it? Did those assholes take Zoey?"

"No, their boat is gone. Like destroyed, gone. But Zoey's unconscious and I have no idea why. She's breathing normally and her pulse is good. I just can't wake her up."

"Hmm. Any thoughts?" Mack asked Mateo.

Mateo shook his head. "Not really. Unless..." He stopped himself.

"What? Unless what?" Panic started to grip me. I had to get myself in check or I'd lose it.

"Well, I have seen Isa like that before when she's used too much of her magic. It takes a while to recharge. If that's what it is, she'll wake up when her magic is full again," Mateo explained.

"We just have to wait? It's going to be hard, but I guess there's nothing else we can do."

Mack nodded, then turned back to Kyro. I understood this was life or death and took priority over Zoey being unconscious. She wasn't going to die.

"We're going to have to move Jack tonight. We need to keep them both isolated to prevent infection. I'll need your help with that, if you don't mind." Mack spoke softly, and I knew it was to mask the flood of emotions he was feeling.

"Just let me know when. I'll do whatever I can to help. I'm going to go sit with Zoey again for a while. Please let me know how this goes." I couldn't watch him poke around inside Kyro's chest any longer. Tears were a luxury I didn't allow myself. I headed back to Zoey's room and sat in a chair staring at her, waiting for Mack to come tell me that our friends would be all right.

FORTY-seven

Jack

I WOKE UP IN pain. My gut hurt like I'd been stabbed. Not stabbed, shot. I got shot. I sat up cautiously and pulled back the bandages to inspect the incision. It seemed to be healing nicely, but that didn't give me a clear indication of how much time I'd lost. I could tell someone had operated, my guess to remove the bullet that had been lodged in my stomach.

I rose to my feet slowly and went to the door. Well, it must not have been too bad, since there wasn't anyone guarding the door or sitting here staring at me. I needed to make sure we got the dodeca and that Zoey hadn't tried to run off. I moved slowly down the hall toward the galley.

I heard voices in that direction and realized it must have been a while since I'd eaten. I was starved. Three heads turned toward me as I stood in the doorway. The conversation stopped.

"Jack! What are you doing out of bed?" Q jumped up and ran over to give me a shoulder to lean on.

"I'm starved. How long was I out?" I leaned on her and she helped me to a seat. Mack brought me a plate of food.

Mateo slid into the chair across from me. "You've been out for two weeks. Kyro's still out, and so is Zoey. We've been taking turns keeping an eye on the three of you."

"Two weeks? How bad were Kyro and Zoey hurt? How did Zoey even get hurt? Did Chris and Katie make it onto our boat?" I had so many questions.

"Kyro got shot twice and almost died. Zoey took matters into her own hands and sank Chris and Katie's boat while Mateo and I operated on you and Kyro." Mack's explanation made no sense.

"How did Zoey single-handedly sink a boat? That makes no sense. What aren't you telling me?"

Q laughed. "She has powers, Jack. Surely you know that, since you grew up with her. She created a massive storm and sank that boat while protecting ours. She drained her magic and has been out ever since."

I finished eating in silence. I had no idea Zoey had powers. She never said anything about it. I guess now I had something to be upset with her about. Once she woke up, we'd be having a long talk about this.

It was another three days before Kyro woke up and a week before Zoey stirred. We all took turns sitting with her and talking, although we weren't sure if she could even hear us. I tried to stop Kyro from sitting with her, because I knew she'd be mad about it. But he insisted, and the others backed him up on it, using the excuse that we all had to take turns, and I was needed elsewhere.

Both Kyro and I were still moving pretty slowly. But almost dying will do that to a person. I began training with Mack and Q while I waited for Kyro and Zoey to wake up. Once Kyro came back, Mack decided that it would be a pretty even match for Kyro and me to train together. Training was more like physical therapy, but that was fine with me.

The day Zoey came to, she kicked everyone out of her room. She wanted to be alone for a while. It made me wonder what had happened to her while she was out. After giving her a couple of days to adjust, I went to talk to her. I knocked on the door and waited for her to respond.

"Who is it?" She called from inside the room.

"It's Jack. We need to talk."

"I don't feel like talking. Go away." She was extra salty today.

"I'm not going anywhere. You are going to talk to me, or else." I wasn't backing down. Not this time.

The door flew open, and I was face to face with Zoey. Anger and grief were written all over her face in the expression she wore and the tear streaks down her cheeks.

"Or else what? You'll lie to me again? You'll hide more stuff from me? You'll treat me like I can't be trusted? What, Jack? Tell me."

"Or else I'll break down the door and sit on you. You know I'm not the only one here who's lied, right? I'm not the only one who's hidden anything. You're just as guilty as I am on that front. You may want to consider that when you're working on your 'holier than thou' routine." I shoved my way into the room.

I was pretty sure we were evenly matched in our anger. Even though I felt guilty over the years I had spent hiding things and lying, I wasn't going to let her off the hook for her part in any of this. I sat on the edge of the bed and waited for her to close the door and walk over.

"OK, you're here now. You want to yell at me, go ahead. I have no idea what you think I've lied about, but I'm done trying to play nice. I almost died because of the lies. I'm finished here. I'll be contacting the Patrol and turning myself in once we make port."

She was so stubborn. Of course she would decide to turn herself in for a murder she didn't commit.

"No, you're not."

"And just why not? You can't stop me. All I have to do is make a call, and they'll come get me."

"Zoey, you can't turn yourself in for a crime you didn't commit. That's crazy."

"Oh, so you're calling me crazy now? Great. The guy who's supposed to protect me decides I'm a nut job. I don't know why you care."

"I'm not calling you crazy. I'm calling your idea crazy. Because it is. Have you discussed this with Ian? Does he know you're giving up?"

"I'm not giving up. I'm removing myself from the equation. You and the others can finish the quest without me. You're all perfectly capable, so don't try to guilt me."

"I'm not trying to guilt you. If I was, I would say 'think about how your mom will feel if you turn yourself in' because that would be the most effective guilt trip. I'm trying to convince you to not abandon your friends. We need you." I hadn't planned to beg, but I wasn't going to let her do this.

"I don't know, Jack. I don't want to turn myself in, but I don't want to continue being lied to either. I can't take it anymore. It's too painful."

"Yeah, I get that. Now imagine that your best friend failed to tell you that she has magical powers. Then she had nerve enough to get pissed at you for keeping things from her, all while she knows she's keeping that giant bombshell to herself. I'd say that makes us pretty even, wouldn't you?" My voice was harsher than I had intended, but maybe that is what it would take to get through to her.

"You're right. I should have told you. I just didn't know how. I wasn't trying to lie. And you're right, we should be even now." She sounded defeated and looked as though she might start to cry again.

"All I'm asking is that you talk to Kyro and keep that in mind when you do. He wasn't trying to lie to you or deceive you. We've had a lot of time to discuss it since you've been out. Please give him a chance to explain. Don't give up on us yet." I walked away, but not before I heard her sobs. It broke my heart, but I had to set her straight.

FORTY-EIGHT

Zoey

A PART OF ME wished I hadn't woken up from whatever stasis I had been in. It was the most peaceful dreamlike state I'd ever experienced. I could pick flowers in the field, or I could walk down a country road, take a nap on a beach, or be at home with my parents. Anything I wanted was within reach. There was no Patrol, no Order, no reason to worry or fight.

I felt bad for yelling at Jack, especially after he called me out on what I'd been hiding from him. I wasn't trying to keep secrets; I just didn't think to tell him. It wasn't the same as what he'd been doing or as what Kyro had done. I knew I had to talk to Kyro, I just didn't want to let that hurt in again.

I found him in the galley, though I wouldn't have our conversation there. I wanted to make sure we had privacy. "We need to talk," I said from the doorway.

He looked at me hopefully. "Come and sit with me, then." He gestured to the seat next to him. I shook my head.

"In private." My eyes met his, and it was like he could see into my soul. As much as I wanted to talk to him in private, I was terrified I would just give in and forgive him instantly. A part of me wanted to run as far and as fast as I could away from Kyro and the quest that had entangled us. But I knew I couldn't do that. I'd already made my choice.

He stood up to follow me, and I moved out of the way for him to lead. I trusted him just enough to find a place to talk. He led me to his room. This definitely wasn't going to be easy.

"I'm not trying anything, I promise. This is the only place I know of where we can talk in private. I have a silencing cone that can be activated so no one else can hear us." He opened the door and gestured for me to go inside.

I gave him a skeptical look as I entered his room. I walked over to the small table and took a seat in one of the lounge chairs next to it. I wasn't about to go near that bed. I felt my heart start racing at the thought of being in his bed with him. My cheeks turned purple from the flush I felt at those thoughts.

I took a moment to compose myself. He had to know how difficult this was for me. And it seemed like he was set on making it even harder. His white shirt was unbuttoned halfway, which was his usual style, with the sleeves rolled up to just below his elbows. It was untucked but didn't hide the way his jeans fit just right. It was hard to focus when we were alone like this. His brown eyes were sad, and his chestnut curls begged to have my fingers tangled in them. I watched as he closed and locked the door, then walked over to a crystal cone that was sitting on his dresser. A shimmer circled the room.

"I know you're mad at me. I should have told you about the pearl. I'm sorry." He started the conversation I knew we needed but couldn't figure out how to approach.

"I am mad. And hurt. I don't understand why you can't trust me." I told myself I wasn't going to cry, but I knew it wouldn't take much to break that promise.

He took a couple steps closer to me. "It's not that I don't trust you. When you first came to me, I didn't remember I even had the pearl. Then when I realized I had one, we'd already begun looking for the others. Ian gave us all kinds of places to look, but never once indicated he thought I had one. It seemed a little shady to me."

I nodded. "So, you're saying you didn't trust me to keep it from Ian. Hmm."

I could see the panic in his eyes. This obviously wasn't going the way he had hoped. "That's not what I'm saying at all. I should have told you. There's nothing I can do about that now. Hindsight is twenty-twenty. I just don't want this to be the reason I lose you. I know I'm to blame. And if you don't want me anymore, I understand. I don't know how to fix this." He looked as if he might cry.

I had to focus on being angry. I couldn't let his tears distract me. Yet I found myself standing in front of him, placing my hand on his cheek and wiping the tears that had just begun to fall. "I don't know how to fix it either. I don't know if I even want to."

I could see that I'd hurt him with that statement, but I wasn't going to lie about it. This was a difficult situation, and I wasn't going to make any rash decisions.

He reached up and put his hand over mine still on his cheek. "Please don't give up on me yet."

I couldn't have pulled away if I had wanted to. My mind screamed for me to run, but my body refused to move. Even when I realized he was going to kiss me, I stood there and let it happen.

His lips met mine ever so gently. One hand still covered mine on his cheek, and the other wrapped around my waist to pull me closer. The kiss was so tender and held every bit of emotion neither of us could express. For a moment, I gave myself over to it.

Then I pulled back, placing my hands firmly on his chest. "I can't do this right now. I want to, but I need time. I can't just brush off that you hid things from me. It's going to take time to get over that."

He nodded; his arms still wrapped around me. "All I'm asking is that you give me the time to make it right. I'll prove to you that you can trust me. We can take things really slowly. Whatever you want. Just don't leave. I need you here."

"Jack told you I was planning to leave? Why does that not surprise me? I didn't think you two liked each other. What's that all about?" I scoffed at the realization they were working together on this.

Kyro gave me a sly smile. "Maybe I won him over. I mean, I did take two bullets so he could get down to the sickbay and Mack could save his life." He shrugged, still not letting his arms drop from around me. It was frustrating and adorable at the same time.

"I'll give you time. But I'm not making any promises. I can't guarantee we'll end up together. I'm not going to agree to something just because it's what someone else wants."

He nodded and pulled me into a hug. "That's all I want. Just time with you. Everything will fall into place, you'll see." I wrapped my arms around him and gave myself over to the hug for a moment, then pulled back and walked out of the room.

FORTY-NINE

KYRO

IT SEEMED AS THOUGH Zoey and Jack were attached at the hip since her return from the magical stasis. They had their heads together whispering secrets more often than not. She claimed I had no reason to be jealous, but I suspected there was more to their relationship than she let on. I was trying not to let it interfere with us, though. I had to try and let it go since she needed time to decide what she wanted. I told myself it made sense they were spending so much time together, since he'd been her best friend almost her whole life.

Once Zoey was back, Ian was much more cooperative. He promised us a map of the next location we needed to search for clues. Calling it a map was a bit of an exaggeration. It was a crude drawing of the globe with basic shapes used to symbolize the countries that existed in Ian's time. Most of the countries still existed, but some of the continents had been combined to make larger factories. Of course, Ian wouldn't know this, and I wouldn't have either, except for my mermaid friends reporting back to me from their journeys. Because of them, I knew Canada and Greenland had become one continuous mass of land, both natural and manmade, and the same thing had happened with Japan, except that it had taken over Korea.

Ian had both Greenland and Japan marked on the map, as well as the United States and Madagascar. Obviously, his intel wasn't great, since there were only two more pearls to find. Since we were currently sailing pretty close to Madagascar, it made sense to start there.

"So, Ian thinks one of the pearls is in Madagascar?" I didn't like the way Ian was controlling things and was having a hard time trusting him without an explanation.

Zoey looked flustered, "I have no idea. You can ask him, you know. Just say it out loud and make sure he knows you're talking to him."

"Ok, I wasn't sure if he would be OK with that since you're back now," I responded. "Ian, are you listening? We have some questions about the information you've shared with us this morning."

Yes, Kyro, I'm here, and I can hear you. I know it's hard to trust someone when you aren't sure what their motives are. I'm in the same boat with all of you. I'm not sure if it's a pearl or a clue in Madagascar, but my scrying is showing a large power source. I think it's best to look there first. If you can find one of the pearls, I've been told it will lead you to the others. The pearls are about 5 inches in diameter and, other than being larger, will look like a regular pearl. Through my research, I've found that once all three are together, they can be put on a necklace and will change in size to proportionally match their holder. I have no indication that the three are together right now, so that will actually make finding one a little easier. I'm not really sure what will happen once they are introduced to the dodeca.

"Good to know. So, we'll adjust our path to make it to Madagascar, and then what? Search the whole island?"

My information shows the power surge to be in the southwest of the island. You should start there.

"Got it. We'll check back in once we've searched the island. Thanks." And with that, Zoey closed the book.

Jack looked concerned. "Do you think it's a good idea to get these pearls together with the dodeca if we don't know what will happen? What if it's like the transporter all over again?"

"I don't have a good answer for that, Jack. All we can do is find the pearls, then decide if we want to risk putting the four pieces together." I still wasn't sure how I felt about him, but he did seem to be more interested in his daily conversations with Elena than in Zoey. We had talked about it, and he said he had no interest in Zoey other than to protect her and make sure the mission was a success. I just needed to put aside the jealousy and try to work with him. Although I saw the way he looked at her when he thought no one was looking and the way he looked at me when she paid attention to me. It wasn't hard to see that he was dealing with the green-eyed monster too.

Mack and I went to adjust the sails and change course. We estimated it would only take an hour at most to get there from our location.

FIFTY

Zoey

WE GATHERED SUPPLIES AND weapons for our trek. There was no way to be sure of what we would encounter, so we made sure to have some healing herbs, a casting machine that would splint and cast a broken bone (Q was a whiz with tech), and some throwing knives, just in case. Of course, Mack had his axe strapped to his back; I don't think he ever went anywhere without it. We met on the deck and prepared to go ashore. None of us had a clue where we were going or what exactly we were looking for, so Kyro decided to lead the way, walking carefully to avoid alerting anyone who was on the island of our presence.

I followed him with Q and Mack behind me. Jack walked next to me. We headed southwest as Ian had suggested. After walking for an hour or so, I noticed the air had changed. It smelled of soot and ash, and a sour smell that I had never experienced before. Mack called it sulfur. I glanced around, not seeing anything, then decided to climb a nearby tree to get a better vantage point. It only took a couple of minutes to get to the top, and the view was breathtaking.

When I turned to face the direction we were heading, I gasped. There was a mountain with smoke coming out of it, and we were walking straight for it.

"Wait! Stop!" I called out to my friends below, who had continued to walk slowly as I climbed.

"What is it, Zoey? Is something wrong?" Q responded to my warning first.

"There's a volcano ahead. We have to be careful." I said as I climbed down the tree and thudded onto the ground.

Kyro and Mack looked concerned, but we headed forward anyway. Neither Jack nor Q voiced an opinion. We had to find that magic source, whether it be a pearl or just a clue to its location. Kyro had another amulet today that he had set to look for magic. It was supposed to glow when we got close. Hopefully we didn't have to enter the volcano to find the magical object.

Kyro and Mack had been having a discussion of the most direct path to sail toward the next destination, so we could make the best time in our journey. Kyro was still talking when Mack stopped short. Q and I halted a few steps behind.

"Ky, what is it?" I wasn't sure why he suddenly stopped. I didn't see anything.

"Mack? Are you ok?" Kyro then turned his head and saw why Mack had stopped. Standing almost directly before them was a nine-foot-tall beast that looked to be made of lava rock. There was lava flowing over it like blood vessels in a human. It had a rock head with glowing molten lava eyes. Almost before we realized what was happening, the monster threw a lava chunk at us. We each jumped in a different direction to get out of its path. The monster then focused its efforts on the person who landed closest to it. Unfortunately, that was Q.

The lava beast threw another chunk of flaming goo at Q. She managed to avoid the worst of it, but the lava struck her left leg, sticking on her just below the knee. She shot a fireball in return, but it had no effect on the monster. With it being made of lava, it seemed to absorb the flames and just keep going. Mack rushed to Q's side to pull her out of the beast's path and into the nearby trees. As he did so, the monster attacked again, this time with its giant lava rock hand. It swatted Mack away like batting a fly. He flew a couple of feet, landed in some brush, then stood up and shook it off.

Kyro tried using his water powers on it, blasting it with a stream of liquid, but all he managed was to make steam. This turned the beast's attention to him and away from the rest of us. I helped Mack pull Q out of the line of fire, then turned to see Kyro about to be smashed by the lava monster. I cried out and threw my hands in front of me, wishing I had some magical ability that would help us against this beast. Suddenly a shock of cold flew from my hands, and the monster was blasted with ice. It froze over and was stuck there. I didn't waste any time gathering my friends and retreating to the jungle once again. I knew the ice wouldn't last long against that lava.

We decided to attempt going around the volcano, since of course Kyro's amulet had started to glow. It was rough terrain, and with Q's injuries, it was difficult to maneuver. Once we were far enough away from where the monster had been, we stopped to evaluate Q's injuries. We had Jack and Kyro keep watch while we checked Q's leg. Mack and I cut the leg of her jeans away to reveal charred skin covering her calf, almost completely from her knee to ankle. The burns went deep in spots, leaving marks that looked like she had been gashed with claws. It seemed to be healing slowly, which was odd, but may have had something to do with her having the ability to control fire. She seemed as surprised as we were about it. Mack applied some herbs to help with the pain, and we wrapped her leg in strips made from an extra shirt he had brought. I wondered if he knew it was visible to others that he was in love with her but figured now wasn't the time to bring it up. It was really sweet watching him carefully ripping up his own shirt to mend her wounds.

Once her injuries had been dealt with, we continued around to the other side of the volcano. We continued as quietly as possible, trying to avoid another run-in with that lava monster or its friends. We weren't sure if there were any more, but didn't want to find out.

We had headed straight west after the encounter with the beast. Kyro's amulet glowed brighter with each step we made. It seemed like we had been walking for hours when the amulet suddenly stopped glowing. We each looked around to see if there was anything hidden in this area of the jungle. Mack and I searched the ground near the trees, looking under grass and leaves on the ground. There was nothing here. Jack searched the woods a few feet away from us and came up empty-handed. Q looked in hollowed-out trees, calling Kyro to help her move one because she could see something odd inside. Kyro picked the fallen tree up, lifted it over his head, and set it down on the other side of Q.

"Show-off," Q chided him. "Look!" She was as excited as a child during the holidays, sitting by a pile of gifts. She jumped up and down a little, then winced at the pain from her charred leg. Mack moved quickly over to her side so she could lean on him for relief.

There was something in the mud where the tree had been. It could have been round or star-shaped. It was hard to tell with it also being caked with layers of mud and muck. But the glow was unmistakable. Whatever this was, it was magical. I wrapped it in a scrap of material and put it in my bag.

"Let's get out of here. We've got what we came for." I turned to the others and patted the bag. They nodded, and we began to head back toward the boat. We didn't make it very far when our lava friend showed up again. I tried to freeze him like I did earlier, but it didn't work. I planted my feet, threw my hands up and tried again, but to no avail. I could not control my power, and it terrified me.

The beast started throwing lava chunks at us again, seemingly at random. A small one hit my right foot, burning instantly, because I wasn't fast enough to duck completely out of the way. I cried out in pain, and Kyro rushed to my side. I saw the rock that hit him in the back just as the monster released it. I couldn't stop it from hitting him, and he went down instantly. I screamed and threw my hands out as I had before. The monster froze again, and this time, Mack took his axe and made sure it wasn't going to thaw. Or rather, he tried. It turns out frozen lava rock is harder than dwarven steel, so Mack was able to knock chunks out of the monster, but not fully decapitate or dismember it. Jack took a few swings at it with no luck either. We had to move quickly, so Mack and I carried Kyro, and Q kept up the best she could. When she started to fall behind, Jack picked her up and carried her. We cleared the edge of the trees, making our way back to the beach. As we started down the dock to the boat, we heard crashing behind us. There was no need to turn around, we all knew it was the beast. It threw lava chunks as we ran to the boat. One flaming chunk hit the dock, almost exactly where we were. The dock splintered and caught fire, and we all fell into the water.

Fortunately, with Kyro being the son of Poseidon, as soon as he hit the water, he turned into a merman. He also wasn't burned very badly by the lava rock. It seemed as though his water powers helped with that. Unfortunately, he didn't wake up, so we had to drag him with us back to the boat. I managed to get him to the side of the boat, but I had hit the point of exhaustion. Jack climbed onto the boat first and helped the rest of us. Q climbed up onto the boat, then reached down and pulled Kyro up with Jack's help. Mack helped me climb up as well. There, with the lava beast just out of reach, we collapsed on the deck. Kyro went through his transformation again to regain his legs. It was fantastic to watch, even with him unconscious. Mack treated his wounds and helped me get him into bed. I would be caring for him once more, again because he tried to save me. It didn't matter that I was still mad at him, I would do what needed to be done. Mack treated my foot and told me to stay in bed until morning as well. He said he was going to tend to Q, then they would be getting some sleep as well. Since Mack and Jack were the only ones who hadn't been hurt, they were stuck taking care of the rest of us.

Jack headed to the galley to prepare a meal for everyone. He delivered the meals and checked on all of us before heading to his room for the night.

FIFTY-ONE

Mack

AFTER GETTING KYRO AND Zoey settled in, I helped Quinn back to our room and onto the bed. I gathered up some fresh water and bandages, along with medicines and herbs to help with her burn. I knew she had some healing capabilities but figured I should check it out anyway.

I thought I might need some help holding her down, so I found Jack and asked him to help.

"I just need you to hold her down if she tries to fight me. I have to get that wound cleaned, or it'll get infected."

"No problem, man." Jack followed me to my room and sat beside the bed as I got everything together.

Once I had everything beside her on the bed, I handed her a small bottle of whiskey. "You're gonna want some of that before I start, love." She nodded and took a swig. Then she gritted her teeth as I started peeling the makeshift bandages off her burned leg as gently as I could.

"OK, Jack, hold her shoulders down for this part."

He did as I asked, and I could tell from his face that he wished he'd refused to help.

She did her best not to scream, though I could only imagine the amount of pain she had to be in. Layers of skin came off along with each bandage. Her leg was a bloody, blistered mess. There were large chunks of flesh missing from where the lava had melted them away. There were places where the bones may have been exposed, but I couldn't tell for sure without cleaning the rock and gravel from the wound. I did my best to hide the fear I was feeling. I wasn't sure I could do anything to heal her, and without Gill, I didn't have anyone to help me with the healing.

As I pulled the last piece of bandage from her calf, Quinn screamed then passed out from the pain. I felt like that was probably for the best. I went to work gently cleaning and disinfecting her wounds, making sure to get all the soot and volcanic rock out of the raw places. It was difficult and took a couple of hours. I was pretty sure it looked even worse once the soot and rock were all removed. There were indeed places where the bone was exposed. I felt like she'd be lucky if she was ever able to walk again. It broke my heart. I laid a damp cloth underneath her leg and draped another one over top of it.

When she passed out, Jack loosened his grip on her shoulders, but didn't let go. When I was finished cleaning and draping the cloth over it, I turned to him.

"That should be it for tonight. Thank you."

"I'm happy to help, but I hated that. I'll see you in the morning."

Then I started preparing herbs into a salve to calm the burning and encourage healing. I did the best I could to remember what Gill had taught me. I hoped it was enough. Once the salve was prepared, I gently rubbed it all over her leg from the knee down. I made sure to make it a thick layer, then wrapped her leg with a clean, damp bandage to keep the salve moist. When I finished, I cleaned up my own wounds, then crawled into bed beside her, careful not to hit her leg.

FIFTY-TWO

Zoey

I WOKE IN THE morning to a throbbing pain in my right foot. I checked on Kyro, who was still unconscious beside me. His breathing and heartbeat were both steady, so I figured he'd be ok if I got up. I took a shower and cleaned my foot. My usually blue skin was purple and marred on the top of my foot. I hoped Mack had something to help it heal, and I hoped he had a way to wake Kyro up. I went to find Mack and ask about both.

I gently knocked on Mack's door, figuring he would have brought Q here instead of staying in her room. Mack answered instantly, as though he was waiting for me. He came out of his room with a small jar and closed the door behind him. We walked to the galley so we could sit and talk.

"I've already told her she has to stay in bed. It's bad, Zoey, really bad. I'm not sure I can help her. This salve will help your foot, though. How's Kyro?"

I took the jar he offered. "Thank you. He's still out. His breathing and heartbeat are steady and strong, but he won't wake up. I'm sorry about Q. Is there anything I can do?"

"Not unless you know a medic or some healing magic."

"I don't think I know any healing magic, and the only medic I know is still on the space station."

At that moment, Jack walked into the galley. "I'm not helping you with medical stuff again. Don't even ask. That was too much." I laughed because I knew that as tough as Jack was, he had the weakest stomach.

"Well, we will just have to do the best we can. With any luck, Ky will wake up today, and maybe he'll know what to do." Mack responded.

"Do you think it would be ok to check out what we found last night? Or should we wait for everyone else?" I wasn't sure which answer I wanted. I was anxious about the whole situation.

Mack considered for a moment, then replied, "We can check it out ourselves, then show it to them later. C'mon, we'll go to the galley. I'm sure it's still caked in mud like when we found it. We'll clean it up and see if it's what Ian wanted."

I followed him to the galley, stopping to get my bag with the book and the orb in it. I placed the bag on a table and pulled out the orb wrapped in fabric. Then I pulled out the book and set it aside. I wasn't going to talk to Ian until I knew what to tell him.

Mack brought a pan of warm water, and we began to peel away the fabric and clean up the mud. The more we cleaned, the more anxious I became. It looked just like a regular pearl, but much larger. This had to be what Ian sent us looking for, but there was no way to know which pearl it was or what it did. Even Ian claimed to not be sure what they would do. I wasn't sure if he was giving us the whole story, but I didn't push it. I was happy enough to have found Kyro.

Through this process, Jack stood back against the wall with his arms crossed. He obviously wanted to make sure we were safe but didn't want to get too close to anything magical.

Mack turned the pearl over in his hand, rubbing it gently. "I wonder what this one is for."

"I feel like Ian should have told us what the pearls do. I'm sure he had reasons not to, though."

"Maybe we can figure it out. Let's concentrate and see if we can make it do something." It wasn't a bad idea, but I wasn't sure how we'd figure it out.

Mack tried holding the pearl while meditating on what it might do. I'd never seen a dwarf meditate; it was actually rather calming. However, it didn't yield any results, so we were still at square one. He suggested that I try next, so I got comfortable and tried what I had just seen Mack do. Unfortunately, I had the same results he did. Since we were getting nowhere, we decided to put the pearl back in my bag and go check on Q and Kyro.

FIFTY-THREE

Mack

WE CHECKED ON Q first, because I didn't want to risk her trying to get up. I brought her a tray of fruit and toast with some juice, hoping she would feel like eating. She was awake when we arrived, trying to sit up, and groaning in pain.

"Wait, I'll help you. Just sit still for a minute, would ya?"

"I don't have much choice, do I? What happened?"

"How much do you remember?" I was certain she meant after she passed out, but it didn't hurt to ask.

"You were cleaning my leg, and then I was out. Did I pass out, or did you drug me?"

"I didn't have to drug you, your leg was pretty rough. I had Jack hold you down until you passed out. Can I take a look? Or would you rather eat first?"

"You brought food? That would be great." At this point, she noticed we weren't alone. "Oh, hey, Zoey. How's Kyro?"

"He was still out when I left him. I think I'm going to check on him now."

She excused herself, leaving Q and me alone. I watched her eat, then checked her bandages. It looked the same as it had the night before. I carefully peeled away the bandages again, cleaned the blisters, applied more salve, and rebandaged her wounds. She managed to stay awake this time, which I took as a good sign. "You need to stay in bed today and rest so you can heal."

"I don't like it, but since I'm sure I can't walk, I'll have to do what you say. Thank you, Mack, for taking care of me."

"It's nothing, love."

"Would you have Jack come see me? I have something I need him to do while I'm laid up in here."

"I'll send him right down."

I leaned over and kissed her gently. Then she laid back to relax, and I left her alone. I went up to the deck and started the work I knew Kyro usually did in the mornings. Jack was already up there, so I asked him to go see Q. I had no idea what she needed him to do, but it had to be important if it couldn't wait until she was healed. I figured I'd give Zoey some time with Kyro before I went down to check on his condition.

FIFTY-FOUr

Zoey

I FELT AWKWARD IN Mack's room when he went to check on her, so I decided to check on Kyro. I went back to our room, hoping he had woken up while I was gone. Unfortunately, he was still in the same condition. His heartbeat and breathing were both steady, so I guessed he was as OK as possible. I hoped Mack had something to help him.

I sat on the bed next to him, watching him breathe. I ran my fingers through his hair, speaking softly to him. "Please come back to me. I can't do this without you." I leaned down and kissed his forehead, then sat back against the headboard.

I wasn't sure how long I sat there like that. Before I knew it, Mack was at the door. "Can I check on him?"

"Of course. Do you need me to leave?"

"No, I may need your help. If you can."

"I'll try." I was hoping he'd have the answer, but he seemed as uncertain as I was. He walked over and put his hand on Kyro's forehead.

"Well, for starters, he's warm, but not hot. That's a good sign. And I could tell from across the room that his breathing was good." He placed one of his large hands on Kyro's chest for a minute. "Heartbeat is strong. This is good. But I don't know why he's still knocked out, which is bad."

"What do we do? Can you wake him up?" I was feeling particularly desperate at the moment, panicking at the thought of Kyro staying like this for much longer.

"I have enough knowledge to make potions or salves that can heal, but I don't know what I can do with him unconscious. We may have to wait it out. I'm willing to try a couple of spells, though they're long shots at best." With that, he hung his head, disappointed in himself and upset that he couldn't help his friend.

"OK, let's try it. I'm pretty sure it can't make things worse. Right?"

"I certainly hope not. I'll get my spell book and be right back." He exited the room, walking with purpose.

I turned to Kyro, "I really hope this works. I don't know what we'll do if it doesn't." I could have sworn that he stirred when I said that, but it was so brief, I couldn't be sure. I turned toward the door when it opened again. Mack was back, but he was practically carrying Q with him. "She insisted on being here too, so I couldn't let her walk on that leg."

I cleared my spot on the bed for her, and we settled her in, propping her leg up. "I'm not going to let the two of you save him and take all the credit. I want to help. Since I can't do anything else, at least let me lend some magic to the cause."

She made a valid point, which I'm sure is why Mack carried her in here. The more magic we had access to, the better. He was getting everything set up for the spell, candles, the book, some herbs and oils. Suddenly there was a loud noise on deck that sounded like a bomb had gone off. Mack and I rushed to the stairs to see what had happened. He yelled over his shoulder, "Stay in that bed, Quinn, and keep an eye on Kyro. I mean it." To my surprise, she simply nodded and asked us to be careful.

FIFTY-FIVE

Mack

WHEN ZOEY AND I ran out of their room to the stairs, I half expected to look back and see Q following us. But when I looked, the hall was empty. Good, she had decided to listen for once. I needed her to watch Kyro anyway. We could handle whatever was going on up there ourselves, I was certain of it. I grabbed my axe and led the way up the stairs. "Do you have any weapons on you?" I didn't think to tell her to grab something when we passed my room. I had plenty of weapons to spare. "I have these throwing knives we've been practicing with. Is that good enough?" At least she had something. "It should be. We're about to find out. We have to protect Q and Kyro, no matter what. Understood?" I knew her answer before she nodded her head. A blind man could have seen the way she loved him. We would do whatever necessary to protect those we loved. I poked my head out of the door and took a look around.

"Where the hell is Jack?" Zoey asked. I shook my head in response. He must have been in the cargo hold working on whatever Q needed him to do, or he would have heard this commotion.

I didn't like what I saw, but I was glad it hadn't seen me. I pulled my head back in and carefully closed the door. "It's a gbahali, a crocodile-like monster native to this area. I knew we were sailing too close to land." It looked like a croc, but its snout was shorter, its legs were longer, and though I'd never admit it to anyone, it was the most terrifying thing I had ever seen. "We have to go out there and defend the boat. Just don't get eaten. And be careful, we still don't know what made that bomb sound."

I slid the door open just enough to slide through and went the opposite direction of the monster. I motioned for Zoey to follow me, and she did, carefully closing the door behind her to protect the others. We silently decided to try to flank the beast and attack before it saw us. I felt like that was going to be our best chance to defeat it. I went to the left, Zoey went to the right, and we both prayed to our gods that we could kill this thing before it killed us.

The gbahali was sniffing around looking for something, probably its next meal--there was no way to be sure. We both came upon it from behind, flanking the beast and assessing the best spot to attack. I motioned to Zoey to wait for a count of three, when she jumped on the monster's back and started stabbing it in the ribs with two of her knives. The beast bucked and tried to throw her off, but she already had one blade thrust deep in its back, which allowed her to hold on.

I ran forward with my axe, ready to slice the beast in two, when it flipped its tail around and knocked me across the boat, slamming my axe out of my hand and just out of reach. "Ah, shit. This isn't good." The monster then turned its attention to me, walking over with its jaws gnashing. Just as I was within reach of its terrifying jaws, Zoey thrust another knife into its back, twisting and jamming the knife as far as the hilt would allow. This caught the beast by surprise, and it stopped, screaming in pain. It began to turn in circles, trying to buck her off. I took this opportunity to go for my axe, which meant diving right in front of the gbahali. I grabbed my axe in my right hand, just as the beast chomped down on my left arm. I let out a scream of pain and slammed the axe down on the monster's neck, slicing a large gash. The croc-like creature let go of my arm, screaming in pain.

Zoey pulled her knife from its back and thrust again in a different spot. The creature screamed again, bucking for its life. This time it managed to throw her off. She landed a few feet away, on top of some crates. The crack of her landing was sickening, and I was certain she had broken something, though I couldn't tell what. I silently prayed she would be OK and went after the beast before it could attack her again. I held my axe in my right hand and used my left to steady it, even though the blood running down my arm made it somewhat slippery. I slammed the axe into the beast's neck once again, feeling the bones break as the blade sliced through, separating its head from its shoulders. This particular gbahali would not be feasting on my family tonight. I threw the body overboard, keeping the head to harvest the teeth of the beast as a trophy. I secured it to some crates on deck, then rushed over to Zoey. I could tell from where I was when the beast went down that she was breathing, so I knew she was alive.

As I made my way over to check Zoey's injuries, I heard a noise over the edge of the boat in the water. I checked her pulse and breathing, then made my way over to where the noise had come from. It was Mateo, swimming next to the boat. "Mack, is everything ok? I've been trying to contact Kyro but haven't heard anything in response. I started to worry."

"I don't know, Mateo, things are bad. Can you come up?"

"Sure, can you throw me a rope?" I tossed him a rope, and he pulled himself up, standing on two legs when he hit the deck. He saw Zoey lying where she had landed and rushed over. "Is she OK? What happened?" Without being asked, he picked her up effortlessly and started to carry her down below.

"We'll check her out, but I think she's OK. Take her to Kyro's room, that's where the others are. I'll get bandages and salve. I'll need your help with my arm as well." Mateo nodded and did as I requested.

FIFTY-SIX

q

THE DOOR OPENED, AND I summoned a fireball, holding it in my hand. I had to protect Kyro. It was Mack's request, and I was beginning to think I would do anything for that man, within reason, of course. He must have known I would react that way, because as soon as the door opened, he pushed through it, swinging it wide for the guy carrying Zoey to follow. It took me a minute to realize it was Mateo.

"What happened? Mateo? Is she OK?" I couldn't tell if she was breathing, but I knew he needed a place to check her out, so I jumped out of the bed, standing on one leg, and hopped out of the way. "Put her down here. Thanks."

He nodded, laying Zoey down on the bed next to Kyro. "I'm sorry, Q, I hate to shove you out of the way. She's unconscious. What's wrong with him?" He gestured to Kyro, who was in the same condition he had been since our encounter with the lava monster.

"We're not sure what's wrong with Kyro. Physically he's fine, but we can't wake him up." I kind of hoped he would have an answer for us.

Mack pulled the table beside the bed, then moved a chair over for me to sit on. I sat down and helped him organize his supplies. "Let me clean up your arm, then you can take care of her. Please." I hated seeing him put himself last, which he was prone to do.

"Aye, lass, that would be nice." He stepped over where I could reach to cut his sleeve off and start cleaning his wounds.

"What was out there? This is a huge set of teeth marks wrapping all the way around your arm!"

He explained about the crocodile monster and how they had defeated it. The story was terrifying. By the end, I was silently thanking the gods that my friends had survived this encounter. "But how did it get on the boat?"

I didn't understand the logistics of it. It wasn't the type of creature that could climb up the side of the boat on its own. Mateo spoke up, "I think it was dropped onto the boat magically. I heard the boom and swam over as quickly as I could. But by the time I got here, Mack had already hacked its head off."

I shuddered to think that we weren't safe no matter where we went. There had to be a cloaking spell for the boat. I'd have to ask Mack about it later. After I cleaned up his arm, I put a few rudimentary stitches in the worst wounds, and he used a mild healing spell to close up the rest. It didn't look pretty, but it would keep the wounds from getting infected.

Then he turned his attention to Zoey. He checked her pulse and breathing and searched her body for injuries. She had a knot on her head, but he said that wasn't too bad. Other than that, she had no injuries. I gave Mack my right hand, he took it with his left, and placed his right hand on Zoey's forehead. There was a warm blue glow that ran through me, then Mack, and hit Zoey. It seemed to fill her from head to toe. She began to stir. Her eyes opened, and she gasped. "Mack, is it dead? Did we beat it?" He brushed a hand over her forehead, and she instantly calmed. It seemed that he had more magic than I originally thought. "Yes, little one, we defeated the monster. Now rest so you can heal."

Zoey leaned over and kissed Kyro gently on the forehead. She began to glow again, just as she had when we healed her. Then Kyro began to stir. He didn't wake up, but he did get close. His eyes fluttered, then he sighed. "I think we're close to figuring out how to heal him." Mack was optimistic, which was a change from earlier. It was a good sign.

Mateo stepped over to the bed, placed his right hand on the amulet he wore, then his left hand on Kyro's chest. He concentrated for a moment, and an orange glow surrounded Kyro. "He will wake with the sun. He may be sore yet, but he will be fine."

"What did you do? How do you know that?" I didn't understand what was happening.

"I only scanned his body for injuries, I didn't heal him. She did." He pointed at Zoey, who looked confused.

"I didn't do anything, just kissed him." Then she realized that it was just as Ian had told her. The powers would be there when they were needed.

"Is this what Ian was talking about?" She asked Mack.

"It may be. We can ask him later. We need to check you over now and see how well the healing worked." He was adamant that he needed to check her foot, which was the worst of her injuries.

When he removed her boot and sock, he looked impressed. "It's fully healed. This is amazing."

FiFTY-seven

Zoey

WHEN MACK REMOVED MY boot and sock, I expected to see the blistered mess that had been there this morning. Instead, my foot looked as though the incident with the lava monster had never happened. I didn't understand what had just happened. "Mack, how did you do that?"

He looked puzzled. "I didn't do it, you did."

Mateo cleared his throat, "Uh, I've actually seen this once before. A few years ago, there was a mermaid and a merman who had powers, but they weren't fully able to use them separately. Their powers only worked fully when they used them together. I'm guessing that Kyro cares for you as much as you do him. Don't be embarrassed, it's truly obvious, just like with these two."

He motioned to Mack and Q, who both blushed, but didn't argue. "He must have reached out with his magic at the same time you pushed yours forward to him." It made the most sense of anything I'd heard since meeting this bunch.

"So, our powers work together, and that's how I'm healed? Why isn't he awake then?"

"I really don't know, but my power tells me he will wake in the morning. Maybe he will have more information about what happened." Mateo sounded more certain than I felt. Mack suggested that Mateo stay with us for the night, and he agreed. He settled into my old room across the hall. Mack waited until he left to ask me for a favor. He pulled me to the side and kept his voice low.

"Can you try to heal Quinn? I know her leg is bad, and she's in a lot of pain. I've tried to heal it, and nothing is working. Will you please just try?" He sounded desperate, and I could see the concern in his eyes.

"I can try, but I'm not really sure how. Maybe if I hold Kyro's hand and ask him to help me. That might work. Let's try it." We walked back to the bed, where Q was still in the chair sitting next to Kyro. "Hey, Q, do you mind if I try something?" I figured it was better to ask than to just do it.

"What are you talking about?" She seemed a little skittish.

"I'd like to try to heal your leg, if that's OK with you." She relaxed a little bit. "You can try if you want. I hope it works. I hate being an invalid."

I turned to Kyro, took his hand, and said, "If you can hear me, I need your help. Q's leg is badly burned, and I need you to help me heal it. Please try." He squeezed my hand gently, so I knew he could hear me.

"OK, he's in. Let's try this." I had Kyro's left hand in my right, then placed my left on Q's leg, just above her knee. I figured it was close enough to the burns without actually touching them. Mack stepped over and picked up Q's hands in his. We were planning to give it all we had. The three of us concentrated on healing thoughts, knowing that Kyro was trying to do so as well. I pushed as much blue healing energy into Q as I could. Her leg started to glow, and I figured that meant it was working. I held the energy for as long as I could, but it became too much to handle. I had to release it before it exploded. I wasn't sure how I knew it would explode, but I was certain of it. "Mack, I have to let it go. I can't hold it anymore."

I dispersed the energy into the air above us, releasing my hold on Q and Kyro when I did it. The blue puff of energy dissipated, leaving behind a heavy feeling. I wasn't sure if it had worked at all. I practically held my breath while Mack carefully peeled back the bandages from her leg. "Oh." That was all he said.

"What does that mean?" Q was as impatient as I was to see if it had worked.

"It worked, but not as well as I had hoped." He lifted Q's leg to show us what he meant. It was still marred with deep scars where the worst wounds had been. But other than scarring, it was healed.

"Mack, it's ok. It feels a lot better now. Just sore. I'm sure I can walk on it now. And I'm not afraid of a scar." Q was looking at the bright side. Mack helped her to her feet and stayed close while she carefully took a few tentative steps to make sure she was right.

She seemed satisfied with her first few steps. Q turned to me and said, "Thank you, Zoey, and you too, Kyro—if you can hear me. And Mack. Thank you." She leaned down and kissed him hard on the mouth, then turned back to me.

"Now if you'll excuse us, I want a shower, and he'll be wanting to help. He hovers; it's cute." And with that she patted Mack on the cheek, winked at me and sauntered away, leaving him standing there with his mouth gaping open.

"You'd better follow her. I think she was serious." He nodded at me and hurried out the door after Q.

FIFTY-EIGHT

KYRO

I WOKE THE NEXT morning as if pulling myself out of quicksand in a swamp covered in fog. I wasn't sure how many days I had been out, but I had an idea of what had happened in the meantime. I knew Zoey was brokenhearted they hadn't been able to heal me. I had sensed something had happened to her and pushed as much energy out as I could when she kissed my forehead. Then I heard her asking me to do it again for Q. I wasn't sure why she needed it, but it was enough that Zoey had asked. I fully accepted the fact I would do anything for her. I may not have been ready to tell her yet, but it wouldn't stop me from taking care of her.

I turned my head to the left and relaxed when I saw her sleeping beside me. I was sore, for sure, but thought I could manage to get up and move around some. I raised up on my elbows and turned toward Zoey. She was so beautiful sleeping next to me. I leaned over and kissed her gently on the lips. She smiled, then sat up in a panic.

"Oh, gods, Kyro, you're awake! Just like Mateo said! Oh, I'm so glad you're okay!" She grabbed me and kissed me like I had come back from the dead. It was fantastic. We spent some time catching up on the details of the past few days, starting with how they got me back on the boat, and ending with the healing last night. Once I was fully up to speed, we decided there was no time to waste on our journey. We plotted the quickest course to Japan and planned to head out today. It would take a few days to get there, but we would be vigilant about protecting each other and the boat.

Once everyone was up and about for the day, I asked Mateo if he wanted to join us on this quest. He agreed, but said he wanted to spend most of his time in the water. I figured he was more comfortable out there and agreed. We decided to continue training while we traveled but at a lower intensity, because, with the exception of Mateo, everyone had been injured at some point over the past few days.

Nobody had seen Jack in days, and we'd begun to wonder if he'd somehow left the ship when we weren't paying attention. Then suddenly he was standing next to me, holding some weird contraption and grinning from ear to ear.

"Q, I think I got it. We can test it out when we stop for supplies."

"That's fantastic, Jack. Are you sure it'll work?"

"What exactly are you two going on about? What is that thing?" I broke in, trying to get answers.

"It's an electronic protection device for the boat. I'm not sure if it'll work or not, but like I said, we can test it when we stop for supplies. I can stay on the boat and activate it, then we'll know if it works without risking anyone else getting hurt."

I wasn't sure how I felt about that, but if it would protect the boat, I guessed it was a good idea.

FIFTY-NINE

Mack

WE HAD TO STOP in India for supplies. We all ventured into the marketplace together, then split up to get what we needed. It was mostly an open-air market, with vendors set up on the street for clothing, blankets, food, and other necessities. The vendors had canopies to keep the sun or rain off their wares and tables covered with goods. There were several with the latest clothing options, ranging from fancy dresses and suits to hoodies and jeans. Others had blankets in every color of the rainbow and in multiple textures, thicknesses, and patterns. Still others carried canned foods and farmer's market goodies. Fresh-grown food was rare with the state of the planet, so we knew those would be expensive.

There were stores inside buildings that carried electronics, communications, and other tech stuff. They had items stuck in windows to show them off. We could see keyboards, circuit boards, computers, communicators, and other gadgets on display.

Of course, the tech stuff is where Q wanted to go, while Zoey and Kyro looked for clothing and food, and I concentrated on weapons and supplies of that nature.

I met with a farrier who allowed me to rent his forge for a few hours. I was able to create two small daggers each for Kyro and Zoey and made repairs to my own weapons, including sharpening my axe. Before I was finished, Q met me at the forge and kept close until I was finished.

"Did you get what you needed?" I wanted to make sure we had everything before we left the market. It would be less than ideal to get where we were going without the right weapons.

"I did. I got some cool new parts for some interesting devices, but I don't think I'll have them ready for this trip. You?"

"I got my axe sharpened and made some goodies for our friends. I figured you've got it covered, since, well, you know...fire and all." She nodded and proceeded to tell me all about her tech thingy, while I pretended to follow. I really didn't understand all that. I was much more comfortable with a forge and a hammer.

We met back up with Kyro and Zoey and headed back to the boat with our wares. It was time to get moving. This quest wasn't going to finish itself.

As soon as we got back on the boat, Jack rushed up to Q. "I can't get it to work right. I can keep working on it, but it just won't do what it's supposed to."

They huddled together discussing possible issues with his design and ways to fix it. I didn't stick around because nothing they were saying made any sense.

SIXTY

Ian

I WOKE IN A cold sweat at three in the morning. That dream had been so realistic. Was it a dream? Or could it have been a vision? I needed to write it all down before I forgot anything. I would need to warn Zoey and the others as soon as possible.

I sat up slowly, so I didn't bother Kara. The poor dear was already struggling to sleep, and it seemed to get worse the further along she was. It wasn't good for her or the baby to be constantly bothered by my inability to control my powers. I silently climbed out of bed, replaying the dream as I walked to my office.

The battle raged, with bombs sounding in the distance, blades slicing through the air, gunshots pinging off metal shields. It seemed as though magic was having little effect on the weapons the enemy had brought. For a while, it appeared as though we might have the upper hand. I watched as they fought valiantly. I was confident we were going to win this battle. Then Kyro cried out and put his hand to his chest, the redness spreading as he fell.

Zoey instantly ran to his side and was cut down by a blade slashing across her back. Jack rushed forward only to be blasted by an explosion and fall. Glancing around the battlefield, my eyes settled on Mack, lying face down with a red puddle beneath him. Nearby, Q was releasing fireballs faster than anything I'd ever seen before. Suddenly she was hit by something flying through the air. She gasped and grabbed her stomach, falling to her knees, her hands coated red, and a puddle forming under her as well. It was then she realized that the others had fallen. She cried out in pain and anguish, as a figure walked through the wreckage and stood over her. As I watched, he brought his katana down and finished her off.

I had to make sure they didn't try to go up against The Order. Watching the Chairman kill everyone who was helping me made me sick. Writing it all down so I could share it with them made it even worse. How could I tell them that I had seen all of their deaths? Could I be that cruel to let them know their ends were so near? Or was it more selfish to keep the dream to myself and hope it didn't happen? I needed some time to think about what I needed to do.

If I stopped them from going against The Order, would I be stopping them from completing the mission I had sent them on? I was so conflicted by the whole thing; I wasn't sure which decision would have better results. I had been so focused on fixing everything while finding a way to keep my powers, that I hadn't stopped to consider I might become fond of those I recruited to help me.

I locked my office door, sat cross-legged on the floor, closed my eyes, and regulated my breathing. I calmed my mind as much as I could, and then went searching for the answers I needed. I had to find out if there was a way to change what I had seen. I became desperate to figure out what had gone wrong in the timeline from that vision.

In the past, I had been able to call forth visions when I had questions. For some reason, it wasn't happening today. I pulled myself up from the floor and went to my supply cabinet. Maybe if I cleansed the area with sage and crystals, I would be able to concentrate and pull the truth from the vision.

As I walked to my supply cabinet, the room began to spin. It was the strangest sensation, as though my soul was being separated from my body. I fought to remain intact, but the onslaught was too much, and I couldn't resist. The room went dark, and I felt my body fall away. When my vision cleared, I was standing in what appeared to be a holding cell. I had no idea how far I had traveled or if I would be able to return to my body.

In front of me, there was a door, standing slightly ajar. I took a chance by walking over to it, then through it. The room I had come into was at the end of a long hallway. There were doors every few feet on either side of the hall, and it felt like this was a vision, but I was actually experiencing it first-hand. I cautiously walked down the hall, looking into the small windows in each door as I passed.

Each room was empty but appeared to be an interrogation room. It was eerily similar to what was depicted by television shows. I turned the corner at the opposite end of the hall from my entrance. There was a commotion happening in front of me, and it took me a moment to realize that the people involved couldn't see me.

There were three armed men in uniform wrestling a large, obviously alien person who seemed set on escape. The alien was tall, with gray skin, and tentacles in place of hair on its head. It was wearing a shirt and pants, but I couldn't tell if it was male or female. To be honest, I had heard of some species who weren't classified as either one. I watched for a minute more before casually walking past them.

I felt as though I was being pulled down the hall. It was an uncontrollable urge to move forward. Something was calling out to me from around the corner. I was intrigued and terrified at the same time. I tried briefly to resist the siren song that was leading me down the hallway, but I couldn't stop myself. It felt as though my feet had a mind of their own, and I was just being brought along for the ride.

I turned the corner and saw another opened door. There was a faint light coming from it. My feet finally stopped right outside that door. My curiosity got the better of me, and I pushed the door open more to get a better look. In the center of the room was an altar, which looked to be set up for a ritual.

I shivered at the thought of what could be happening here. To the left of the altar was a metal table. It had streaks of something on it. If I didn't know better, I would think it was blood and that this ritual was a sacrifice. But that couldn't be, since people didn't actually make sacrifices anymore. That had been outlawed a few years back, when it became obvious that the sacrifices weren't willingly giving themselves up.

I stepped closer to check the table more closely. It did appear to be blood, but that didn't mean the sacrifice was human or humanoid. It could have been an animal. I didn't want to let myself assume anything. I wasn't even sure where I was. This could be the headquarters for The Order, but it could just as easily be the main base of the Patrol.

A noise behind me caused me to jump. I turned suddenly to see the same guy who was being practically dragged in the opposite direction a few moments ago. Now he was being brought in here. I stepped back against the wall, though I was fairly convinced at this point no one could see me. The guards strapped him to the table, injected him with something, then left.

As soon as they closed the door, I moved closer to take a look at the rather large person who was now unconscious on the table. The moment I got close enough, a hand shot up and grabbed my arm. The alien being looked right at me with hollow eyes and mumbled something I couldn't understand.

"What did you say?" I asked aloud.

The being looked at me again. "Run while you can. Save yourself. This is the end for me. But you can stop all of this." The words were breathy and strained.

"How can you see me when no one else can?" I didn't expect an answer but had to ask.

"It's my power. I brought you to see this. Get the other pearl. Combine them all with the dodecahedron. Fix what was broken. Save them before it's too late."

"What do you mean?"

"It's too late for me. My time has come. Now go!" With those words, the being thrust me back into my body. I regained consciousness to find myself lying on the floor with a knot on my head. There was no time. I had to get to work.

SIXTY-ONE

Zoey

MACK AND I HAD been trying to figure out exactly what each pearl could do but hadn't gotten anywhere. We'd been spending a few hours every day on it, and the frustration was starting to show. Especially with Mack. He wasn't a patient person anyway. I think part of his frustration had nothing to do with the pearls, but I wasn't going to ask him about his relationship with Q. They'd been fighting a lot lately, which meant they'd been having lots of makeup sex. Great for them, horrible for the rest of us. The boat wasn't exactly soundproof, so we knew when they were fighting, and when they were making up. And sometimes it was hard to tell which was which. But I guess when you throw two people with fiery tempers together, that's bound to happen.

He'd been cranky all morning, so I sent him off to spar with Kyro. I kept turning the pearl over in my hand, as though I was waiting for it to do something amazing. I knew it wouldn't, since we'd spent days trying to figure it out up to now.

I caressed the deep red pearl with my left hand as I held it in my right. I was running out of ideas relating to discovering which power this thing held. I opened the book. Maybe Ian would have some suggestion of what to try next. "Ian? I'm pretty new at this magic thing. Can you help me out? We can't get this thing to work."

I don't know much about the pearls specifically, but most magical artifacts require the use of a trigger word or phrase. I would guess it's based on the power of each item. Which I know doesn't help much right now, since we don't know what each pearl does.

"But maybe that does help. At least now I know I'm looking for a word or phrase to activate it. And we already know the other one shows the user what they most desire, so this one has to either teleport or freeze time. Unless your original intel was wrong, that is. I'll let you know if I figure it out." I closed the book and put it back in my backpack. Even knowing that we're safe now, I feel better having it put away where it's easy to hide. I don't want to take any chances.

I pull out a notebook and start to brainstorm possible trigger words to activate the pearl. At some point, I must have dozed off. A loud noise startled me awake. I looked around the room for the source of the noise. I didn't see anything. I took a moment to carefully put the pearl I'd been working with away and ward its hiding spot before heading up on deck.

My jaw dropped when I ran up on deck and saw what had caused the noise. There was a giant squid attacking the boat. It had Mack in one of its tentacles and was starting to crush the boat with another one. I looked around to see where everyone else was and noticed Jack knocked out next to the mast. That must have been what made the noise. Kyro was nowhere to be seen. Just as I started to panic about having to fight this monster on my own, a fireball flew past me and nailed the beast in its left eye.

At least I wasn't alone. I grabbed my bow from its holder next to the training area and started shooting arrows at the squid. I wasn't sure I even had any that could penetrate the beast, but I had to try. I concentrated on the tentacle that was wrapped around Mack, shooting the monster in the same spot over and over until it released Mack. Q kept beaming it with fireballs to distract it so I could help get Mack out of its reach.

By the time I got him out of the way, Jack had regained consciousness and was chucking harpoons at the squid. Suddenly the monster let out a scream and dipped below the surface. It held onto the boat as if to keep from going under, but whatever was pulling it down was too powerful. The boat slipped from the tentacles as the giant squid was pulled under one last time. Bubbles rushed to the surface in the spot where the beast was just attacking. The water turned red with the monster's blood, and then Kyro shot up out of the water onto the deck of the boat.

"What was that? Are you all right?" I was in his arms the moment he transformed from a merman to a man, even though he was covered in blood.

"That was unfortunate. But I couldn't distract it. I didn't want to kill the squid, but it didn't give me a choice." The grief in his voice was obvious.

"You defeated that thing on your own?" It wasn't that I didn't believe him, but there were four of us fighting it up here, and we weren't really getting anywhere.

Kyro smirked at me. "I wouldn't say on my own." He nodded his head toward the side of the boat. My gaze followed his nod, and there in the water was the most beautiful merman I'd ever seen. His white hair was long and flowing, his chin covered with a full beard to match. The instant I saw him, I dropped to one knee.

"Poseidon, it's an honor." I was in awe. I'd never met a god before, and the stories of Poseidon were some of my favorites. I wanted nothing more than to ask him if any of it was true but figured that would be rude, so I just stayed where I was.

"Rise, child. You've no need to bow to me." His voice was deep and rich, exactly as I had imagined it. A single tear slid from my eye.

I raised my head to look at him. "You're the god of the seas. Of course, I need to bow. Thank you for helping Kyro save us."

He smiled, his eyes lighting up with amusement. "You are most welcome, Zoey. But honestly, Kyro did most of the work."

Kyro laughed at his father's statement. I noticed I had been the only one to bow, but I still didn't stand. Poseidon deserved every bit of respect I could show to him. After all, I was in love with his son.

Poseidon laughed along with Kyro, as though they were sharing an inside joke. His expression became serious a moment later. "Kyro tells me you're having trouble with one of my pearls. Is there anything I can do to help?"

My eyes went wide with shock. "They're YOUR pearls? Like, you created them?"

He nodded. "My son tells me you're searching for three of them and already have two. There are many more, though. It might help to know which ones you need. Then I can point you in the right direction."

"That would be amazing. I can't believe Poseidon is helping us. This just keeps getting more exciting!" I couldn't help but fangirl a bit. I had to get myself under control.

Mack stepped forward and explained to Poseidon we'd been trying to activate what we thought was the transportation pearl. Kyro guided me away as they discussed how to activate it.

"Are you all right? I know that beast was scary, and you don't like to harm anything." It was sweet that he was concerned for me.

I nodded. "That's true, but I'm fine. It's unfortunate, but that monster would have killed us if you hadn't taken care of it."

Mack and I headed back to the library to try what he had learned on the pearl. "He told me all of the pearls work on the basis of desire. This one should take you where you need to go, but you have to say the word, too."

"What word? We never figured that out," I said as I held the pearl in my hand gently.

"Pigaíno."

Mack said the word, and the world went dark. Suddenly I was surrounded by a swirling vortex of colors. I had no idea what was happening to me.

"Mack? Where'd you go?" In an instant, the vortex stopped, and I was dropped in front of a small house on a quiet street.

I looked around and realized the pearl had worked. I wasn't on the boat anymore. But where was I?

SIXTY-TWO

Ian

I HEARD A THUD on the porch outside my house. I ran to the window and looked outside. It was too early for Bay to show up with this week's shipment. Even she had some limitations. As I opened the blinds and looked out, my jaw dropped. This wasn't possible.

There was no way that Zoey was actually standing on my front porch holding one of the pearls. I was hallucinating. That was the only explanation. But I had to be sure. I threw open the door.

"Zoey? Is that really you?" I asked cautiously. If this was a trap, I wasn't going to fall for it.

She looked at me confused for a moment. "Ian? Oh, shit. This is so much worse than I thought."

I motioned for her to come inside, and she ran through the door. I closed it quickly behind her.

"So, it looks like you figured out how to work the pearl. That's a good thing. But I don't understand. How did this happen?"

She laughed. "I wish I knew. One minute I was standing there with Mack, concentrating on the pearl sending me where I needed to be, and the next, I'm in front of your house. I didn't even know the pearl could send me through time. I thought it was just a different location."

I offered her a glass of water. "It's going to be fine. We'll figure it out. I promise we'll get you back home soon. My wife will be home from work in a few hours, and maybe the three of us can come up with a plan."

She looked at me strangely.

"What?" I felt a little paranoid, like something else was going on here I didn't know about.

"I had no idea you were married. None of us did. I guess we really don't know much about you at all. It just caught me off guard. Do you have kids?"

I smiled. "Not just yet, but Kara is pregnant. We should meet our little one in just a few months."

It was obvious Zoey wasn't sure what to do with that information.

Once Kara got home, it seemed as though there were more questions than answers. But I had faith that my girl would figure it out. If anyone could, it would be her.

"Do you remember anything else?" Kara prodded Zoey for the fourth time.

Zoey shook her head. "As I said, we were just standing there. I was holding the pearl, and Mack was telling me about his conversation with Poseidon on how to activate it."

She paused, then her face lit up. "That's it! I know the word! Mack said it, but it worked anyway."

Kara grabbed her shoulders and gave her a small shake. "What is it?"

Zoey looked around as if checking something before she spoke. "Pigaíno. That was what Mack said. I had to make sure neither of you was touching the pearl. I didn't want to risk sending you off somewhere."

"Well, there's really only one way to test this. But I'd feel better about it if we used the book and talked to the others first. That way if it doesn't work right, we'll know immediately." I hated being the buzzkill, but Zoey's safety was my top priority.

SIXTY-THREE

Kyro

I COULD HARDLY BELIEVE it when Mack told me Zoey had vanished. It was so unbelievable that it had to be true. Mack and Zoey had been working on that pearl for the longest time, with no results. It was still surreal for her to just disappear. We searched the boat, but she was nowhere to be found.

"I have to see if Ian knows where she went," I told Mack. I was starting to panic. This girl just kept disappearing.

Mack grabbed the book and rushed back to the galley, where we all gathered around it. I opened the book and called out to Ian.

"Ian, we need your help. Zoey has disappeared again. Please tell me you know where she is." I begged.

It took a few minutes for the pages to glow, indicating Ian was there.

Kyro, yes, I do know where she is. Although I have no idea how to explain it. It appears that she figured out how to use the teleport pearl. She popped up on my doorstep a few hours ago. We're trying to figure out how to send her back now.

"Oh, that's a relief. Unless you can't send her back. Then what?" My relief threatened to turn into panic.

Trust me, I have one of the best minds on it. If there's a way to send her back to you, we will manage it. I'll keep you updated, but for now, I have to go.

We closed the book, and Mack put it away. There was nothing to do but wait and see if Ian could send her back.

A few hours later, when everyone was in bed, there was a glow in the center of my room. It got brighter and brighter, then Zoey stepped out of the center of it. They had figured it out!

"Zoey! You're back! But how?" I ran to her and pulled her into an embrace.

She kissed me hard, as if she'd been gone for weeks instead of just a few hours.

"That was insane," she said, pulling the pearl out of her pocket. "Let's put this somewhere safe, where we don't accidentally do this again."

I nodded and took the pearl from her, placing it in the safe and locking it up, then securing the magic that hid it from view.

I could tell she was wiped out, and there would be time to discuss everything in the morning, so I ushered her to bed. She fell asleep as soon as her head hit the pillow, but still stretched her arm out to find me. I pulled her close and held her while we slept.

SIXTY-FOUR

Gill

TRAV AND I HAD been experimenting with spells to create fresh water for three days. I knew if we didn't get out of this cell and get his wound cleaned soon, Trav risked losing his leg. The infection was getting worse. I was glad it hadn't started to spread yet, but he couldn't hide how painful it was.

"You're sure there's no way to break out of here?" Trav asked me again.

I shook my head. "I've already told you four times today. There is no way out of here unless the Chairman orders it. And I'm pretty sure he's decided we're still useful or we'd be dead."

Trav cocked an eyebrow and smirked. "What if the Chairman orders us to be freed?"

Great, now the infection had gone to his brain. I was going to lose the love of my life because I was stupid and got mixed up in something I couldn't handle. "That's not going to happen. What part of that do you not understand?" I hated that I was getting frustrated, but I couldn't help it. He was making no sense.

"Just give me a minute to explain. I think you'll like it," Trav continued. He motioned for me to join him where he was sitting on the floor. Once I did, he started to explain his idea in hushed tones so no one would hear us.

"I was thinking—I can't remember the spell for creating water. ..but I can remember the glamour spell for making myself look like someone else."

I could see where he was going with this, and it might work. It was a long shot, but it may just be exactly what we needed to get out of here.

"Even if it works, neither of us knows the way out of the catacombs. How will we escape?" I had to play devil's advocate so Trav would think of all the options.

He pursed his lips and scrunched his face in thought. "Well, I think I have a tracking spell that can be reworded to find an exit. But once we're out of the building, we may need to steal a boat or a car. Do you think you can handle that?"

I nodded. "I'll take care of transportation. If you can get us out of here, I can do that much."

We sat there in the middle of the floor for hours, planning our escape. By the time we were finished, Trav had me convinced it would work. He would need a couple of days to write out the spells we would need, then we'd be ready to go. That gave me two days to work out a protection spell to make sure nothing happened to him.

Trav spent the next week working on the spells to help with our plan. Unfortunately, it looked like the plan might be a bust, since he couldn't get any of the spells to work right. I'd never admit it, but it may have been in part because I kept disrupting them.

I couldn't take the chance of him getting hurt, especially with the infection from his leg starting to spread. He wouldn't be able to run, and I wasn't physically strong enough to carry him.

Being held in the dungeon was so much more difficult than being a spy for the Chairman. It was becoming harder to keep track of the days. At least Trav and I were together.

While working on the other spells, he had managed to remember the wording for the water spell finally, and we had cleaned up his leg. It was starting to heal, and for the first time since I returned, I actually thought he was going to be all right.

I wasn't sure how we would get out of here. Even if we could escape, there was nowhere we could go. My betrayal of Kyro and Mack made sure of that. Trav and I would have to figure it out on our own. For now, that meant staying here and not even trying to find a way out. I talked Trav into holding off on our attempt until the right time.

I knew the Chairman had been planning something big and figured we'd know when it had come to pass. I couldn't let Trav masquerade as the Chairman without risking his life, so I had to find a way to stop him from going ahead with that plan. I would have to come up with a better idea and wait for the perfect moment to execute it.

SIXTY-FIVE

Zoey

Having never been to Earth until a few weeks ago, I marveled at each location our quest led us to, taking in every detail. It was all so beautiful, and tragic. I remember reading in my books about how it had all looked before the latest industrial revolution.

I had seen pictures of the beauty of Japan and wished that was what I was seeing right now. What I wouldn't give to see the cherry blossoms and hydrangeas from the pictures in my books. It reminded me why we were on this quest. There was a chance we could bring it back. Ian just needed the pearls and the dodeca to get us there.

What lay ahead of us was a huge mass of land, the island of Japan, that had been attached to the countries closest to it by metal, cement, and brick. The Sea of Japan no longer existed. It had been covered by manmade material, which was then covered with factories.

Men had basically run out of room for factories and decided to pave over the sea. It broke my heart. I longed to see the Earth as it had been before humans ruined it. I was impressed with how much of the plant and animal life was still trying to come back. If they could keep going, so could I. I wasn't going to give up. We would fix this.

Where there was once a beautiful mass of water with wildlife flourishing, now stood a dozen or so buildings. It seemed to be deserted, which was even more painful to see. At least if there had been people working, it would have made sense to expand the city the way they had. But like this, it just seemed like a huge waste.

It made me sad to see that industrialization had taken over the country. Each building was several stories high, with windows that had been caked with grime. I could imagine how they must have glowed when they were new. The windows would have allowed natural light to illuminate the factories as the workers ran machinery to create whatever it was they were making here.

The buildings were spectacular but decrepit. It appeared as though no one had been in the area for quite some time. Decay like this could only happen over a period of years or decades. The whole country looked as though it was one mega-city, with factories at the heart of it all.

Though the buildings were indeed works of art, it made me sad there was a lack of plant life in this area. It seemed like the plants were faring better in Africa than Japan. The native Japanese plants were beautiful, and I would have treasured being able to see them in person. Sadly, it was too late for that, unless we managed to complete our mission and stop what had happened here.

It was beginning to feel like a long shot, but Kyro remained positive we could do it. He even convinced Jack we were getting close to finding exactly what we need. I felt bad leaving him on the boat, but we would need someone to have everything ready to leave the moment we returned. Since Jack and Kyro were the only ones who really knew how to work the boat besides Mack—we needed him for this part of the quest—that left Jack as the odd man out. He didn't seem to mind it that much. I think he was planning to call Elena again.

They had the cutest long-distance thing going. It seemed like they were on the comm device every time we turned around. It helped that Mama had put Elena in charge of Jack and his mission to protect me. That fact alone gave them an excuse to talk daily.

A movement ahead of us caught my attention, dragging me from my amused thoughts. I grabbed Kyro's arm and pointed. There was something out there, and it was enormous. With the size of the buildings in the city, it was hard to tell exactly what we were coming up on, but I was suddenly terrified.

I fought the desire to race back to the boat where I knew I'd be safe. *I have to do this. For Ian. I promised to help him. I can do this.* I had to try to convince myself I wasn't really scared. I needed to find the pearl that was hidden here or the next clue that would lead me to the pearl.

Something crept across the street, darting between buildings. It was hard to make out the shape of it. The beast was zigzagging from one building to the next, heading directly for us but keeping just out of sight. When I pointed, Kyro nodded, then motioned to Q and Mack to be ready. We figured there would be a fight for the pearl, but I'm not sure we were ready for this.

Kyro moved to the front of our group, making sure I was in the middle. He held up a hand for us to stop. The moment we did, each of us turned our backs against each other and searched the block with our eyes. The movement had stopped. I wondered if that meant the beast had left.

I didn't figure that whatever it was would give up that easily, but I was hopeful. Not seeing anything, we resumed moving in the direction of the magical signature.

SIXTY-SIX

Kyro

WE WERE IN THE heart of the city when I saw the first beast. It was close to seven feet tall, with the head of an ox, great horns stretching out close to two feet on each side, and the body of a hulking man. The beast was clad in a loincloth and was covered in dark brown fur. I had heard tales of the Ushi Oni as a child but had never seen one in person. It was terrifying.

Mack and Q decided to hold it off while Zoey and I kept heading toward what we hoped was the location of the pearl. I had enchanted a pendant to help us locate the next piece of our puzzle. It was glowing brighter the further inland we went. We could see an abandoned factory at the north end of the city and headed in that direction.

We watched as Mack and Q worked in harmony to fight the monster. Mack distracted it with his axe, and Q shot it with fireballs. While its attention was on Q, Mack would strike out again with his axe. The beast charged, and they both had to jump out of the way. The way they worked together to fight and protect each other was phenomenal. It was like watching a choreographed dance. But we had to keep moving, or we'd never find the pearl and get out of here.

Zoey stopped short a couple of blocks from our destination. She didn't speak but pointed to the west. There was another Ushi Oni, but this one looked different from the other. It had the same head of an ox, with horns closer to a foot long, a shorter snout, the mid-section of a fur-covered hulk of a man, and the body of the largest spider crab I had ever seen. It was tan in color, with tufts of beige fur around its head.

We quickly turned to the east and continued toward the factory that seemed to be the location of something magical. It was hard to pinpoint the pearl exactly, when none of us had ever seen it. If we were being led to something else, it was a large source of magic and would likely be of use anyway.

We made it another three blocks before spotting another of the Ushi Oni beasts. This one was markedly smaller than the other two, with an ox head and the body of a yellow tabby cat. Its horns were probably only six inches long on either side of its head. This one didn't have the humanoid torso but looked more like a large cat with an ox head.

I was less worried about this one than the other two, but we decided to detour around it anyway, just to be safe. That made three of those monsters, and we hadn't even made it to our destination yet. There was no way to tell how many more we would find, or how much longer we could avoid a fight.

Zoey and I quietly entered the factory as my pendant glowed brighter and began to vibrate. I knew we were getting close. The pendant seemed to be leading us toward the center of the building. We followed its guidance as carefully as we could. I began to feel a warmth pulling me toward a chest in the middle of the central room we had just entered. "I think it's in that chest. I'm going to take a look. Cover me."

Zoey pulled out her crossbow, nocked a bolt, and nodded. I hunched over and crept out into the center of the room, heading toward the chest. Of course, I didn't see the fourth Ushi Oni until it knocked me off my feet. I fell face-first into a stack of crates. I heard it grunt as it caught a bolt in the shoulder.

This one looked a lot like the first one we saw, except it had one broken horn and was gray in color. It wore a vest and shorts that may have been pants at some point but were shredded below the knee. The horn it had was about a foot and a half long; the broken one was maybe eight inches long. I got back to my feet, wiped blood from the corner of my mouth, and prepared for the next attack.

sixty-seven

q

MACK AND I DISTRACTED the first Ushi Oni we ran into so Kyro and Zoey could follow the pendant. I hoped they would find what we were looking for so we could get out of here fast. I knew from experience that where there was one Ushi Oni, there were usually several. They were almost pack-like in nature, working together, fighting together, eating together.

During my training with the Resistance, I spent some time here in Japan and Korea, and had battled these monsters before. I wasn't sure how much Mack knew about them, but he seemed to be doing fine fighting this one.

He swiped at it with his axe, ducked out of the way of its horns, then swiped at it again. As he had its attention, I flanked it and started chucking fire at it. Each one that hit singed and burned its flesh and fur. The smell of charred beast was horrid, and the fire wasn't doing as much damage as I had hoped. We needed to find another way.

The beast charged at me, anticipating my move to avoid it, and caught me with one of its horns. It ripped my shirt and tore into my left arm. Mack, seeing this, made a feral sound and jumped on the beast's back, beating it with the handle of the axe. He stood up on the monster's back and planted his axe into the broad shoulders of the creature. The Ushi Oni cried out in pain, and I saw movement out of the corner of my eye. It was another beast, but this one looked more like a crab with an ox head. Crabby was even uglier than his friend.

I started shooting fireballs at the crab monster, trying to give Mack a chance to get the one he was fighting under control. Suddenly he was flying through the air and landed on me, knocking us both to the ground. His axe had fallen on the other side of the beast he had been bucked from. There was no good way to get to it with both of these monsters in the way.

We were backed into a corner, up against a building that was barely standing. When we hit it, bricks fell from the top. This gave me an idea. "Get ready to jump and run out of the way. We just have to get it closer first." I pointed up, and Mack seemed to understand what I was thinking.

We guided the two beasts closer to the building. When I thought they were both in range, we jumped, rolled and ran, as I shot fireballs at the base of the building to bring it down on the monsters. It didn't take much encouragement for the building to fall, and it landed exactly where I had planned. What I hadn't considered, though, was that one of the beasts was part crab, and had a hard shell. The first Ushi Oni was flattened, but the second was barely fazed by the building clamoring down on it.

I was able to buy Mack enough time to get his axe, which helped more than the building had. We went to work flanking the crab beast, alternating between axe chops and fire shots. It took a lot more energy than I was used to expending, but it was satisfying to watch the monster fall and take its last breath. Mack and I ducked around a corner to wait for the monsters' friends, as I was sure there would be more beasts coming after us.

SIXTY-EIGHT

Zoey

Just as the beast came out of the shadows and plowed over Kyro, I shot, then nocked another bolt. My first shot hit, and it didn't look happy. I had to keep it busy so Ky could find the pearl, or whatever magical item it was we were tracking. Lucky for him, it worked, as the beast started to chase me.

I quickly jumped on some crates and climbed the scaffolding overhead to buy some time. I had to keep shooting to get the monster to focus on me. It tried to jump at me but couldn't get off the ground enough to reach. Then it tried climbing on crates to get up on the scaffolding. It couldn't get a good foothold once it was on the scaffolding, though, and fell through before it could reach me.

I saw Ky take a defensive stance, then realize what I had intended. He turned his attention back to the crates. I kept nocking arrows and shooting at the monster until I ran out of bolts. It was strange to me that the beast could still be standing after taking seven bolts to various parts of its body.

It had three in its left shoulder, one in its right, two in its back, and one in its left thigh. I hadn't done too bad for someone who had never really had any hunting experience. We had spent a lot of time training, and shooting practice was my favorite.

It was harder to keep the beast's attention without ammo. I had to pick up random things and throw them at it, or flip myself over the railing of the scaffolding, letting myself dangle for a minute, then pull up just out of reach. The weight training Jack had added was helping too.

I ran along the scaffolding just above the monster's head and had it chase me all around the room, trying to keep it focused on me instead of Ky. I saw him pick up something the size of his palm that looked to be wrapped in cloth. He gave me a thumbs-up, and I decided to stop playing with the Ushi Oni.

I jumped down in front of it and pulled out my dagger. I threw it at the beast's chest, and my aim was true. The monster stumbled, obviously hurt. Kyro blasted it with a shot of water, and the beast went down. We didn't stay to make sure it was dead. I would have to get another dagger the next time we were in port.

We ran out of the building and straight into the other two beasts we had seen on our way to this building. The Ushi Oni tabby cat didn't look too intimidating, so I attacked that one first. I had underestimated the kitty. It slashed me across the left cheek with its claws. I stabbed it in the chest with a second dagger I had pulled from my boot. It fell and laid motionless, not even breathing. I pulled the blade from its chest and headed to help Kyro with the other one.

SIXTY-NINE

Kyro

As Zoey ran to attack the cat monster, I drew the crab beast to me. I pulled a staff from my back and tried to get a good whack at this thing. My staff proved to be ineffective, so I blasted the giant crab with water to push it back. It barely had an effect. I knew my magic wouldn't be as useful as I had hoped. I couldn't see a way to defeat this beast.

Between Zoey and myself, we had three blades, a crossbow with no bolts, and some unreliable magic. The beast came at me, knocking me a few feet back. The next thing I saw was Zoey come out of nowhere and land on the beast's back. She held onto its horns as it bucked, waiting for the right moment to strike.

I ran over to distract the beast by whacking it with my staff again. I just needed to get it to come after me so she could kill it while it wasn't paying attention. The monster started to chase me. I climbed the drainpipe of a building, hoping I could get out of its reach, while still keeping its attention.

I watched as Zoey let go of the beast's horns, brought her blade over her head and slammed it down into the back of the monster's neck. The blade went clean through, sticking out the underneath of the beast's neck, where a puddle began to form. It stumbled, then fell. I ran over to help Zoey off its back and make sure it was dead. We took turns slashing it with our blades and managed to cut the head off the Ushi Oni.

"Do you think you can do that freeze magic you did with the lava monster?" I didn't want to push her, but figured if we could freeze these things, we'd have an advantage against the last one.

"I can try, but I just don't know how to control it yet, or even how to make it happen." No sooner had she said the words, than the beast with the broken horn came crashing out of the building. "No time like the present to try," I said in a hushed tone. I wasn't sure the beast had seen us yet, as the crab monster was obscuring its view.

We knew as soon as she tried to summon the magic the monster would see us. She stepped out from behind the fallen crab monster, and I took my place beside her. The broken-horned beast saw us immediately and began to run toward us. It was now or never. I had faith that she could do it. I just needed her to believe it as well.

Zoey took a couple of deep breaths, centered herself, and threw her hands out in front of her. Nothing happened. Her face fell. "Let's try something else. I'm going to shoot a cannon of water at it, and you see if you can freeze the water, OK?" She nodded, and I was glad she was willing to try again.

I shot the water out at the beast, who had begun to head our way. She looked at me, then held her hands out at the water coming from mine. Nothing happened at first. The beast was getting closer. Suddenly the water coming from my hands started to freeze, trapping the monster in a solid block of ice.

"You did it!" I was beyond proud of her, scooping her up in a twirling hug.

"We have to go before it unfreezes. And we did it, not just me." She planted a kiss on my lips, then pushed away from me so I would set her down.

We ran off in the direction we had come, looking for our friends. I hoped they had fared as well against the Ushi Oni they had been fighting. We turned a corner to see Mack, covered in blood.

"Mack, are you ok? Where's Q?" Zoey and I frantically looked around for Q, who was nowhere to be seen. Then she popped her head around a corner. She looked as bad as Mack, covered in blood.

"What happened?" Zoey was freaking out.

"It's OK, most of this belongs to that." Q pointed to what had been an Ushi Oni until they had managed to flatten it by dropping half a crumbling building on it. "Or that." She then pointed to a second beast that we hadn't seen before. It was similar to the one we had fought with the crab body. It looked as though Mack had hacked it up with his axe, and Q had fried it with fireballs. "That one was more difficult."

"Yeah, we fought one of those as well. But there's no time to revel in our win. We have to go before that big one thaws." There was no need for an explanation, we all just ran for the boat. Just as we were pushing the boat off the dock, Zoey got our attention and pointed at the shore. The beast had thawed and was heading to the dock.

I used my ability to control water to move us far enough away to deter the monster from following. I wasn't sure if it would be able to swim after us, but I didn't want to take any chances. I kept the water pushing us forward away from Japan for as long as I could, then I collapsed onto the deck from exhaustion.

seventy

Zoey

I KNEW WE HAD to get out of there quickly when the Ushi Oni managed to break free of my freeze. I was glad that Kyro had a way to move the boat faster, but once he collapsed on the deck from expending too much magic, I knew we had to find another way. Q and I had a talk about finding someone to repair the boat.

"Do you think it's possible?" After discussing it for a while, I wanted to cut to the chase. If it wasn't possible, we'd have to consider another boat. Kyro didn't have the supplies to fix it ourselves.

"Maybe? I'm not an engineer, but I don't see why it couldn't be done. I mean, if we were talking about upgrading the comm system, I'd be your girl. I just don't know enough about sailing to know how to do it."

She was receptive to the idea, but lacked the knowledge for the project. Great, now what? It was too bad I didn't know someone...

"Q, give me your comm device. I think I know someone who can help."

She handed it over without arguing. I dialed Mama's number and waited for her to answer.

"Yes? Who is this? What do you want?"

"Mama, it's Zoey. I need a favor."

"Zoey? Where are you? What happened? Are you ok?"

"I'm fine, Mama, really. But I can't tell you where I am. I need your help with something."

"You know the Patrol is still looking for you. It's not safe for us to be in contact."

Q broke in, "What's she talking about? Why isn't it safe to talk to your mother?"

"It's Race. He's dead, and they think Zoey killed him. I'm surprised she and Jack didn't already tell you."

Q's face turned pale, and I almost dropped the communicator. "What?" She coughed out.

"Someone choked him to death. We found him in his office right before we realized Zoey had left. The authorities assumed that since she left and didn't come back, that she had killed him. They're trying to track her down now. They have pictures, and her accounts are most likely frozen."

Jack and I had decided not to tell the others about Race when we first made it back to the boat. At that moment, I figured it would be easier to let Mama explain. The looks I was getting from the others were enough to make me want to hide. I didn't do anything, but their looks seemed to accuse me of it anyway.

Q had taken the communicator from me when I almost dropped it, and was holding it for me. She picked up the conversation with Mama, since I had all but walked away.

"Ok, so that's all we have to do? You're sure it'll work? Man, you're awesome. Thank you so much. We really appreciate you helping us with this, especially since you really don't know what's going on down here." She had taken it off speaker, so I couldn't hear Mama's reply.

"Yeah, I'll tell her. And we'll make sure she's safe." Q listened again, nodding, "Yeah, I'll make sure she checks in with you again in a few days. And we're sorry about your friend." Another pause while she listened, "Ok, we'll talk soon. Bye." She closed the connection and powered off the communicator.

Q turned to me, "So your mom thinks we should be able to handle the tech mods pretty easily. That's good. But you're wanted for murdering your ex-boyfriend? That's bad. What are we going to do?"

I shrugged in response. "There's nothing I can do, except avoid the Patrol. I didn't do it, but that won't matter to them.

Jack shook his head. "I'm sure it was the Chairman who killed him. And I've told your mother as much. But I have no proof, so we can't move forward with going after him for that."

Q nodded her agreement. "I understand that. We have other reasons to go after him though. And by chasing him down, we may find the proof you need to pin your friend's murder on him. You know what I mean." She must have realized that didn't sound right.

"We aren't going after him, though." Kyro broke into the conversation. "We're going to have repairs and upgrades done on the boat, and we're going after the other pearl. End of discussion. Understood?"

Q's eyes widened. "But—"

Kyro cut her off. "I mean it. We aren't here to chase him down. Our goal is to help Ian fix his mistake. I'm not putting any of you in more danger for some wild goose chase. Especially not to chase after someone as powerful as the Chairman. Not happening."

Q started again, "But Kyro, just hear me out—"

Kyro held up his left hand, cutting Q off again. "No. If you want to leave us and chase him down, I can't stop you. But I won't let you endanger Zoey with your haphazard planning. If there's a way to take him down once we have the pearls and dodeca together, fine, we'll do it. Until that moment, I'm not going to even consider it." Kyro turned and walked away without giving Q a chance to respond.

It was no surprise when Q stormed off in a huff, heading toward her room. What was surprising was the fact that she didn't slam her door when she entered it.

seventy-one

q

I HAD MORE THAN one reason for storming off after talking to Zoey's mom and trying to reason with Kyro. With the information she had just given me, I knew we would have a chance to run into the Chairman and his goons.

From Zoey's mom, I learned that there was a place in India that could outfit Kyro's boat with some new tech that will make it faster and more practical for our purposes. She said she would contact her people there and set it up for us. It would take Geo two days to get it done, which meant we would have to keep Zoey hidden and safe until then. I had a feeling that was going to be easier said than done. I used the communicator to call James and asked him to contact our agent in India. I made sure no one was around for that particular conversation.

"James, it's Q. I need you to contact India, near the midwestern coast, around Panaji. We need a safe place to stay for a couple of days. There's four of us. Yes, I know what I'm asking. I need you to do it.

The usual signal will be great. I can't explain right now. I promise I'll call again when it's safe. Thanks."

I didn't even give him a chance to respond. I wanted to make sure the call wasn't traced, even though I knew it was a secure connection. I couldn't be too careful. I knew Zoey's life was in danger if she was caught. There was no mercy when it came to murder charges. It would be one of two choices, prison camp or death. I'm not sure which was worse, honestly. My organization had done a lot of research on the subject and had yet to figure out how to break someone out of one of those camps.

Prison camp was a secure location where they basically dump murderers and leave them to survive on their own, with no shelter or weapons. There were no guards either, except on the wall surrounding the camp. Their sole purpose was to prevent escape. The whole thing was an island, with a twenty-foot wall surrounding most of it.

Other than the guards on the wall, there were only murderers inhabiting the island. There was no food or supplies dropped for the inmates, only the guards on the outside. It was very much kill or be killed, with no one to protect an innocent who got caught up in something and found themselves on this island.

I knew she wouldn't last there, especially if they found out about her powers. If that happened, she'd be chipped and would have no way to protect herself. They had taken to chipping killers, which blocked their use of powers, when they realized there was no other way to keep them in prison. Chipping was what they called the process of implanting a microchip in the spinal column, just at the base of the skull. The microchip prevented the nerves that controlled someone's powers from connecting and allowing that person to use their abilities.

It made sense but seemed really cruel given that Zoey was innocent. Proving she didn't do it would be more difficult, since I didn't think we had anyone inside the space station. I'd have to contact headquarters and find out what they could do. But that would have to wait until we had a secure location in India to stay.

I'd make the call from there, with my friends safely underground. That would protect everyone—my cover would stay intact, Zoey would keep her freedom, and Mack wouldn't freak out about the whole situation. I knew if I continued to see him, I'd have to tell him at some point. I just didn't feel like now was the time.

seventy-two

Kyro

We turned the ship and headed back to India. Q was convinced a guy there could outfit my boat with some brand-new tech, which would get us where we needed to go faster than the sail, and with less magical energy usage from me. We would have to lay low to keep Zoey from being captured. I knew she was innocent, but given how difficult it would be to get us on Calliope now, I didn't think there would be a way to prove it.

The thought of losing her broke my heart. I didn't think I could take watching her die or worse, being shipped off to the prison camp. There was no choice, we had to keep her safe. It wouldn't be easy to disguise her, though. Her blue skin made for a very distinctive look. I'd have to talk to Ari again and see if there was anything we could do. I took a few minutes and wrote her a note.

It would take us at least a day to get to the port where we were headed. Q said she had a contact in Panaji. We would have a safe place to stay underground for the time we were there, and she would make sure the boat was repaired and outfitted with the tech Jack had suggested. I really hoped we could trust him. Zoey did, but she really was naive sometimes, always thinking the best of people. It was sweet, but not very practical.

We made sure she wasn't left alone. Since her mom broke the news to the rest of us, we were determined to show her our support.

I wondered why neither she nor Jack had mentioned what happened to Race, but I didn't dwell on it. There was no point in making her feel more guilty than she already did.

I didn't know much about the guy who got killed, but it seemed like they were pretty close. Of course, they must not have been too close if she left him to come to Earth for this quest. Which is what we needed to be worried about, not keeping her from going to prison camp for a murder she didn't commit. The whole situation made me angry. I was determined to keep her safe, no matter what.

I walked around the corner and up the stairs to the deck. Mateo had taken Zoey out on the deck to get some fresh air while Jack, Mack, and I listened to Q's plan. Zoey's face lit up momentarily when she saw me, then looked concerned.

"What is it? Are you OK?" I hated seeing her look so terrified.

"I'm fine. I guess I'm just worried you all will think I did this. And I didn't. I promise. I wouldn't."

I wrapped my arms around her and pulled her close, so her head was on my chest. "Baby, I know you didn't hurt him. I don't know how we'll prove it, but we'll find a way. I promise." She broke down in tears at this point, which was probably a good thing. She needed to let it all out.

"Did you and the others figure out what we need to do?" Mateo asked, including himself in the group to show he was all in at this point. He wanted to keep Zoey safe as much as the rest of us.

"I think so. But I need you to do something for me. I have a note I need to get to Ari. Would you mind? You know where we're heading, so you'll be able to catch up."

He nodded, "Of course, anything to help this beautiful creature." He patted Zoey on the back, and she managed a small smile.

I handed him the note, he placed it in a small bottle on a cord around his neck, and quickly hugged Zoey and me, since I was still holding her. Then he slipped into the water. There was a faint blue glow as his legs turned to a tail, and off he went. I knew he would make the best time possible and bring me back answers. I just hoped it wasn't too late.

seventy-three

Zoey

I WAS SO RELIEVED Kyro believed me. I couldn't think of anyone who would want to hurt Race, much less kill him. I wondered if Jack was doing all right. I didn't even ask him. He'd been quiet the past few days. It was easy to forget how close he and Race had been with everything going on. I felt so badly about the whole situation. I had to find a way to find Race's killer. I just had no idea how. Maybe Ian would be able to help. I'd have to make sure I asked him later.

It was so nice to be in Kyro's arms. I wanted to be with him so badly, but given the events of the day, I didn't expect the feeling to be mutual. There was no point in bringing it up either, because there was too much to do getting the boat ready for its transformation and preparing to head south to Australia, since we had decided that the dodeca was top priority.

I eased back from Ky's grip so I could look at him as he watched the waves. "You want to be out there in it, don't you?"

He looked down at me with a grin. "I want to be just where I am. I'd rather have you than anything. But yes, the sea is my home. It's where I feel the most myself. What about you? Where do you feel the most at home?"

I caught a tear as it slid down my cheek. "I haven't had a home for a long time, but I feel the most at home when I'm with you. So as far as I'm concerned, right here is home." As I spoke, I laid my hand on his chest.

He leaned down and pressed his lips to mine, gently at first, but with passion behind it, building with each moment. I sighed and relaxed into him, allowing my tongue to play with his. Before I knew it, my hands were fisted in his hair, and it was the exact moment I had envisioned when we met. I gasped and pulled away.

Of course, he looked confused. "I'm sorry, that was too much, right?"

I shook my head, trying to find the right words to explain it. "No, not at all. I just got overwhelmed, that's all. It's just...I, I saw this moment when we first met." My cheeks turned purple with embarrassment.

"What? How?" He was just as confused as I had been when I had the vision.

"I don't know. I honestly thought it was just a little fantasy because of how gorgeous you are." Cue even more purple cheeks.

"You thought I was gorgeous when we met?" I think he was enjoying my mortification again.

"That's not the point. I didn't know it was a vision. It's just like when Ian got his powers. He didn't know at first what was a vision and what wasn't. I didn't even know I could have visions."

He grabbed my hand and held it. "It's OK, we'll figure this out too. Don't worry about it. Have you had any other thoughts that could have been visions? Something that seemed out of place at the time, or felt different than a usual thought?"

He was so sweet, trying to help me figure out this new power, even after I completely embarrassed myself with it. "Not that I can think of right now. But I didn't think that one was unusual at the time, either." Now I had two powers I needed to learn to control.

Wait, I guess that meant I had three, since I had heard his thoughts that day as well. "Um, Ky, I have to tell you something."

He nodded, "Go ahead, you can tell me anything."

I took a deep breath, "Well, if that thought was actually a vision, then I don't have two powers, freezing and visions, I have three, freezing, visions and mind-reading. Because when we met, I heard your initial impression of me. I just thought I was going crazy at the time. But now, maybe it means something. Ian said I would have the power I needed at the time I needed it most. Maybe that's what he meant. Maybe I won't ever be able to do any of this stuff again."

Kyro studied me before responding. "You heard my thoughts? Hmm...well, I can't apologize for my initial impression of you, because it was right. You are amazing. As for the powers, you've used the freeze more than once, so I think they're sticking around. We just have to help you learn to control them."

seventy-four

Zoey

AFTER DISCUSSING MY CONFUSING and growing powers with Kyro, it was late, and everyone else had already retired for the night. He said Mateo would meet us in India, because his journey to deliver the note would take him longer than our trip. We walked downstairs to our room. It felt funny to say our room, but that's what it was. I was still upset he had lied to me and had hidden a pearl from me, but it was impossible to deny the way we were being pulled together.

And at some point, we would be done with Ian's quest. Then we would be free to be together and spend our lives exploring the world. That is if I could find a way to clear myself of the apparent murder charge hanging over my head.

As soon as the door closed, I grabbed Ky and kissed him hard, softening the kiss into heated passion. He was caught off guard for a second, then matched my passion before taking over. His kiss took me to places I'd never been before.

There was more love in this moment than there had been in years with Race. That thought made me sad for a moment, but I didn't let it linger. Ky brought my thoughts back to him by biting my neck gently, teasing me back into focus. I ran my hands up his arms, over his shoulders, finally tangling my fingers in his hair. I pulled his mouth back up to mine, and our tongues tangled once more.

I couldn't take it anymore, I had to have him. I moved my hands to his cheeks, then slowly ran them down his chest, unbuttoning his shirt as I went. Once his tan and chiseled chest was exposed, I reveled in touching every part.

He caught on to what I was thinking as I pushed his shirt off his shoulders and slid it off his arms. He moaned, then pulled my shirt over my head, exposing the lacy lingerie underneath. I sighed, because it felt so good having him touch me finally, and he moaned once more, apparently being more aroused by my sigh.

He pulled my pants off, revealing the mate to the lingerie top, and his eyes got dark with need. I slowly unbuttoned and unzipped his pants, making sure not to touch anything important just yet. I wanted this to be torture for us both. I removed his pants, then kissed him again, with so much feeling we both seemed out of breath.

I trailed kisses down his neck, over his shoulders and chest, down to his finely chiseled abs. I dipped my fingers beneath the waistband of his underwear, and his breath caught. I licked him where my fingers had just been, and he groaned. I liked having this kind of control over him.

I enjoyed seeing what my touch did to his usually calm demeanor. When I was done teasing, I found him rock hard and ready. Before I could do anything else, he flipped me over and began to tease me.

He reached around my back and unfastened my bra, throwing it across the room. His mouth trailed kisses down my neck, adding a few little bites, before settling on my breasts. He ran circles around my nipples with his tongue, causing me to arch my back and pant.

He chuckled and continued the torture by suckling gently at each before moving on. He trailed little bites down my taut blue flesh, until he reached the top of my panties. He slid back up next to me, taking my mouth with his, while his hand slipped under the thin fabric. I knew I was already moist with anticipation. His fingers played, stroking, teasing, entering, until I couldn't take it anymore. Then he teased me even more.

We took our time exploring each other's bodies before I pulled him on top of me. I needed to feel him inside my throbbing center. He understood and entered so slowly that it was torture. We both groaned, enjoying the slow, teasing pace. He seemed to want to continue at that speed, and I let him for a while.

It was relaxing and exciting at the same time. When I couldn't take it anymore, I flipped him over and rode him to the finish, managing to end us both together. Neither of us was concerned by the beacon of light that shot up as we climaxed. We collapsed in a tangle of body parts, kissing sweetly.

Before long, we both fell asleep, still wrapped around each other. With everything that had happened recently, neither of us expected to get a good night's sleep. I was glad we were wrong about that.

seventy-five

Kyro

I HADN'T INTENDED TO make love to Zoey last night, but I was extremely satisfied that it had finally happened. I knew I had to find a way to protect her. By the time we got up, we were almost to Panaji, the port where we would meet Zoey's mom's contact and then go to the safe house Q had arranged. I still wasn't clear on how she managed that, but I trusted she would help me keep Zoey safe.

I had hoped that Mateo would have gotten back to us by now, but I knew it was a long shot. Even if Ari had a way to help, it would take him longer than one night to get there, get her answer, and return. I had to take steps to make sure he could find us when he returned. I knew he had his amulet around his neck all the time, as I did. I went to my safe and pulled out another stone. This one was pink, rose quartz, and I put a charm on it for protection as well as connecting it to my amulet and Mateo's. Now he would be able to track Zoey as long as she wore the pink necklace, and I would as well. It was the best insurance policy I could come up with. Especially after our fishing boat fiasco.

It was late afternoon when we pulled into port. We had each packed up what we would need for the next few days before we hit land. When we got to the workshop, Q went out, with Mack at her side and Jack trailing behind, to find Geo and get directions for bringing the boat to him.

After they left, I turned to Zoey and pulled the new amulet out of my pocket. "I made this for you. I hope you like it and will wear it."

Her face knotted up for a minute, then she threw herself at me, wrapping her arms around my neck and kissing me hard. "I love it! I'll never take it off! Thank you!"

She let me tie the cord around her neck, and the amulet hung perfectly just above her cleavage. It had a slight glow to it, which I found odd, but didn't say anything. I hoped that meant it would work if it was needed.

We waited patiently for Q and Mack to return, talking and joking around to lighten the mood. She told me a bit about her childhood, and I told her some about mine. From her stories, it appeared that my childhood was more normal than hers. At least my parents had been around for the whole thing. Hers had all but abandoned her on the space station with Race.

The stories helped me understand why he was so important to her, but she hadn't ever been in love with him. They would have passed for a normal couple just hanging out if it wasn't for the annoying feeling that something just wasn't right.

Almost at the moment I began to worry, they came around the corner, bringing someone with them. I assumed that was Geo. He was average height, with broad shoulders and long dark hair pulled back in a low ponytail. He looked huge compared to Mack, but Jack made him look small. If I hadn't known how Zoey felt about me, I might have been jealous of the way he looked at her.

He didn't try to hide the fact that he found her attractive and seemed encouraged by her giggling when he told her as much. I moved over and put an arm around her, giving him a look that should have told him we were together. He didn't seem to notice, or he noticed but didn't care.

Either way, it really didn't matter, since we just needed him to outfit my boat with the new tech, so we could continue our quest. So I bit my tongue and put up with his flirting. I knew once we were finished here, we'd never see him again.

seventy-six

q

WHEN MACK AND I got up in the morning, we could tell something was different between Kyro and Zoey, but nothing was said. We discussed it as we walked to Geo's shop, deciding it was a good thing for them to have found each other. It had been obvious they had feelings for each other. Jack sulked, but I couldn't tell if it was because of Kyro and Zoey, or if he was just missing Elena. Either way, he was quiet and didn't want to join in the conversation.

We found Geo's shop easy enough, and he was happy to help once he heard Zoey's mom had sent us. He walked back to the boat with us and made a big show out of flirting with Zoey. It was plain to see that Kyro and Jack both got a little jealous, but Zoey seemed to not even realize Geo was flirting.

It made for an adorable scene. I thought for a moment Jack was going to punch the guy before Kyro had a chance. I wondered if Mack would make that face when someone flirted with me. I guess if we lasted long enough, I'd find out.

While Geo was talking with Mack and Kyro, I stepped away and pulled out my communicator. I knew I'd have privacy since Zoey and Jack had taken a walk around the shop to check out Geo's other projects. I had to call James and see if he had arranged our safe house. Although James was my most trusted agent, and I knew he had. He never failed at anything. I made the call. "James? It's Q. Did you get it all set up?" I waited for his response.

"Do you doubt me? Of course, I got it all set up. I'm sending the file to you now. It has a map of the town showing where to go. Your contact is Jayne. You'll be staying under her house. It's a secure panic room built under her house by our guys, so I'm sure it's safe. She was in my class at the academy. I'd trust her with my life. Which is why I trust her with yours."

I was impressed, even though I'd had no doubts he would take care of it. "I'll contact you later. I need to call headquarters while we're here and my friends are safe. Also where no one will hear." James agreed, and our call ended. Within moments I had the file he sent and was able to see where Jayne's house was in relation to Geo's shop.

It turned out Jayne's house was just around the corner, so we could all ride on the boat to the shop, then depart on foot for the house. I walked back to the others and explained this. We finished getting the boat ready and headed toward the shop, with Geo at the wheel, and the rest of us hanging out on the deck, waiting. I was hopeful he would be able to do the job in less time than Jack had estimated.

We got the boat settled, and Geo assured us it would be done as quickly as possible. He seemed to understand the need for a speedy job, though I was certain it was the extra credits I promised him for getting us on our way sooner than anticipated.

seventy-seven

Zoey

Once we arrived at Geo's shop, we left for Q's contact's house. She said the lady was a friend of a friend, and her name was Jayne. I hoped we would be safe while the boat was taken care of, but I didn't expect what we found once we got there. I don't think any of us were prepared for what happened here.

Jayne's house wasn't just a house, it was a mansion. The house was three stories tall and looked to be in pretty good shape. It didn't stand out, though, because all of the houses in this area were similarly built, with between two and four stories. All of the houses looked to be well kept, which was very different from the state of most places we had been so far. Each house looked to have at least half an acre of land around it, with groves of trees, and barns on the properties as well. Seeing the house, I wasn't sure what to expect from Jayne.

The front door opened before we got to it and standing there was a petite girl with dark skin and caramel hair that was tied up in a knot on top of her head. She looked to be around my age, but seemed more grown up, like she had been on her own for a long time. I felt like I had always had someone taking care of me, making it hard for me to feel like a real grown-up. She smiled at us and extended her hand when we got to the door. "Hi, y'all, I'm Jayne. This is my place. Welcome, come inside. I'll show ya around." I knew instantly I was going to like her. She was warm and welcoming when we got inside as well. There were tea and cakes set up in the formal dining room, just to the left of the entrance. We were escorted in and took seats in the chairs around the table.

"I hope y'all'll be comfortable here. The safe room is downstairs, underground. There are no windows, but I've tried to make it as homey as possible with no sunlight." She served tea and cakes to everyone, then took a seat at the table as well.

"Thank you for your hospitality. We really appreciate it." I spoke before anyone else had a chance.

"It's all part of the job, honey. And I love my job. Right, boss?" She said the last part to Q, who looked visibly annoyed. "Oh, I'm so sorry, I thought since you brought them here they knew. Oh, no. I'm sorry." And she ran off, leaving Q to deal with the aftermath of the bomb that had just been dropped.

"What did she mean? Why did she call you "boss"? What aren't you telling us, Q?"

seventy-eight

"WELL, SHIT. I GUESS we're having this conversation now." I took a minute to compose myself. "This isn't the time to explain everything, OK, so just bear with me. I'm not even sure how much I can tell you without getting into trouble myself." I could see they were all varying degrees of angry and confused with me right now.

"Q, maybe you should tell us what you can, so we can decide if we can trust you or not." Kyro's voice was as cold as an ice storm in winter.

"Fair enough. And just so you know, I am sorry that I had to keep things from you all. You've become like family to me in such a short time. I was actually going to discuss this with headquarters tonight and see if I could get clearance for all of you. I guess we'll do this a little backward." I stood up to pace while I talked, because it helped me think.

"When you came to find me, did you think it was odd that you had to go through a process? That when you asked about me, it set people on edge? Well, that's because I'm a part of an organization.

It's a big part of the rebellion against The Order. And I'm actually a Captain in the Resistance. Jayne and James work under my supervision." I realized I would get questions about all of this, and I was not prepared at all. But I was even less prepared for what happened next. No one said anything.

"Are you guys OK? Look, I'm sorry I couldn't tell you. And I'm sure you have questions. I'll do my best to answer what I can, but there are some things I can't talk about. No matter how badly I want to."

Still nothing. Any response would be better than this. This was awful. I couldn't take it. "Mack? Kyro? Zoey? Please someone say something."

"I'm not sure what to say. You didn't directly lie, but you did hide things from all of us. Which is bad enough, but you actually slept with me. Or did you do that with the others, too? I'm not sure what I think right now. But I do have a question. Was what happened between us part of your cover? Was any of it even real?" He didn't even give me a chance to respond, he just stood up and stormed off.

"Mack, wait! Please, let's talk about this!" Calling after him did no good, he didn't even turn around.

"I guess you both feel the same?"

"Not really. Or at least, I don't. You've been there for us since the day we met, and I feel like you wouldn't have kept anything from us if it wasn't important. I, for one, don't feel any different about you. It does hurt that you couldn't tell us, but I understand why." Leave it to Zoey to be the most understanding person I'd ever met.

"I'm with her. Everyone has secrets. But we aren't the ones you started a relationship with. Don't worry, he'll come around. He just needs time to process the news. You might want to think about telling him that you actually do love him. Just my thoughts, though." Kyro made perfect sense.

"I'll give him a bit to cool off, then I'll talk to him. But I need to hunt Jayne down and let her know it's not as bad as she thinks. She takes things really personal and will beat herself up over this one big time. if you'll excuse me?" And with that I walked off, heading upstairs to Jayne's room. Luckily for me, James was thorough, and had included a map of the house in the file. I knew exactly where to find her.

seventy-nine

Zoey

"Do you really think they're in love with each other?" I had to know what Ky thought. I had seen the signs myself but didn't realize that's what was going on.

"I think it's pretty obvious. Like I'm sure it is with us. Think about it. He got unreasonably upset that she didn't tell him in particular. I think they'll work it out. Mack is stubborn, but he doesn't love easily, so when he finds love, he won't give it up without a fight." Kyro seemed so certain, I had to believe him. After all, he had known Mack the longest.

A few minutes later, Jayne came back downstairs. "I'm really sorry about all of that." It was obvious she had been crying. "I'm usually a better agent than that. I hope I didn't cause you too much trouble." She seemed more delicate and fragile now than she had earlier.

"It's OK, really, you didn't know. I hope things are OK with you and Q?" I wanted to make her feel better but wasn't sure if anything would.

"I'll be fine. She's more understanding than she lets on. Let me show you to the safe rooms. Follow me, please."

We followed her downstairs to the fortress-like area known as the safe house. The walls were reinforced steel, and though it was dark, it seemed somewhat homey. She had done well decorating to make it feel less like a dungeon and more like a safe place to stay.

"So can you tell us anything about this organization you work for, if you don't mind us asking?" It was easier to ask her than to wait for Q to come back.

"We generally refer to ourselves as the Resistance. I'm not sure how much Q told you, but we fight against The Order, trying to undo the horrible things they do to people. We want to make the Earth a better place for everyone."

It sounded a lot like what we were trying to do, which was good. But there really was no way to know for certain if they were telling the truth. I felt like Q was being honest with us, so I decided to go with it. She had already saved my life and Ky's as well. I wasn't going to accuse her of anything unless I had proof.

"So, do you two want a room together, or separate? Normally we'd separate everyone, but Q told me upstairs that if we were breaking rules, we were gonna do it big. She's going to share a room with Mack, which means you can share as well, if you'd like." It really was obvious to everyone that we were a couple, even people we just met.

"That would be perfect, thank you." Ky answered before I could, so I just nodded. She showed us to a room with a queen-sized bed and a bath attached. It was spacious and comfortable. We couldn't have asked for more.

"Q and Mack will be across the hall, just there. And Jack, you'll be over here," She told us, pointing to a room a few feet away, then showing Jack to the room next to ours. Once we were inside, she explained that dinner would be brought down to us, and she went back upstairs. Jack followed her, and I heard him say he'd like to know more about the Resistance.

EIGHTY

Mack

I WAS SHOCKED AND hurt by the revelation I may have just been
part of a cover. How could she have done this to me? I had fallen
for Quinn hard and didn't know how I was going to handle this. I
knew I was being unreasonable by not giving her a chance to defend
herself, but I just couldn't stand there in front of my friends and
hear her say it was all a lie. How dare she make me love her, then not
feel the same? My heart couldn't take that. I went out the back door,
into the yard behind the house. I walked for a bit into a small grove
of trees that were at the back of the property. I was sitting under one
of the trees when she found me.

"Please just let me explain."

I didn't even look up. "Why should I? So you can lie to me more?
What reason do I have to trust you?" I knew my words would sting
her, and maybe part of me wanted to hurt her, like she had just hurt
me.

"I know you're upset with me, and I understand why. Please just
give me a chance. I'd like to explain."

I gestured to a tree root across from the one I was sitting on. "Then explain."

She sat across from me and tried to get me to meet her eyes. I couldn't, because I knew if I did, I would instantly forgive her. I'd been in similar situations, so I knew from experience. I had to remain calm and not look her in the eyes.

"Mack, please. Just look at me. No? OK, I guess I deserve that." I remained focused on her feet. "I know I should have told you. But in my position, we're sworn to secrecy. It's hard to know who's trustworthy, so the Resistance takes that decision away from you. There are penalties for telling others about us without permission from higher up. And I'll be the one to pay for Jayne's slip today."

The thought of her being punished for someone else's misstep hurt me, and I made the mistake of raising my eyes to hers. "So, you do care. Good. Don't worry, it won't be that bad. Just a few lashes with a whip on my bare back, no big deal."

I stood up, "They'll hit you over my dead body." I'd had it with people being abused and mistreated in my presence.

"Oh, Mack! I was only kidding. It will be a verbal lashing, I'm sure. Once I explain that you've all become important to me, and that I was going to ask to tell you today, I'm sure it won't be that bad."

I felt a little silly for getting so upset, both over her news and over her teasing me. But at least my feelings seemed to be out in the open now. If only I knew hers. "So, tell me, was this all a cover? Us, everything that's happened?"

She looked as though I had slapped her, which normally would have been enough for me, but this time I wanted to hear the words. "Well, to be perfectly honest with you, I didn't even want to like you when we met, much less fall in love with you. But we don't always get what we want."

My jaw dropped at her words. "What did you just say?"

She stopped, tilted her head to the side, and thought for a moment. "Hmm, that could have gone better." She chuckled, "I said I'm in love with you, you moron. Or did you not understand?"

My eyes went wide. She did say it. I didn't think she would. "I'm not ready to completely forgive you yet. Just so we're clear." She nodded solemnly; her face instantly sad. "But I'm in love with you too. I may not admit it to anyone else, but I suspect they knew before I did." Her face lit up, and I felt as though a weight was lifted from my shoulders.

In an instant, she was in my arms, raining kisses down my face. "Please say you'll stay with me here. It's totally against the rules, but I told Jayne we were going to do it anyway. I may get fired or worse, but I don't care. I need you with me. Well?" She continued to kiss all over my face, not giving me a chance to answer. I grabbed her hands and held her still.

"You have to give me a chance to answer, silly girl. Though I think you already know the answer." I kissed her hard, showing her all the passion I held for her. I knew this one was different than the past. This had a chance at being my forever.

EIGHTY-one

q

I KNEW I HAD broken so many rules, I would be lucky to not be locked away, but I didn't care. For once there was something I wanted more than to achieve the goals of the Resistance. I wanted Mack. If that meant losing the position I had fought so hard for, then so be it. It didn't seem like that big of a sacrifice at this moment. He insisted on being there when I called the Commander to explain. It was probably not going to be an easy conversation. But better to get it over with than to drag it out.

We headed upstairs to Jayne's communications room. She had everything set up on a secure line, so we did the video call together, with Jayne insisting to stay in the room as well. As soon as the Commander picked up, he visibly tensed at seeing Jayne and some man he didn't know. I'm sure he thought we'd been discovered and Mack was our captor.

"Sir, I have some things to report. But first, I have some things to tell you," I began.

Jayne broke in, "It was all my fault, sir, please don't punish the Captain. She didn't do anything except clean up my mess."

I held up a hand for her to stop, and she did. "If I may explain, sir. It concerns the mission I had James tell you about. This is Mack, he's one of the people I've been helping on the quest. I had to bring them here for a few days because of a hiccup we've encountered. Jayne took that to mean that they had been filled in about the Resistance, and well, she kind of spilled the beans, so to speak. I had to tell them what I could about us." The Commander relaxed a bit.

"Is that what this is about? Oh, that's a relief. I thought he was with The Order, and you were calling to tell me we'd been found out."

I shook my head, "No, sir. Our mission is still a go. I haven't told them everything, but I was going to call tonight and ask permission to bring the four of them in. I feel like they could be extremely useful to us. Your call, sir. And my apologies for going out of procedure on this."

He held up a hand for me to stop, the same way I had for Jayne. "Q, you know I trust you. Your judgment is sound, even if you don't trust it. One time does not make for a pattern. You are free to bring all four in as much as you see fit. If they wish to join, that will be permitted. If not, they will be permitted to use our resources to complete their mission, then be released. So long as they keep our secret, they'll not be detained. And there will be no formal punishment for this incident, for you or for Jayne. Understood?" Jayne looked relieved.

I nodded, "Thank you, sir." I proceeded to tell him about what we had dealt with so far and to ask his opinion on what we should do next. He advised that our plan was sound, but we needed to be cautious getting Zoey back to the boat. She would be difficult to disguise, and The Order would be searching for her as well as the Planet Patrol. It would be bad if the Patrol found her, but much worse if The Order got to her first.

EIGHTY-TWO

Zoey

I WOKE UP ALONE in the dark. The room was damp, and my head was tender. I didn't remember how I got there. I stood up and realized I must have taken a blow to the head. The throbbing and dizziness came on as soon as I was vertical again. My hand instinctively went to my throat where Ky's amulet should be. I breathed a sigh of relief when my fingers touched the stone. I left it under my shirt for safekeeping, since I wasn't sure about my location or who my captors were.

I hoped that he was safe and not being held here somewhere. The last thing I remembered was Q getting the call from Geo that the boat was done. We had all gathered our things and headed back to the shop. Kyro had insisted on carrying my backpack for me. We were walking to the shop when we got ambushed. Oh, no! The others! I had to find them.

I rushed over to the door, feeling my way along the wall of the minuscule room. This had to be a dungeon cell of some sort. When I found the door, it didn't surprise me it was locked. There was a small window, but the bars on it prevented me from sticking my fingers through. I wasn't tall enough to see out, but maybe my voice would carry down the hall into any other cells nearby.

"Kyro? Jack? Q? Mack? Are any of you here?" I called out in a hushed whisper because I was terrified of drawing attention from my captors. I waited for a response. Nothing but silence touched my ears. I fought the tears that threatened to fall. "Please, is anyone else here?" I called out a little louder this time.

"Zoey, is that you?" Ky's voice was a source of both relief and sadness. I was glad to not be alone, but I was horrified that he was here too.

"Ky? Where are you? Are you OK?" I needed to ask about the others but wasn't sure who was listening.

"I'm fine. Are you? Have you seen or heard anything to know where we are?" I let the tears fall out of fear and relief.

"No, I guess I was knocked out. I don't know where we are or who took us. What about the others?" I was hoping they'd be able to get us out of here, wherever here was.

Before Kyro could answer, I heard a noise from behind me. I wasn't as alone in my cell as I had thought. "Oh, ugh, what happened? Where am I?" I rushed over to Q as quickly as I could in the darkness. "It's OK, we're together. It's going to be OK." It was easier to reassure her, since we were together, and I was much more confident about our chances now. I guided her to the door, where she was tall enough to see out. "Ky, Q is over here with me. Mack may be over there with you."

Kyro checked and confirmed that both Jack and Mack were indeed in the cell with him. OK, this wasn't as bad as it could have been. We were together, more or less. "Do you have any idea who is holding us?" I directed my question at Q, who looked seriously pissed at the whole situation. "I can't be sure, but this looks like the holding cells used by the Planet Patrol. This isn't good. But at least I think we still have a chance. I'm not sure how to convince them you didn't kill that guy, though. But I don't really know, we could be in a Resistance dungeon. Maybe they decided to punish me for violations after all. Wait, I hear something. We may be about to find out who has us."

The footsteps grew closer, echoing down the hall. A group of guards stopped at Kyro's cell and began to round up the guys. Fortunately, they were cooperative, so nobody got hurt. Then a second group of guards came to get Q and me.

"Please don't fight them," I whispered to her as they opened the door.

"I don't even know who they are. I'm not going to give them a reason to separate us," she whispered back.

The guards ushered us out of the cell and down the hall in the same direction the guys had just been taken. We were shoved into a room and heard the heavy iron doors close behind us. All five of us were looking around trying to figure out where we were being held and who had captured us. I was relieved to see Kyro still had my backpack. Q and I walked over to where Jack, Kyro, and Mack were standing. The guards had backed off and given us some space.

Looking around, the room looked like something from a book I had read years ago. The book was about the Renaissance, and the room I was in reminded me of a throne room from a castle. There was a huge ornate throne across the room from us and strange banners hanging on the walls. The only thing missing was the king.

Just then, a door opened in the back of the room. A figure wearing a dark, hooded cloak entered the room. The cloak was floor length but was hanging open, making it obvious this was a man entering the room. He was wearing dark pants and a gray button-up shirt. The cloak hung loose on his shoulders and the hood obscured his face.

From Q's expression, this wasn't anyone she knew from the Resistance. I had a feeling it wasn't anyone Mama worked with either. He strolled over to stand in front of us.

His hood fell back as he turned to face us, and my jaw dropped. Jack had a similar reaction, because the face in front of us was far too familiar.

I knew it had to be a trick or a spell, but there was no mistaking that purple fringe that hung just over those almond-shaped eyes. I looked up at Jack, and from his expression, I knew we were thinking the same thing.

It wasn't possible—Race was dead. There was no way he could be standing in front of us right now. He walked over and placed his hand on my cheek, gave me a smirk, and spoke to us while my eyes were searching his.

"Ah, so nice of you all to finally join us. I'll take you to meet the master now. Follow me."

Thank you for reading Betrayed! Please consider leaving a review. They help more than you realize. It only takes a sentence or two to convince someone to give a new author a chance.

Check out the thrilling conclusion to Zoey's adventure in book 3:

The Story Continues...

Don't miss out on the rest of the story!

Saved: Forged by Magic – Book 3

Now imprisoned by the Order, we might all meet our end.

I'm forced to stay here, in this series of caves, held prisoner by a man who looks like my dead ex. It can't really be him, can it?

If only I knew for certain. Now I face life at his mercy. After he separates me from my friends, my memories start to fade. I can't remember their faces anymore. I can barely remember anything.

Despite Race trying to turn me into his perfect wife and keeping me from remembering who I am, nothing can stop me from discovering the truth. The all-consuming attraction I have toward a prisoner in the mines should feel wrong, but it doesn't. His amber eyes entrance me, and I have flashes of intimate moments with him--of a life I need to remember.

I have to remember and find a way out of here. Not only do the people I care about need me, so does the world. If I don't get the artifacts to the rift and close it on the Solstice, there will be no way to stop the Order from taking over the world. All will be lost. The Order can't win.

Click below to get Saved:

https://books2read.com/forgedbymagic-saved

About the Author

romance that transforms

M.P. Starkweather is a wife, mother, author, poet, casual on-line gamer, self-proclaimed fan-girl, and full-time nerd. She writes free-form poetry, paranormal romance, sci-fi romance, reverse harem romance, omegaverse romance, and is branching out into contemporary romance. In her free time, she enjoys writing, reading, Dungeons & Dragons, table top games with her husband and friends, and playing with her son. M.P. also enjoys tv, movies, and music across various genres.

To get the most up-to-date information about her latest releases and book signings, check out www.mpstarkweather.com or follow her on your favorite social media site.

Also By M.P. Starkweather

Standalones – Contemporary RH

Finding Fiona
Standalones - Contemporary RH OV

Forsaken Omega – free with newsletter signup

Cold Princes

Knot My Valentine
The Pack Next Door – Contemporary RH OV series

Princess or Knot

Fiancée or Knot

Queen or Knot

The Pack Next Door: The Original Trilogy

Christmas or Knot
Standalones – Paranormal RH

The Wayward Girl

The Cursed Blade Series – Paranormal w/ different pairings

<u>Digital Blade</u> – RH

<u>Elemental Blade</u> – RH
Vampires at Midnight - Paranormal RH series

<u>Blood Moon</u>

<u>Blood Lost</u>

<u>Blood War</u>

<u>Vampires at Midnight: The Complete Trilogy</u>
VaM/HoF Crossover Novella - Paranormal RH

<u>Blood Wolf</u>— free with newsletter signup
Hunters of the Forest - Paranormal RH series

<u>Wolf Bane</u>

<u>Wolf Caged</u>

<u>Wolf Moon</u>

<u>Hunters of the Forest: The Complete Trilogy</u>
Forged by Magic - Sci-fi/Fantasy M/F series

<u>Hidden</u>

<u>Betrayed</u>

<u>Saved</u>

<u>Forged by Magic: The Complete Trilogy</u>
Daydreams and Sunsets - a collection of poetry

Daydreams and Sunsets